THE TALE OF THE
LADY OCHIKUBO

Ochikubo Monogatari

THE TALE OF THE LADY OCHIKUBO

A tenth-century Japanese novel

Translated by
Wilfrid Whitehouse
and
Eizo Yanagisawa

An Arena Book
Published by Arrow Books Limited
17-21 Conway Street, London W1P 6JD

An imprint of the Hutchinson Publishing Group

London Melbourne Sydney Auckland
Johannesburg and agencies throughout
the world

First published in Great Britain 1970
by Peter Owen Ltd
Arena edition 1985

© Hokuseido Press Ltd Tokyo 1965

Reproduced, printed and bound in Great Britain by
Hazell Watson & Viney Limited,
Member of the BPCC Group,
Aylesbury, Bucks

ISBN 0 09 935300 8

UNESCO COLLECTION OF REPRESENTATIVE WORKS
JAPANESE SERIES
This book has been accepted in the Japanese
Series of the Translations Collection of the
United Nations Educational, Scientific and
Cultural Organization
(UNESCO)

FOREWORD

THE 'Tale of the Lady Ochikubo' dates from the last quarter of the tenth century. It is therefore one of the earliest of that long line of **monogatari** which are the special glory of Japanese literature of the tenth and eleventh centuries—the Heian Era. The earlier tales are fairy stories or accounts of wonderful and miraculous adventures or are strings of short and disconnected anecdotes and poems; there is nothing which could be called a novel. 'Ochikubo' is the first novel; here for the first time we have a vivid and realistic chronicle of life, related with a wealth of natural dialogue. In no story of the Heian Era, either earlier or later, are there so few poems; in none such a complete absence of descriptions of the beauties of nature. The author keeps close to the human story he is chronicling. Further, in this story, dramatic situations succeed one another continuously, yet throughout the plot is wonderfully consistent. Each incident has its place in the mosaic of the plot; there is not a detail inconsistent with another, with the chronology or with the characters he is portraying. 'Ochikubo Monogatari' also is the first which attempts any kind of characterisation. The author is strikingly successful in delineating the characters even of those who take but a minor part in the plot. As we might expect in a story of a 'wicked stepmother,' there is emotion and pathos but a more prominent characteristic is the wit and humour. Such are the marks of this masterpiece of Heian fiction; these are the merits which make it of outstanding importance in the history of Japanese literature.

CONTENTS

THE FIRST BOOK

ONCE there was a Chūnagon[1] who had several daughters, the two eldest of whom were already married and living in grand style in the east and west wings of his mansion, while his third and fourth daughters, now near to the age of 'putting on the skirt'[2], also lived there in his loving care. Besides these there was in his mansion a daughter by a princess, now dead, whom he had formerly been in the habit of visiting occasionally. The Kita no Kata[3] of the Chūnagon was of a somewhat peculiar nature, and always treated this step-daughter of hers as inferior even to the servants. She was made to live in a part of the mansion leading off from the main building where there was a small room on a lower level than the rest.[4] She was not addressed as 'Lady,' still less was she allowed to be called 'Princess.' The Kita no Kata would have had her addressed as the servants were, but in deference to what the Great Lord might have felt had she done so, she had her called by everyone 'Ochikubo no Kimi.'[5]

---

[1] One of the three State Counsellors of Middle Rank. Personal names are rarely used, and individuals are referred to always by their titles. (See Appendix II.)

[2] The ceremony of First Putting on the Skirt (mogi) at the age of twelve or thirteen.

[3] The title of a noble's wife.

[4] 'ochikubo naru tokoro.'

[5] The Lady of the Lower Room; but kimi was used of upper servants also.

Ever since her childhood not even the Chūnagon had treated her with affection, and moreover as the Kita no Kata had her own way in everything in the house, the Lady Ochikubo had had to suffer many indignities. She had never had a foster-mother; no one had ever cared for her except a very sharp-witted girl named Ushiromi who had been the Lady's special attendant since her mother's death. The Lady and this attendant of hers were very devoted to each other and were never apart.

Now the Lady far excelled her lovingly-cared-for step-sisters in beauty, but she had never been outside among people, and no one knew of her existence. As she learned more of the world, and understood the sadness of her situation, she composed this sorrowful poem.

> As the days pass by,
> Each brings me new troubles;
> In this world of care,
> How can I live on, when
> Filled is my heart with despair.

It was unfortunate that the Lady Ochikubo had never had anyone to teach her to play the kin;[1] she would certainly have been an excellent player, as she was very sensitive and intelligent. Her mother, however, had taught her to play the sō no koto until she was five or six years old, and as she played exceptionally well, the Kita no Kata allowed her own third son, a boy of about nine years old, to be taught occasionally by the Lady Ochikubo, as he had taken a great liking to playing this instrument.

---

[1] A kin had seven strings; a sō no koto thirteen.

In her spare time, the Lady Ochikubo had learnt to sew, and did this work very skilfully.

'Good!' her step-mother had said to her. 'It is very good for people who are not pretty to learn to do things.'

She was kept busy making robes for the two sons-in-law and had no leisure at all, and as time went on, she had to work harder and harder, until at last she did not even have time enough for sleep at night, and if she worked a little slower than usual, her step-mother would reprove her.

'If you do even this trivial task in such a languid manner, what do you think you are here for?' she would say, and cause the Lady Ochikubo to burst out weeping.

'Why is it that there is no way for me to die?' the Lady Ochikubo would say to herself.

The ceremony of 'putting on the skirt' was performed for the Third Lady, and soon afterwards she was married to the Kurōdo no Shōshō.[1] This caused infinitely more work for everyone; the Lady Ochikubo had even less leisure now, and her existence became more and more dreary. Few young and lovable people have to work as hard as she! She was despised by all; she felt forlorn and she wept over her sewing.

> No longer do I
> Wish to live in this world, but—
> I can find no way
> To put an end to this my
> Miserable existence.

---

[1] A Vice-Director of the Imperial Archives.

As Ushiromi had long hair and was very pretty, she was forced to go into the service of the Third Lady. She felt very sad at this.

'It was to serve you and you alone that I refused to be adopted by my aunt. Why then must I leave you and go to serve another?' she said with tears.

'What's that?' exclaimed the Lady Ochikubo. 'As long as we live in the same house, everything will be just the same as it is now. And you will have much more elegant clothes than you now have; you should be very glad about that.'

As the Lady Ochikubo loved this attendant of hers very much, she felt very lonely without her, and being accustomed to serve her, Ushiromi was very sorry to see her so sad and was always going to her room to see her; the step-mother treated the Lady with infinite cruelty because of this.

'Ochikubo is always getting that girl to go back to her,' she would say angrily, and so the girl was unable to talk with the Lady in peace.

(As Ushiromi[1] was now not an appropriate name, she was given the name Akogi.)

The Kurōdo no Shōshō's attendant, Kotachihaki,[2] a very sharp-witted fellow, had written letters to Akogi for

---

[1] Ushiromi, a guardian.

[2] Really a title, Bodyguard of the Crown Prince; his personal name is given later as Korenari.

several years, and now they became lovers. When they
had an opportunity of intimate conversation, they were
always speaking of the unfortunate situation of the Lady
Ochikubo, her beauty, and her feelings at the cruel attitude of the Kita no Kata towards her.

'Oh, how I wish that I could persuade some paragon
of a man to carry her off!' Akogi exclaimed with tears.
So it was that they thought of her and spoke of her always in her unhappiness and loneliness.

Tachihaki's mother had formerly been in the service of
the Sataishō[1] as nurse to his son who was now Sakon-e
no Shōshō.[2] This son had not yet married and often
asked people to tell him of suitable ladies. On one such
occasion, when Tachihaki told him of the Lady Ochikubo,
he was very interested and afterwards in private had an
intimate talk with Tachihaki about her.

'How pitiful! What must she feel! And she is the
daughter of an Imperial Princess too! Do enable me to
meet her in secret,' the Shōshō said.

'At present she is not thinking of such things at all;[3]
but I will do what I can,' answered Tachihaki.

'Do find an opportunity for me to visit her secretly,'
the Lord said. 'You tell me that she lives apart from
the rest of the household, so it should be easy.'

---

[1] Commander of the Bodyguard of the Left.
[2] Major-General of the Bodyguard of the Left.
[3] The Lady was fifteen or sixteen years of age.

Tachihaki told Akogi of the Lord's desire, but she answered coldly, 'The Lady does not think of such things; and besides I have heard that the Shōshō is of a very dissolute character.'

In answer to Tachihaki's continued entreaties, however, she said, 'All right. I will see what the Lady says.'

Akogi had been given two exterior rooms next to the Lady's room, but thinking it presumptuous on her part to live in rooms on the same level as the Lady's, she had furnished a room on a still lower level for herself.

It was about the First Day of the Eighth Month; and the Lady alone in bed and unable to sleep cried out, 'Oh, mother, come to me and take me away from this world. I am so miserable.' And in the vain attempt to soothe her feelings, she composed this poem—

> If but as the dew
> Your compassion falls on me,
>   Come back to me now;
> And from this harsh world, let us
> Then dry away together.

Next morning, in the course of conversation, Akogi told the Lady what Tachihaki had said about the Shōshō wishing to see her. 'What shall I do about it?' she asked. 'You cannot continue to live all your life alone in this way.'

The Lady made no answer, not knowing what to say, and just then someone called out, 'Bring the Third Lady's washing water,' and Akogi had to leave.

'Whether I do this or not,' thought the Lady, 'what will be the good? My mother not being here, my sole desire is to die and end this my unhappy existence. To leave this house, even to become a nun, is impossible. And to live here is misery. Oh, how I wish to die and leave this world!'

When Tachihaki went to the Taishō's mansion, the Shōshō asked him how he was progressing with the affair. Tachihaki told him what had been said, and added, 'It seems that it will be a very long business. In these matters, it should be the lady's parents who worry about bringing the matter to a successful conclusion. But the Chūnagon is so hen-pecked that he will do nothing to help her to find a lover.'

'It was for that reason that I told you to take me to visit her in secret; it would never do for me to become the son-in-law of that Chūnagon. If, when I meet her, I find that she is beautiful, I will bring her here; if she is not, I shall stop going to see her on the excuse that people are talking.'

'Then I ought to know more of what your intentions are before I do anything further,' said Tachihaki.

'I cannot decide anything about my intentions until I see her. How can I decide on hearsay alone? Exert yourself faithfully for me, and I shall not forget it perhaps.'

'"Perhaps" is not a pleasant word to hear,' said Tachihaki.

'I meant to say "for ever"; I said the wrong word,' said the Lord with a smile. Still smiling, he handed a letter to Tachihaki who took it reluctantly and went to the Chūnagon's house and gave it to Akogi.

'No, I do not want to take it. What is the meaning of it? We ought not to allow the Lady to see anything improper,' Akogi said; but she took the letter eventually.

'However, persuade her to write an answer to the Lord. I do not think that any evil will come of it.'

Akogi therefore took the letter to the Lady with the remark, 'This is a letter from the Lord of whom I was speaking the other day.'

'Why do you bring me this? If my step-mother hears of it, will she approve of it?' the Lady asked.

'Does she approve of anything you do? You need not worry about what she will think of it.'

The Lady Ochikubo made no answer to this, so Akogi lighted the chamber-torch and read the letter. There was written only this poem—

> When first I was told
> Of the bitter life you lead,
>   Pity filled my heart;
> It is filled with love for you
> Even though yet we have not met.

'What fine handwriting!' commented Akogi, as if to herself, but seeing that the Lady took no notice of what she said, she rolled the letter up again and put it in the comb-box.

'Well, what happened?' Tachihaki asked her later. 'Did she read the letter?'

'Alas, she did not so much as answer me. So I left it there and came out.'

'Well, if she consents, she will be happier than she is now. And we shall be better off too.'

'Well, if he remains constant in his love, the Lady cannot possibly refuse to ———.'

The next morning, the Chūnagon, on his way from his sleeping-chamber, happened to look into the Lower Room. He felt very sorry for the Lady; her hair hanging down was most beautiful, but she was very poorly dressed.

'Your clothes are very shabby,' he said to her. 'I feel very sorry about it. But I have so many children to look after that I cannot care for you as I ought. If you should meet a man who falls in love with you, you can act as you think best. I am sorry to find you still living alone like this.'

The Lady, feeling shy, did not answer, and the Chūnagon went out.

'When I looked into the Lower Room,' he said later to the Kita no Kata, 'I found the child clad in one thin white lined robe only. Have the other children no old clothes? If they have, give her some to wear. She must be very cold at night.'

'She is always supplied with clothes,' the Great Lady answered, 'but she does not take enough care of them. She soon tires of them and then she does not wear them again.'

'Very strange! However, she lost her mother when she was very young, and that seems to have made her very dull and stupid.'

The step-mother ordered the Lady Ochikubo to make a Court-hakama for her son-in-law, the Kurōdō no Shōshō. 'Sew this better than usual and you shall have a robe as a reward,' the Great Lady said, to the Lady's infinitely great delight.

As the hakama was finished very soon and was very well made, the Kita no Kata was very pleased, and gave to the Lady as her reward some damask wadded robes of her own, but which were almost worn out. The cold winds were then beginning to blow and the Lady had begun to worry about what she could wear in the winter, and so this present, poor as it was, made her very happy—so humble of spirit had she become.

It was the Kurōdō no Shōshō's nature to use extravagant language whether in praising or in blaming, and he praised the sewing of this hakama very much. 'This is very well made, extraordinarily well sewn,' he said.

The Kita no Kata, however, when she heard of this from the servants said, 'What nonsense! Do not say anything like that to the Lady Ochikubo, or it will make her vain. It is better for such a person to be kept humble, for a humble spirit is most needful in one who must serve others.'

'What a cruel thing to say! And she is such a nice

girl!' the servants said behind her back.

The Shōshō sent another letter to the Lady with this poem and a stalk of miscanthus grass—

> If the desires that
> I have expressed, have any
> Hope of flowering,
> Then like a miscanthus flower,
> In gentle breeze, nod to me.

To this, he received no answer.

One rainy day, he sent another letter, chiding her for not being as sympathetic and responsive as he had heard that she was. Together with this letter he sent this poem—

> In the autumn time,
> Season of days of drizzle,
> Gloomy skies and grey;
> Overcast with gloom of doubt
> Is the heart of one who loves.

Still he received no answer.
Next he sent her this poem—

> The river that flows
> Through the heavens may be crossed
> By bridges of clouds;
> To cross you must dare
> Do more than just stamp on it.

He did not write every day, but he did so frequently. And still he received no answer.

'She is rather timid, and perhaps she does not know how to write an answer to such a letter,' the Shōshō commented to Tachihaki. 'I have heard from you that she is responsive to affection, and so it seems very strange that she does not send me an answer, even if it is only a brief one.   Why is it?'

'I do not know,' answered Tachihaki. 'However, I have heard that she is always very retiring, because she fears that the Kita no Kata would be even more cruel to her, if she did anything at all that would not be approved.'

'Well, can't you take me to the Lady secretly?' the Lord again urged him, and Tachihaki feeling that it was difficult to decline his master's request wondered about looking for some opportunity to do this.

No letter was sent for the next ten days, and then the Lord thought that it was time for him to send another. So he wrote—

> Lately,
>   No more do I find
> It in my heart to write you;
>   I will write no more,
> For when I have no answer,
> It does but feed my sorrow.

And in the letter accompanying this poem, he told her how he had tried to cease thinking of her, but had found it impossible; he appealed to her to meet him in secret, even though on account of this request, she might think him a dissolute man.

'Do induce her to answer this time at least. I was blamed very much for not having done as much as I ought to have done,' said Tachihaki to Akogi, as he reported to her what the Shōshō had said to him.

'I told you before that the Lady does not know how to reply and that it would be a very difficult thing to do as the Lord wishes,' she answered, but she went to show the letter to the Lady. However, as she was making a Court-robe for the husband of the Second Lady, the Uchūben[1], who had been suddenly summoned to the Court, no answer was given.

'Well, it seems that she doesn't know what to answer,' the Shōshō thought, but believing so strongly from what he had heard that she was very intelligent and sympathetic, he rather liked this reluctance on her part. Still he reproached Tachihaki for his slowness. However although Tachihaki was always looking for a good opportunity, for some time no such opportunity occurred, as the mansion was always full of people, the ladies and their husbands.

Then the Chūnagon announced that he intended to pay a visit of thanksgiving to Ishiyama Temple. All the inmates of the mansion begged leave to accompany him; even the matron[2] wished to go, being ashamed of being left behind. The Lady Ochikubo was not among the number of those to go, and so the Lady Ben[3] said 'Please

---

[1] The Vice-Controller of the Right.
[2] The old lady in charge of the servants; the housekeeper.
[3] The wife of the Uchūben; the Second Lady.

take the Lady Ochikubo. It would be a shame to leave her behind.'

'No. When was she ever allowed out? How can she sew when she is on a journey? I will not begin to let her go on excursions. It is better for her to be shut up in the house,' the Kita no Kata answered with finality.

Akogi, as an attendant of the Third Lady, was to go and had had given to her incomparably fine new clothes. Nevertheless, feeling very sorry for the Lady left behind alone, she declined to go. 'I have suddenly become unclean,'[1] she told the Kita no Kata.

'I do not believe it,' the Great Lady answered angrily. 'You say that because the Lady Ochikubo is to be left alone.'

'You have no reason for saying that,' Akogi replied. 'If you tell me to go, I will go. Would anyone be unwilling to go on such a pleasant excursion? Even the matron has asked to be allowed to go.'

The Kita no Kata must have been convinced for she allowed Akogi to stay and made her give her fine clothes to one of the other maids.

The party started with a good deal of noise and excitement, and in the deserted mansion, Akogi felt very sad and lonely. Then, while she was chatting with the Lady, a letter arrived from Tachihaki. 'I have heard that you have not gone with the others. Is it true? If it is, I will come and see you,' the letter read.

---

[1] From her bodily condition, she was ceremonially unclean.

'Seeing the Lady's bitter disappointment at having to stay here alone, how could I go?' Akogi answered. 'We are very bored. If you can amuse us, come. Be sure to bring the pictures that you told me of.' Tachihaki had told her that the Shōshō's sister had a large collection of pictures, which she would be able to see when the Shōshō began to visit the Lady.

'Is this your wife's handwriting, Korenari?'[1] the Lord asked, when Tachihaki showed him this answer. 'She writes very well. This is a good opportunity for us. Go and arrange everything.'

'Will you lend me a roll of pictures, then?'

'Yes, when the time comes.'

'The time we have been waiting for has now come.'

The Lord laughed and went to his room. On a piece of white poem-paper, he drew a face with a little finger in its mouth and wrote—

As you order, I send a picture.

I cannot find it
In my heart to laugh with joy,
When I am downcast
By the refusals of her
Who does not return my love.

from a child.[1]

He gave this to Tachihaki and on his way out, Tachi-

---

[1] Tachihaki's personal name.

[2] By signing the poem "from a child", he implies that no answer is necessary.

haki said to his mother, 'Get ready a bag of choice fruit for me. I will send for it later on.'

Then Tachihaki went to the mansion of the Chūnagon and called Akogi outside.

'Where are the pictures?' she asked.

'Here. Show the Lady this letter,' said Tachihaki.

'Well, it is probably all nonsense,' she said and took the letter to the Lady who, unoccupied at the moment, read it.

'Did you tell this lord how I liked pictures?' she asked.

'I expect the Lord read the answer which I sent to Tachihaki. I mentioned it in that letter.'

'Alas,' thought the Lady sadly, 'I am afraid that he thinks me cold-hearted; yet perhaps it is better for such as I to be thought heartless.'

Tachihaki called Akogi outside. She went out and chatted to him.

'Who are left behind?' he asked, as if he had not already learnt. 'How lonely it must be for you! I will send for some fruit for you from my mother,' he went on, and then sent to his mother for the food. She sent in reply a bag of fruit arranged very prettily, and also a larger bag, containing various kinds of fruit and different sorts of rice-cakes, both red and white, and then parched dried rice, separated frorn the rest by a piece of paper.[1]

'Even among us this is strange food to offer,' the message accompanying it said, 'for in eating it, one has to

---

[1] Parched dried rice was becoming a very old-fashioned form of food by the date of 'Ochikubo Monogatari.'

screw up one's face horribly. So what will noble people think of it? I am ashamed to offer it to them. Therefore give this parched rice to the little girl, Tsuyu.'[1] Feeling that her son and his lover were lonely, the mother had sent these things with the object of showing, even in this very trivial manner, her love for them.

'This is very strange!' Akogi said angrily when she saw the fruit and rice-cakes. 'Is it not strange to send fruit and rice-cakes?[2] You are the one who is responsible for this trick, aren't you?'

'I do not know anything about it,' answered Tachihaki laughing. 'Is it done in such a disagreeable manner? It is my mother's idea perhaps. Tsuyu, put these things away,' he went on, calling Tsuyu and giving her the bags.

The two went to bed and talked, as they often did, of the Lady and of how sad she must be feeling. It was raining that night, and so Tachihaki thought that the Lord would not come and he lay down without any anxiety.

Left alone, and thinking fondly of her mother, the Lady lay down and played the **koto** very charmingly.

'I am surprised that she is so accomplished,' commented Tachihaki, charmed with her playing.

'The princess, her mother, taught her to play when she was five years old,' explained Akogi.

---

[1] Tsuyu, the name of Akogi's maid.
[2] The symbolism of this present of fruit and rice is explained later, p. 36.

Just as she was saying this, the Shōshō arrived, having come secretly, and sent one of his men in to ask Tachihaki to return as his master had something for him to do.

'I will go and see him at once,' Tachihaki replied, in some confusion, for he guessed that the Shōshō had come to the mansion himself. So he went outside and Akogi went into the Lady's room.

'I have come here in all this rain, so do not send me away without seeing the Lady,' said the Shōshō.

'Well, you have come here suddenly, without sending a message first, haven't you? And I have not yet been able to find out what the Lady wishes. It is going to be very difficult,' answered Tachihaki.

'Oh, do not be so formal,' the Lord said, patting him on the shoulder.

'Well, at any rate, descend,' said Tachihaki with a smile, and they went in together, the Lord sending away the carriage, saying to the driver, 'Come back again while it is yet dark.'

For a moment or two, they stood at the door of Tachihaki's room, deciding what they should do. There were not many people left in the mansion, so they did not think it necessary to be very cautious.

'First, let me get a peep at the Lady,' the Lord said.

'Wait a little while. You may be disappointed, like the Lord was who peeped in at the Lady Monoimi.'[1]

---

[1] Possibly a character in a novel of the period.

'If I am disappointed, then I shall not even take off my hat; I shall run back home, covering my face with my sleeve,' the Shōshō said laughing.

Tachihaki therefore took him through to the lattice door, while he himself sat on the verandah, so that they should not be discovered by the night-watchman.

The Shōshō looked through; the light was dim, but as there were no curtains or screens, he could see clearly. Directly in front of him there was a woman, whom he took to be Akogi, dressed in white, with a glossy red silk under-robe, and with her hair nicely dressed. The other lying beside her was no doubt the Lady. She wore a worn white dress and was covered from the waist down by a wadded silk coverlet. As he was looking at her from the side, he could not see her face. He was looking at and admiring the beauty of her hair, when the light went out. He was sorry at this, but, he thought, soon he would be able to do as he wished.

'How dark it is! You say you have a visitor; you ought to go,' the Lady said, and her voice sounded very sweet and noble to the Shōshō.

'While my husband is away seeing his visitor, I will stay with you. I am afraid that you will be alarmed, if I go away.'

'No, I am used to being alarmed now.'

The Shōshō then went out.

'Well, what do you think of her?' Tachihaki said to

him. 'Shall I accompany you back to the mansion? Where is your hat?'

'You are thinking about your wife, and think that I am a nuisance here. So you are intent on hastening my departure,' the Lord said smiling. 'Call your wife out quickly and go to bed,' he went on; he smiled but he thought that the Lady would be very ashamed on receiving his visit on account of her shabby attire.

Tachihaki went into his room and called Akogi, but she replied, 'I will stay with the Lady to-night. You can sleep in the guard-room or anywhere you wish.'

'I want to tell you what my visitor said. Come out for a moment.'

'What is the matter? You are a nuisance!' she answered, opening the door and coming out.

'The visitor who came to see me said that it was not pleasant sleeping alone on a rainy night like this,' said Tachihaki seizing her. 'Now come then with me.'

'I thought so. You have nothing important to tell me,' said Akogi, smiling.

Tachihaki forced her to lie down with him. They said nothing further, and Tachihaki lay there as quietly as if he were fast asleep.

The Lady not being able to sleep, lay and played the **koto**.

> I would that I could
> Escape from this world, so full
> Of care and sorrow;

How I wish that I could find
Some cavern where I could hide!

The Shōshō thinking that she would not be going to sleep for some time, and, moreover, that she was alone, pried open easily the lattice door with a piece of wood, and entered. The Lady jumped up terrified, but he went to her and caught hold of her.

Akogi in the next room, amazed to hear the sound of the lattice-door being opened, and fearing that something was happening, tried to get up, but Tachihaki prevented her.

'Why do you do that? I want to see what is the matter; the lattice-door was opened just now,' she said.

'It was a dog or a mouse. Don't be frightened,' Tachihaki said.

'What is happening? It must be something that you know about, or you would not have said that.'

'I have done nothing. Go to sleep,' he said, embracing her and forcing her to lie down again.

'Oh, how miserable! How provoking you are!' said Akogi, but although she feared for the Lady's safety and was very angry with Tachihaki, she was not able to move; he held her so tightly in his arms that it was impossible.

The Shōshō, still holding the Lady in his arms, undid his robe and lay down. The Lady trembled and wept in fear and misery.

'As you think that this world is so full of care and sorrow, I have come to take you to a cavern where you will hear nothing of the miseries of the world,' he said.

She guessed that this was the Shōshō who had written so many letters to her, and she felt ready to die with shame at the thought of how shabby her robes and **hakama** were. The Lord was also distressed at her bitter tears and he could only lie there and remain silent.

As Akogi's room was next to the one in which they were lying, she could faintly hear the sound of weeping; she was now convinced that there was justification for her fears; she tried to rise again, but again she was prevented by Tachihaki.

'Are you playing some trick upon the Lady? I thought you were acting very suspiciously. What a wicked man you are!' she said angrily, breaking away from him and getting up.

'You are accusing me of something which I do not know anything at all about,' he said laughing. 'Would a thief steal in at this time? It is a man visiting her, I expect. And even if you go in now, it will be of no use.'

'Oh, do not talk so cruelly! At least tell me who he is. Oh, this is a terrible thing! How distressed she must be!' she exclaimed and wept.

'Don't be so childish,' said Tachihaki, laughing still, but she only became more and more angry.

'Oh, how awful to be married to a man like you!' she exclaimed.

'Well, as a matter of fact, it is the Shōshō,' said Tachi-haki, for he was now distressed to see the bitter grief of Akogi. 'He has come to talk to the Lady. Why are you so angry? Calm yourself. It is her Fate that it has happened like this.'

'I did not know what the Lord was planning to do. But what troubles me is that the Lady will think that I knew all about it,' she said with bitterness. 'I wish that I had stayed with her for the night.'

'Don't you see that she will be able to tell that you appear to have known nothing about it. Don't be so angry,' he said, dallying with her till she forgot her anger.

'Why are you grieving so bitterly?' the Shōshō was saying to the Lady. 'I am not a man of high rank, but I am not of such low rank that you have to be so sad and distressed at my visit. I have written you many letters, but you have never sent me an answer, although you have read the letters. Thinking it useless to write any more, I had determined not to do so. But since I sent you that first letter, you have become dearer and dearer to me. It must be my Fate to be thus despised by you, and your cruelty now cannot increase my sadness.'

He took her in his arms and lay down. The Lady wished she could die; it would sound foolishly inadequate to say only that she was ashamed, with no outer robe on, dressed only in a **hakama** and a robe that was so worn that she felt that her body could be seen through it in places. She was filled with embarrassment rather than with grief.[1]   Seeing this, the Lord was very sorry for her, and began to talk on various subjects, but she could make no answer. She felt very bitter against Akogi for not having prevented this shame falling on her.

At last dawn came.   Hearing the crowing of the cock, the Lord recited this poem—

> How my heart has ached
> To see you pass the long night
>   In tearful lament;
> And now the cock has crowed to
> Say the dawn has come too soon.

'Speak to me now and then,' he went on.   'If I do not hear your voice, I cannot feel that we are lovers.'

So at last she forced herself to say—

> When my heart is full
> Of misery, I cannot
>   Give answer to you
> With any other accent
>   But the cock's tearful lament.

Her voice was very sweet and the Lord thought that he had certainly erred in treating her as quite an ordinary woman.

Hearing the cry, 'The carriage has come,' Tachihaki said to Akogi, 'Go in and say that the carriage has arrived.'

'If I go in now, not having gone in last night, the Lady

---

[1] The original says, 'She was wet with sweat rather than with tears.'

will think that I surely knew all about the affair. Your trick has blackened my character in her eyes.'

'If she loves you less, I will love more,' said Tachihaki laughing, for he found her childish manner very amusing.

He went near to the lattice and cleared his throat purposely. The Shōshō heard him and rose, and wishing to cover the Lady for the coverlet was very thin, he slipped off his outer robe and covered her with that before he went out. She felt infinitely ashamed.

Akogi's heart was filled with pity for the Lady, but for a long time she could not bring herself to go in to her. However at last, when she felt that she could not remain any longer in her own room, she went in and found the Lady still in bed. Akogi was still wondering what she should say, when two letters arrived, one from Tachihaki and one from the Lord.

'All last night, you continued to blame me very unjustly for things which I knew nothing about,' Tachihaki had written. 'If my visits should cause the slightest inconvenience to you or the Lady, I would never visit you again; for then, how badly you would treat me! Certainly your violent temper causes me to fear for our future happy relations. As it seems that the Lady thinks me a very wicked fellow, this match-making business of mine has become unendurable. However I have to pass on this letter from the Lord. Please ask her to answer. It is customary to answer such letters, don't you think?'

Akogi gave the other letter to the Lady. 'Here is a letter,' she said. 'Last night I fell asleep very strangely in spite of myself, and awoke to find that it was already daylight. In whatever way I may try to make you believe that I knew nothing of the Shōshō's intentions, you will not; and you will think that I am only trying to excuse myself for being the Lord's accomplice. That belief would be quite reasonable, were it not that, as you must admit, if I had known that the Lord was coming, I would have made some preparations for his visit.' Akogi swore with a myriad oaths that she had known nothing, but the Lady answered never a word, and did not rise from her bed.

'I suppose that you think that I knew that the Lord was coming,' Akogi therefore went on. 'I am very sorry if you do think that. After all my years in your service, would I have done such an underhand and mean action? Not wishing to leave you behind here alone, I refused to go with the others, only to find myself now in this very unpleasant situation. If you cannot believe what I say, and understand that I am innocent, it will be hateful to me to remain any longer in your service, and I shall want to go away anywhere out of your sight.'

'I do not think that you knew anything of the Lord's plan to come here,' the Lady said, weeping bitterly in sympathy with Akogi's evident distress. 'It was all a great pity. Everything happened so unexpectedly that it has made me unspeakably miserable, and especially because I had on such very shabby clothes. If my mother were alive, I should not have had to suffer any such indignities.'

'That is very true,' Akogi answered. 'The Shōshō must have learnt that of all proverbially wicked step-mothers, the Kita no Kata is the most wicked. However if only the Lord is constant in his love, how happy we shall be!'

'But that is very improbable. Would such a Lord remain the lover of such as I? And what will the Kita no Kata say, if she hears anything of it? She once said to me, "If you do anything for anyone without my per-mission, I shall not allow you to stay here,"' the Lady said uneasily.

'Well, then, it would be better for us to leave this house. If you continue to live here under her eye like this, you will never be happy. Living here like this, you will not be long for this world. Is it not quite evident that the Great Lady has firmly determined to keep you shut up here and make you work as hard as she can?' Akogi, said, reasoning with unaccustomed seriousness.

'What about the answer?' the messenger sent in to ask, for he was still waiting.

'Please read the letter quickly then. It is useless to lament now,' Akogi said, unrolling the letter. And with-out raising her head, the Lady read it. This was all that was written—

> Great was my longing
> For you before ere we met.
> Why is it then that
> Now this devotion of mine
> Grows stronger and stronger yet?

'I do not feel well enough to answer that,' the Lady said, when she had read this, and so no answer was sent.

However Akogi wrote to Tachihaki. 'Alas, you wicked man!' she wrote. 'What does all this mean? Your behaviour to me last night was infinitely wicked—So evil and so hateful that I have no hope in the present and none for the future. The Lady is so grieved that she cannot write an answer; she is still in bed. I also am very distressed to see her in this condition.'

'Does she think me very disagreeable?' the Shōshō thought when he had been told of this answer by Tachihaki. 'No, it is merely the painful memory of the shame she felt last night at the shabbiness of her clothes which now distresses her.'

So, feeling very sorry for her, he wrote to her again during the same day. 'Why is it that now I have found how cold you are to me,' he wrote, 'you have become even dearer to me?

> When you rebuff me,
> And will not be persuaded,
> Pulling back from me
> Strongly like tangled cob-web,
> My love the more increases.

I am beside myself with love for you.'

'All our efforts will have failed, if the Lady does not answer this letter,' Tachihaki's letter, sent at the same time as this, said. 'Now that he has visited her, it would be best for her to accept his love. He says that he intends to be constant to the Lady, and I believe he will be.'

Akogi therefore urged the Lady to answer 'if only this time!' but the Lady was too sad and too ashamed to do so, for it pained her to think of what the Lord was recalling of her shabby appearance on the previous night. She lay in bed and covered her face with the bed-clothes.

Akogi, not being able to get her to speak, wrote again to Tachihaki. 'The Lady has read the Shōshō's letter,' she wrote, 'but she is in too much distress to answer. You say that the Lord will be constant to her, but how can you be certain of this after such a short time? You know that really he does not intend to be constant, but you say that he will be in order to put our minds at rest.'

'How wittily she writes! As for the Lady she seems to be distracted because she feels so ashamed,' the Lord said with a smile when Tachihaki showed him this letter.

Akogi was alone and had no one to consult. So she was very perturbed about what she should do in preparation for the Lord's visit that evening. There were no screens or curtains, and so there was nothing to do but to dust the room hastily. It seemed a shame to disturb the Lady to make the bed, for she lay there almost insensible. However Akogi roused her and found her face flushed and her eyes swollen with tears. Akogi's heart was filled with pity for her. She asked the Lady to let her do her hair and she dressed it with great care, while the Lady still lay in bed, her heart bursting with sorrow.

The Lady had some very nice furniture, which had belonged to her mother, though the number of articles was very small.

'It is good that she has this at least,' Akogi said admiringly, as she polished the beautiful mirror and set it at the head of the bed. So she worked alone, for she had to do the work both of an upper-servant and a young maid-servant.

It was nearly time for the Lord's arrival.

'It is very rude of me, I know,' Akogi said to the Lady, bringing her one of her own beautiful robes which she had worn only twice. 'I have hardly used this. It is a great pity that you were not wearing it last night. It is presuming on my part, but,' she went on in a low voice, 'it will be all right; there is no one here who knows that it is mine. There is nothing to do but wear it.'

The Lady therefore took the robe and put it on; she had been filled with shame at the thought that she must again meet him in the same shabby robes.

Akogi had used most of the incense which she had received as a present on the occasion of the recent ceremony of 'putting on the skirt.' Now she burnt a great deal of what remained to perfume the robe.

Then she cudgelled her brains to think from whom she could borrow a three-foot screen; and she was also worried about the thinness of the bedclothes. At last she thought of asking her aunt, whose husband had been in the service

of the Court and who was now Governor of the Province
of Izumi.

'Someone has suddenly come to stay the night,' she
hurriedly wrote to her aunt, 'and he cannot stay in the
main building, because that would be in an unlucky direction for him. We are not very intimate with him, and
have no suitable furniture for him. Could you lend me
a screen? And also some bed-clothes? For we should
like him to have good ones. I am always making strange
requests of you, but I am in too great a hurry to explain
everything now.'

'It pains me very much that I hear so rarely from you,'
her aunt wrote in reply. 'Your request does seem rather
strange, but I will say nothing more now as you say that
you will explain fully later. The bed-clothes which I am
sending I made for my own use; I am afraid that they
will not be any better than those which you have. I am
sending a screen also.'

The bed-clothes which she sent were aster-coloured.[1]
Akogi's delight was boundless as she unpacked and showed them to the Lady.

She was unrolling the blind of the screen when the
Lord arrived. She showed him in, and the Lady, thinking
it not proper to receive him as she was, tried to rise.

'Why do you rise when you feel so ill? Please do not
trouble to do so,' the Lord said, lying down too.

---

[1] A suitable colour for the Ninth Month.

That night, as her hakama was well-perfumed and her own robes as well as the bed-clothes beautiful, her feelings were as serene as usual. The Lord also lay down without any feeling of restraint. That night she answered him from time to time and he thought that there was no one like her in all the world. They therefore spent the night talking on all kinds of topics, and when the man called out that the carriage awaited him, he did not rise but called out, 'The rain will stop soon. Wait a little while.'

Meanwhile Akogi was wondering what she could do with regard to serving water for washing and whether she could obtain rice-gruel. She doubted whether it was of any use asking at the kitchen as the people of the house were all absent and rice-gruel would therefore not be being made. However she went.

'A friend of Tachihaki's came last night to consult him and could not return on account of the rain,' she told the cook. 'I should like to give him some rice-gruel, but I have no rice. Could you give me some, and also a little saké? And if there is any dried sea-weed, could you give me a little?'

'What a shame! You must be very worried to know what to serve him. We have a little food here for when the people return.'

'When they return, they will be wanting a great feast to celebrate the end of their period of abstinence,'[1] said Akogi, and seeing that the cook was in a very friendly

---

[1] Their period of abstinence from animal food while on pilgrimage.

humour, she took up a saké bottle which was standing near and began to pour out a great deal.

'Leave a little in the bottle!' exclaimed the cook.

'All right! All right!' answered Akogi.

Then she stealthily wrapped up some rice in a piece of paper, put it in her charcoal-scuttle, and took it away. She told Tsuyu to make the rice-gruel carefully while she went round looking for a nice tray to serve it on and for a basin for the washing-water.

'There must be a basin in the main building. I will go and fetch the Third Lady's for the Lord to use,' she said, letting down her hair again. Having made a grand toilet, with her obi loosely tied around her, and her hair, about three feet longer than her height, hanging down her back, she looked very pretty to Tachihaki as he followed her with his eyes as she went into the next room where the Lady, still in great distress, lay in bed.

'Would it not be better to open the lattice?' Akogi said to herself.

'It is certainly very dark here,' the Lord said, very pleased, for he would be able to see the Lady better when the lattice was opened. 'The Lady asked that it should be raised.'

Akogi therefore stood on something to open it.

The Lord then arose and dressed. 'Has the carriage arrived?' he asked.

'Yes, it is waiting at the gate,' Tachihaki answered, and they were on the point of going out when the rice-gruel was served very splendidly, and the water for washing the hands.

'Strange!' the Lord thought. 'This is very different from their having nothing, as I had been told.'

The Lady also was very surprised, wondering how the things had been obtained.

Then, as the rain had abated a little, and no one was about, they left, but reluctantly, the Shōshō looking back at the Lady as he went, and thinking her so beautiful that his heart was overwhelmed with boundless love and pity for her.

The Lady then ate a little gruel and went back to bed.

The next night being the Third Night,[1] Akogi wondered what she could arrange, and how she could serve them rice-cakes. Again, having no one else to advise her, she wrote to her aunt, the wife of Izumi no Kami. 'I received with great pleasure the things I asked you for,' she wrote. 'Thank you very much indeed. Again, it may seem strange, but I need some rice-cakes tonight for a certain reason. And also I should like a little fruit to serve with them as is usual. We thought that the guest would be staying only a little while, but the main building will be in an unlucky direction for him for forty-five days. May I therefore keep the furniture longer? And also may I have a washing-basin? I am sorry that I am giving you

---

[1] The Third Night of the consummation of the union was at this time most important, for it was customary for the bridegroom then to meet the bride's parents for the first time. If he did not come on the Third Night, therefore, it was understood that he wished the affair to end.

so much trouble by asking you so much, but I have no
one else that I can ask.'

Meanwhile the Lord had sent this poem—

> Absence the stronger
> Has made my love; let us be
> As are a figure
> And its shade in a mirror—
> Ever inseparable.

The same day the Lady answered for the first time—

> Inseparable
> Though now we may seem to be,
> This thought saddens me—
> Your love may be as fleeting
> As a shade in a mirror.

The poem was written so charmingly that when the
Lord read it his face expressed his hopes and his affection.

The answer came from the house of Izumi no Kami
for Akogi. 'Because I love you as I loved the one who
is now dead,' her aunt wrote, and as we have no daughter,
we had decided to adopt you and bring you up, giving
you every attention possible. However to our great regret,
you refused our offer. As for the furniture, keep it as
long as you need it. I am sending you a washing-basin.
It is very strange that you have not one already, for every
maid in a noble's mansion ought to have such things.
Why have you not told me before? As for the rice-cakes,
it will be very easy for me to send you some; I will have
them made at once. Do you need these things, because

tonight is your Third Night[1] when you take a husband?
I should very much like to see him. Oh, how I wish
to see you also! Let me know everything in future. A
governor in power is said to be very wealthy and my husband being a governor now, I can send you anything you
wish.' The letter being in such a friendly strain, it made
Akogi very happy.

'Why do you need rice-cakes?' the Lady asked, when
Akogi showed her this letter.

'Oh, I have a purpose,' Akogi said smilingly.

Two fine basins and a beautiful table had arrived with
the letter, and with it, a bag containing white rice and
fruit and dried food-stuffs, separated from each other by
pieces of paper, and all packed very nicely. In order that
she could serve the rice-cakes to them in grand style that
night, Akogi set out the fruit and the chestnuts.

As night fell, the rain which had stopped for a while
began to fall again in torrents. However just when Akogi
was beginning to think that the rain had prevented her
aunt from sending the rice-cakes, a man with an umbrella
arrived, carrying a chest of magnolia wood. Her joy was
beyond compare! Looking into the chest, she wondered
how her aunt could have done so much in such a short
time. There were two kinds of kusa-mochi, and two kinds

---

[1] That is when the union is regularised. The aunt deduces from the
request for mochi and fruit that it is a question of a Third Night Feast.
This possibly explains Akogi's anger at Tachihaki's present of fruit
and rice; he was possibly hinting that the time was approaching when
they would be required for the Shōshō and the Lady (see p. 17).

of rice-cakes for the Third Night ceremonies and **mochi** of all kinds of shapes, some small and some cut into all kinds of curious shapes.

'Your request was unexpected,' her aunt's accompanying letter read, 'and I am sorry that, having to make them in a hurry, I was not able to make them as I like them.'

The messenger being in a hurry to return on account of the rain, she gave him only some **saké** and sent him back with this note to express her heartfelt gratitude, 'Whatever words I may use to express my thanks, they cannot but sound too commonplace.'

Akogi was delighted that everything was now ready; she took some of the **mochi** in on a tray to the Lady.

As it grew darker, the rain fell even more heavily until it seemed as if it were impossible to put one's head out of doors even.

'What a pity!' the Shōshō said to Tachihaki. 'We can't go in this rain, can we?'

'It is a great pity for the Lady, as you have been visiting her for such a short time only. Unfortunately we can do nothing in this rain. It is not as if your not going were due to any neglect of her on your part. As it is not so, send a letter of apology,' said Tachihaki, evidently in some agitation.

'I will do that then,' said the Lord.

'Just as I was about to go to see you,' he wrote, 'this merciless rain began. As it is not through my fault that I have not come to see you, do not think badly of me.'

Tachihaki also wrote a letter to Akogi. 'I am coming to see you soon,' it read. 'Just as the Lord was starting to go to see the Lady, this rain came on. He is very disappointed that he is prevented from coming.'

Akogi was very disappointed and indignant when she received his letter, and wrote in answer to Tachihaki. 'Alas! The poem says, "Although so heavily the rain continues to fall."[1] You are both heartless. I have no words to express what I think of you. And why do you think it all right to say that you are coming here yourself? To say that you are coming after making such a blunder! The poem says, "If my lord should not come this very evening."[2] Will he really remain away tonight?'

The Lady's answer was this poem only—

> Both my sleeves were wet
> With sad tears at the thought of
> How forlorn I am;
> And once more the cold rain falls
> And wets them again tonight.

---

[1] Quoting from the poem—

> Although so heavily
> At this present time the rain
> Continues to fall;
> Yet I must go and see her
> For she is expecting me.

[2] Quoting from the poem—

> Watchers of the skies
> Say the omens are good;
> If my lord should not
> Come this very evening,*
> When can I expect him?

* 'This very evening' is the Third Night.

It was after eight o'clock when these replies arrived, and the Lord was moved with great pity as he read the Lady's reply by the light of the lamp. Then he read the reply of Akogi to Tachihaki's letter. 'Isn't she spiteful?' he exclaimed. 'It is indeed the Third Night tonight, and it must seem to her ominous that I do not go tonight. What a shame!'

The rain was becoming more and more violent. He continued to sit there, his chin cupped in his hands. Tachihaki also did not know what was best to do. At last with a great sigh, he stood up.

'Stay with me a while,' the Lord said, as he did so, and then guessing his intention, exclaimed, 'What! Are you going?'

'I am going on foot to try to comfort them.'

'If you are going, I am going too.'

'Very well then,' said Tachihaki, feeling very happy.

'Get an umbrella while I go and take off my robe,' the Lord said as he went into his room, and Tachihaki went out to find an umbrella.

Akogi, never dreaming that they were on their way, was full of lamentation and hearing her speak angrily of the rain, the Lady said shyly, 'Why do you speak like that?'

'It would be all right if only the rain were falling more gently. It is a very bad omen that it should rain in such torrents tonight,' Akogi answered.

'"The rain has begun to fall still more heavily,"'[1] the Lady quoted in a whisper. Then she felt ashamed that she should have shown to Akogi what she was thinking. Then they lay down together.

The Lord, wearing only a single thickness of white clothing, went out unattended except by Tachihaki, under the same umbrella, both feeling it very disagreeable to have to go out in such weather. They secretly opened the gate and stole out and made their way with great difficulty along the bad roads in the pitch darkness. Then at the crossing of two narrow lanes, they fell in with a procession of men with torches, evidently the retinue of some great noble.

The road was so narrow that it was impossible to avoid being seen, but they walked on the side of the road, and held their umbrella to screen their faces.

'Stop a moment, you walking there,' one of the men in the procession said. 'This is very suspicious, walking about like this in the rain in the middle of the night. We shall arrest you.'

The two stood still, feeling very embarrassed, while the men brandished their torches.

'They have white legs. Perhaps they are not thieves,'

---

[1] Quoting from the poem—

> This night and this rain
> Shall tell me at last whether
> I am loved or not;
> And now the rain has begun
> To fall still more heavily.

i.e. if my lover comes tonight, the Third Night, in spite of this heavy rain, then I shall be certain that he loves me.

one of them said.

'Upper-class pilferers may have white legs though,' said another, and as he prepared to go on, he continued, 'Why do you remain standing? Sit down.'

So the two had to sit down there, where there was much stinking filth.

'Why do you hide your faces under that umbrella?' another of a rougher character said, pulling aside the umbrella, and moving his torch about to see them as they sat among the filth. 'They are both wearing trousers they are only poor men on their way to visit their sweethearts.'

'That is so,' they all agreed and went on their way.

'That must be one of the Emon no Kami[1] going the rounds,' the Lord said, as he rose to his feet. 'I thought I should have died, expecting every minute to be arrested as a suspicious person. It was funny calling us white-legged thieves,' and they laughed very heartily as they talked over the incident.

'Well, it's a pity, but we had better go home. We are all filthy. If we go to them in this stinking state, they will be very distant with us, said the Lord to Tachihaki's great amusement.

'When you come to her in the rain like this, she will realise how very much you love her and she will think that the smell is the smell of musk. Our destination is

---

[1] One of the Commanders, Right or Left, of the Bodyguard.

near and your house a long way off. I hope you will decide to go on.'

The Lord agreed, thinking that it would be a shame to allow all this labour in coming so far to be in vain.

With great difficulty they opened the door, and entered. At Tachihaki's apartment, they both washed their feet.

'Get up before dawn. We must get away while it is still dark. We must not stay too long or we shall look very funny going home in this state,' said the Lord, who went then to tap on the lattice.

The Lady, meanwhile, had been lying weeping in great distress, perhaps not so tormented with disappointment that the Lord had not come that night as with her fears that the Great Lady should get to know of the affair. Her head was all in confusion with her vexation at the sorrows of life.

Akogi, annoyed that all her grand preparations had been in vain, lay beside the Lady. Suddenly she rose.

'The lattice-door is rattling,' she said as she went up to it.

'Open the door.' She was surprised and delighted to hear the Lord's voice. She opened the door and he entered, drenched to the skin. And when she heard that he had come all the way on foot, she was amazed at the depths of his incomparable love.

'How is it that you have got so wet?' she asked.

'I took pity on Korenari; he was afraid that he would

get scolded if we did not come. We pulled our clothes up over our knees, but we fell down and got all dirty,' he said, taking off his robes.

'I will dry them,' she said, as she offered him one of the Lady's robes to put on.

Having undressed, he went to where the Lady lay.

'If because I come to you in this wretched state, you embrace me the more lovingly, I shall be very happy,' he said.

As he felt around, he found that her sleeves were damp. Evidently, he thought sorrowfully, she had been weeping because he had not come.

> Of what have you been
> Thinking, that your sleeves are wet?[1]

> Both my sleeves are wet
> With the rain that shall tell me
> Whether you love me or not.[1]

'If the rain is to show you whether you are loved or not, you may know that you are loved, because I am come thus,' he said as he lay down.

Akogi then brought in some rice-cakes, nicely arranged on a tray.

'Please take some,' she said.

'Oh, I am too tired,' he said and did not rise.

'However, I beg you to take some this evening,' she said.

---

[1] The question by the Lord and the answer of the Lady forming one poem,

'What is it that you have?' the Lord said and raising his head saw that they were rice-cakes, nicely served.

'Who has prepared all this?' he thought. 'This must have been done in expectation of my visit.'

'Oh, it's the rice-cakes, isn't it?' he said, finding it all rather amusing. 'Is there any special way of eating them? What must I do?'

'Haven't you learned yet what you have to do?' asked Akogi.

'How could I have learned? I have remained single up till now. So I have never eaten them.'

'You must take three,' said Akogi, on hearing this.

'This is like a child's game,' he said. 'How many does the Lady take?'

'As many as she pleases,' answered Akogi laughing.

'Take these,' said the Lord to the Lady but she was too shy to take them.

'The Kurōdo no Shōshō took them like this, did he? he asked, as he ate them, keeping strictly to the rule by eating three.

'Yes, certainly he did,' answered Akogi.

Then as it was already late, they lay down to sleep.

When Akogi returned to Tachihaki, she found him still crouching down drenched.

'You have got very wet. Didn't you have an umbrella?' she said.

Then in a low voice, but with a certain amount of laughter, he told her what had happened on the way.

'There has been nothing like his great love neither at the present nor in olden times. Don't you think it is incomparable?' he said.

'Well, we're rather pleased, but we're not perfectly satisfied.'

'Rather pleased! How wickedly ungrateful women are! If the Lord should turn against the Lady and not visit her, don't you think that you ought to forgive him thirty times on account of what he has done this evening?'

'As usual you are speaking with the intention of putting things right for yourself,' answered Akogi, and lay down to go to sleep.

'If he had not come here tonight, how badly you would have treated me indeed!' Tachihaki said, and he also lay down to sleep.

And as the night was already far advanced, it was long past dawn when they awoke.

'How are we to get out? Is anyone about yet?' the Lord said as he lay in bed.

'What a pity! The people are coming back from Ishiyama today. And someone may come in here.' So Akogi was worrying, as she busied herself preparing the rice-gruel and the water for washing.

'Why are you walking about? What are you worrying about?' Tachihaki inquired.

'How can I be otherwise than worried? The room is too small to hide anyone in, and I am afraid of someone coming in. That is why I am hurrying,' replied Akogi.

'Send for my carriage. I shall be going soon,' the Lord said. But just at that moment the people returned from Ishiyama, making a great disturbance. 'It's no use trying to get out now,' he said and remained inside the room.

The Lady was terrified now, wondering what she should do if anyone should come as there was no place where the Lord could hide.

Akogi was also very agitated but she went on with her task of serving the rice-gruel and other food. She busied herself getting the washing-water, but everything seemed to go wrong, and she wished she had not to do everything by herself.

Soon the Kita no Kata, having descended from her carriage, was calling for Akogi and abusing her for her slowness in coming, so Akogi had to go out, leaving the lattice open after her as there was no time to close it. She then went to the lattice door of the main building.

'The people who have been on the pilgrimage are all tired and must have some rest,' the Great Lady said to her. 'But you have been resting all this while. Why didn't you come out to meet us when we arrived? I have never met anyone so annoying as the people in that person's service. Well, I think I shall have to send you back to her service.'

Akogi was very glad indeed to hear that suggestion, but she answered, 'I was taking off my dirty clothes.'

'Bring the washing-water for us then,' the Kita no Kata ordered and Akogi was left almost too agitated to speak or to move.

When the breakfast was all ready, Akogi went to the kitchen and cajoling the cook by calling her 'My dear,' she was able to obtain some food in exchange for a quantity of white rice. This she served to the Shōshō and the Lady. The Lord, having heard that they were in want even of necessities, found the breakfast splendid, while the Lady wondered how it had all been prepared. Neither the Lord nor the Lady, who was still in bed, ate much, so Akogi put the food into bowls and served it to Tachihaki.

'I have been in service here for a long time,' commented Tachihaki when he saw how splendidly he was served, 'but I have never had food sent down to me before. However it must be because of the Lord's visit.'

'The Kita no Kata has sent it to you to show how delighted she is at the Lord's coming,' answered Akogi.

'Oh, how awful if she got to know!' exclaimed Tachihaki, and both of them laughed heartily.

The Shōshō and the Lady remained in bed till noon. Then the Kita no Kata came to look in at the Lady's room, a quite unusual thing for her to do. She tried the inside door but it was fastened.

'Open the door,' she cried.

Akogi and the Lady were both very troubled to know what to do.

'It is all right,' said the Lord. 'Open it. If she should lift the curtain of the screen, I will hide under the bedclothes.'

The Lady feared that the Kita no Kata might do that; she was rude enough. However there was nothing she could do, so she pushed back the screen and sat in front of it.

'Why are you so long opening this door?' demanded the Great Lady.

'For to-day and to-morrow, going through that door is going in an unlucky direction,' explained Akogi.

'What a fuss to make! How can it be in an unlucky direction? How can you have an unlucky direction in a house that is not your own?'

'Open the door then, dear,' the Lady said to Akogi.

The door was unfastened and the Kita no Kata pushed it open roughly and entered. Then she sat down and looked around, for the room had been changed; it was furnished very well, with even a screen; the Lady herself was well-dressed, and the whole room was filled with the fragrant perfume of incense.

'Both you and the room are changed,' the Great Lady then said in a suspicious tone. 'Has anything happened while I have been absent?'

'What could have happened?' the Lady answered, and blushed.

Meanwhile the Shōshō, eager to see what she looked like, peeped through the joinings of the curtains of the screen as he was lying down. He saw that she was dressed, though not very elegantly, in many white silk damask robes. Her face was flattish; however, the shape of her mouth was charming, and she appeared fairly good-looking and lady-like; but at the corners of her eyes were signs of age which marred her beauty.

'I bought a mirror to-day on my way home,' she was saying, 'And I thought that it would be very nice to keep it in your box. I have come to ask if I may have it for a while.'

'All right,' answered the Lady.

'I am very glad that you have consented so willingly. Give it to me,' said the Kita no Kata and took the box. She put the mirror which she had bought into it and found that it fitted perfectly.

'It is very fortunate that I have been able to find such a nice box for it. Gold-lacquering is not done so well nowadays as that on this box,' the Great Lady went on, stroking the box with her hand.

Akogi watched all this with anger. 'The Lady must have a box for her mirror though,' she said at last.

'I will look for one and send it,' the Kita no Kata answered, standing up. 'But whose is this screen?' she asked in a very good-humoured manner. 'It is very nice. And you have other furniture which is new to me. Something must have happened here.'

The Lady was ashamed that the Shōshō should be listening to this conversation. 'I missed the screen very much,' she answered, 'so I sent for it.'

However, the Great Lady still thought that there was something strange about everything there.

'It is ridiculous,' Akogi burst out when the Kita no

Kata had gone. 'She has never given you anything as a gift, and yet she makes you present her with all your furniture like this. When your screens and other things were borrowed for the marriages, she said that they would be returned when they had been repaired, that they would only be kept for a short while. But now they are being used everywhere as if they were no longer yours. Even your tableware has been taken.[1] I shall go and see the Great Lord and get everything back. Before our very eyes, all your furniture is becoming the property of the people in the main building. You are very generous in allowing them to have all these things. But do they show any gratitude?'

'Whether that is so or not,' the Lady answered, amused at this outburst, 'she will return the things when she has finished with them.'

The Lord, full of admiring wonder at her patience, came out, pushing aside the screen, and took the Lady back to bed.

'The Kita no Kata still looks young,' the Lord said to her, 'Do her daughters resemhle her?'

'Oh, no, they are very pretty girls,' the Lady replied. 'I am sorry that you have had such a bad first impression of her. What will she say if she finds out about your having been here?'

He saw that her reserve towards him was slipping away from her, and he found her very charming; he was glad

---

[1] No doubt Akogi is taking advantage of this incident to 'explain' to the Shōshō why they have so little furniture.

that he had not given up coming to see her when at first
sight she had not seemed so wonderful as he had expected
from what he had heard of her.

Soon Ako, a maid of the household, brought in exchange for the Lady's mirror-box a black-lacquered box
about nine inches long and three inches deep, an old
damaged box from which the lacquer was peeling off in
various places.

'This is not a very good box, but the lacquering is
well-done,' was the message with it from the Kita no Kata.

This made Akogi laugh. She put the mirror in and
found that the box was too large for the mirror. 'It
doesn't fit,' Akogi said. 'Don't put it in that box. It
doesn't look nice.'

'But please do not say that. It is a present to me,'
the Lady said. 'Really the box is very nice,' she added
as she sent away the messenger.

'Where did she find such an old-fashioned thing? All
the things she treasures up are like this—matchless in
their utter worthlessness—and yet she considers them
wonderful,' was the Lord's comment as he examined the
box.

Next morning when the Shōshō left, the Lady got up.
'How did you manage to save me from shame!' she said
to Akogi. 'I am glad that you got this screen.'

Akogi explained fully how she had managed to obtain it.

'One would not have expected a girl of her age to

manage things so cleverly,' the Lady thought. 'What a dear girl she is! Really she acts like a guardian to me.'

Akogi also told the Lady what Tachihaki had related to her of their adventures on the way. 'If he remains constant to you, how happy we shall be in this world, hitherto so hateful for us!' Akogi said with emotion at the end of her story.

On the next night, the Shōshō was on duty at the Court and so was unable to visit the Lady. Next morning, the Lady received a letter from him. 'Last night I was not able to see you as I had to go to the Court,' the Lord wrote very lovingly. 'I therefore amused myself imagining how angry Akogi would be with Korenari because I had not arrived. It is terrifying how spiteful Akogi is becoming through following the example of the Kita no Kata. Last night I was certainly feeling that "tame to me seems that which formerly I thought was love."[1]

> Years did I exist
> In that former state of mine,
>   Ignorant of love;
> But now apart from you, can
> I not pass one single night.

Will you not leave that place which to you is full of sorrows?

---

[1] Quoting a line of the poem—
> Before I met you
> I thought I knew what love was;
>   Now I have met you,
> And tame to me seems that which
> Formerly I thought was love.

I am looking for a house where you can live free from anxiety.'

'Get the Lady to write an answer quickly and I will take it at once,' said Tachihaki.

'You have spoken very ill of me to the Shōshō,' said Akogi to Tachihaki when she had read the Lord's letter. 'But I must resign myself to his abusing me thus when I have only you in whom to confide."

The Lady made this answer to the letter—'Last night, I was thinking, "This shower of rain which now unseasonably—!"[1]

> What course would be best,
> To love you or not, can I
> Still not yet decide,
> Nor can I find a way
> Out of these troubles of mine.

As it has been truly said, "The entrances to this world do seem closed."[2]

---

[1] Quoting from the poem—
> This shower of rain that
> Now so unseasonably
> Wets both of my sleeves
> Doubtless is because your love
> Approaches now its autumn.

[2] Quoting from the poem written by Taira no Sadafumi on losing his position at Court—
> I cannot pretend
> The entrances to this world
> Do seem closed to all.
> Why then do I find it so hard
> To make my way into it?

It is almost impossible to escape. As for Akogi, no doubt, in the eyes of one who is guilty she seems a fearsome person.'

Tachihaki had been given this letter and was about to go out with it when he was told that he was needed immediately by the Kurōdo no Shōshō.[1] Having no time to put the letter in a place of safety, he put it into his bosom and went in to see why he was needed. He found that he was wanted to dress his master's hair, and in dressing the back hair, while they were both stooping forward, the letter fell out unnoticed by him. But the Kurōdo no Shōshō saw it and picked it up quickly. His hair finished, he went to his room and finding the contents of the letter very interesting, he showed it to the Third Lady, his wife.

'Look at this,' he said to her. 'Korenari dropped it. The handwriting is very fine.'

'That is the Lady Ochikubo's handwriting.'

'Who is the Lady Ochikubo? That is a strange name for a person, isn't it?'

'But it is someone's name. She is the person who makes all the clothes here.' With that the conversation ended, and the Third Lady kept the letter, feeling that there was something very suspicious about it.

Tachihaki put away the hair-dressing utensils and prepared to go out to deliver the letter. But when he felt for it, he found that it was missing. Greatly disturbed,

---

[1] The Kurōdo no Shōshō was of course Tachihaki's master.

he shook his clothing and untied his **obi** but could not find it. Horrified to think of what might happen if it were lost, he stood there red with shame and fear.

'I did not go out of the room, so the letter must be here, if I have dropped it,' he said to himself, picking up the cushion and shaking it. But the letter was not to be found. 'Has someone picked it up then?' He was in great distress when he thought of what might happen in that case. He sat there, his chin in his hands, pondering over what he should do, when the Kurōdo no Shōshō passed him on his way out.

'Well, Korenari,' the Kurōdo no Shōshō said to him with a laugh, on seeing him, 'why are you looking so downcast? Have you lost something?'

Realising by this that it was he who had taken the letter, Tachihaki felt ready to die. 'Well, I entreat you to return it to me,' he said, very vexed.

'I do not know anything about it. It is the Third Lady who quoted about you the poem, "The pine-clad mountains of Sue,"[1] his master answered as he went out.

Tachihaki could not say one word in answer. The Lady, he knew, would be unspeakably shocked when she heard, so he went to ask Akogi what he should do.

---

[1] Quoting a line of this poem in derisive allusion to his change of affections from Akogi to Ochikubo—

> Ere you forsaking,
> And another I should love,
> The waves of the sea
> Will mount and roll over the
> Pine-clad mountains of Sue.

'As I had to go to the Taishō's mansion,' he said to her, 'I was just on the point of going to take the answer to the Shōshō, when I was called by the Kurōdo no Shōshō to arrange his hair. While I was doing this, I dropped the letter and he picked it up. I am very sorry that this has happened.' He was in great distress.

'How terrible!' exclaimed Akogi. 'What harsh words the Kita no Kata will use! She is already suspicious and this will make her scold the Lady even more harshly.' The two worried about what they should do until they were in a cold sweat.

The Third Lady took the letter to her mother and explained how it had been found.

'Well, you see,' said the Kita no Kata, 'I had my suspicions. To whom can it be addressed? Can it be to Tachihaki; he had the letter on him? It seems that the man, whoever he is, has tempted her to leave this place, for she says here that it is impossible for her to escape. I am very sorry that this has happened. I had made up my mind that no man should know of her. Now if she has already found a lover, it is certain that she will not stay here; the man will be sure to carry her off. It will be very troublesome if we lose her. I was very glad that I had someone to work for my daughters. What rascal is it that has plotted to steal her away? If I had known before, I would have prevented anyone seeing her at all.' She kept the letter, and watched for developments, and as she said nothing, Akogi and Tachihaki in suspense were all the more worried.

Akogi told the Lady how the letter had been lost. 'We cannot excuse ourselves for our carelessness. Would you please write the letter once more?'

To say only that the Lady was made very miserable by this information would be a foolish understatement of her feelings, especially because she knew that the Kita no Kata would be certain to see the letter.

'No, I shall not write again,' she answered, feeling infinitely depressed.

Tachihaki also was so distressed that he shut himself up in his own room and did not go to see the Shōshō.

'Why did you not answer my letter?' the Sakon no Shōshō asked when he arrived that night.

'Because the Kita no Kata was here at the moment,' the Lady said.

They went to bed. Too soon the day dawned, and the Lord prepared to return, but it was already too late and people were about, so instead of going out, he returned to the Lady's room and went back to bed and lay peacefully talking to the Lady, while Akogi was busy getting the food ready.

'How old is the Fourth Lady?' he asked.

'Twelve or thirteen. She is very pretty.'

'No doubt then it is she whom the Chūnagon plans that I should marry. Her foster-mother knows one of my household and she brought a letter saying that the Kita no Kata also favours the marriage. Her foster-mother pressed the matter forward very strongly. What do you think about making public now how far our relations have gone?'

'I should be very grieved if you did.'

This answer sounded to him very childlike. 'It is obviously inconvenient for me to come here,' he went on. 'Will you not move to some place which I shall find for you to live in?'

'Just as you like.'

'Good,' he said and still continued to lie there.

The date was about the twenty-third of the Eleventh Month. The husband of the Third Lady, the Kurōdo no Shōshō, was selected at very short notice as a dancer at the festival of the Kamo Shrine, and so the Kita no Kata was very worried and excited. Akogi feared, and rightly, that there would be sewing to be done; the Great Lady sent a **hakama** cut out ready to be sewn.

'Have this made at once. And there is more work still which will be sent later on,' the message with it said.

The Lady was lying in bed on the other side of the screen, so it was Akogi who took the message.

'I do not know what is the matter with the Lady,' she answered the messenger, 'but she is still in bed; she has felt ill since last night. I will give her the message when she gets up.'

The messenger went away and the Lady tried to rise to do the sewing but the Shōshō prevented her. 'How can I lie idly in bed alone?' he said.

'How did she set about the task?' the Kita no Kata asked the messenger when he had returned to her.

'She did not begin it. Akogi said that she was still deigning to take an honourable rest"[1]

'"Deigning to take an honourable rest." Do not use such honorifics in speaking of that person. That person must not be spoken of in the same terms as we are. I do not want to hear it. And to think of a young girl sleeping in the afternoon! How unpleasant it is to see people putting on such airs!' she said, with a scornful smile, and taking up some under-robes, already cut out, she went to the Lady's room. The Lady was startled and came out from behind the screen.

The Great Lady could see that the **hakama** had not yet even been commenced, and she was furious with anger. 'You have not even put your hand to the work yet. And I thought that you would have finished it by now. It is very strange that you should disobey my orders like this. Recently your mind has not been on your work at all. It has been occupied only with making your toilet.'

The Lady was ashamed at the thought of the Shōshō's hearing this abusive speech. 'As I felt very ill, I have been delayed a little. I will get it done quickly.'

'Don't take hold of it as if it were a nervous, prancing

---

[1] The messenger uses the honorific 'ōtonogomori' which is used very rarely indeed in this book; Akogi had not used it in the speech of which this is a report. The only other occasions it is used in the narrative are in the description of their going to bed on the previous night and immediately in the servant Shōnagon's talk of, and to, the Lady Ochikubo which follows.

horse,' the Kita no Kata said. 'It is only because we have no one else to sew these things that I have given them to you to do, in spite of your being so unwilling and unreliable. If these robes are not finished quickly, I shall not allow you to stay here any longer,' she went on angrily, throwing down the under-robes and turning to go out. Then she caught sight of the skirt of the Shōshō's Court-robe projecting from behind the screen.

'Oh, whose robe is that?' she asked.

'It has been brought here to be sewn,' Akogi replied, fearing that everything had now been discovered.

'She does work for others first and neglects ours! It counts for nothing with her that we have taken care of her all these years. What an ungrateful world this is!' cried the Kita no Kata as she went out, full of anger. From behind, her hair looked very thin for she had had many children.

'How fat and ungraceful she looks!' the Lord thought, as he lay and peeped through the joinings of the curtains of the screen.

Hardly knowing what she was doing, the Lady began to pleat the folds of the **hakama**, but the Shōshō caught hold of her skirt and urged her to go back to bed. Smiling, she went back to bed for there was nothing else to do.

'How hateful she is! Do not do any more sewing. Let her become more angry still. What horrible language she uses towards you! Has she been as abusive as this all these years? How have you been able to endure it?' he exclaimed.

'I am a "flower of a wild pear tree,"'[1] the Lady quoted in answer.

Night came, and the lattice door was shut and the room lighted up. The Lady was wondering how she could finish the Skirt, when the Kita no Kata came stealthily along to see if the Lady was doing the sewing. She looked in; she could see the light burning and the sewing scattered about, but no one was to be seen. She was very angry at the thought that the Lady had gone to bed and called out for the Great Lord to come.

'Please, Great Lord,' she cried, 'come and speak to the Lady Ochikubo. I cannot stand her insolence. These robes are needed urgently. But she is always lying down behind a screen which she has got from somewhere.'

'Come nearer and tell me what you are saying,' the Chūnagon answered, and the Shōshō and the Lady could not hear the rest of what she told him, as she went out of their hearing.

'What does she mean by "Ochikubo"?' asked the Lord, for he had not heard the name "Ochikubo no Kimi" before.

---

[1] Quoting the last line of the poem—

> Although in this house
> I am able to find nought
> But care and sorrow;
> Yet it seems that nowhere else
> Can I find a hiding-place.

The reference to the 'pear-flower' disappears when the MEANING of the poem is considered.

'I do not know,' answered the Lady, feeling much ashamed.

'Why do they call someone by that name? It must of course be someone very unimportant; it is certainly not an elegant name. The Great Lady talks badly of people out of spite,' said the Shōshō as they lay in bed.

A Court-robe cut out ready for sewing was next sent in. The Kita no Kata, fearing that it would not be finished quickly enough, told the Great Lord everything and urged him to go to speak to the Lady. The Great Lord therefore went to her room. 'Why are you behaving so badly and neglecting to do what you are told, Lady Ochikubo?' he asked her, opening the door. 'As your mother is dead, I have been anxious for you to gain the love of the Great Lady. Why have you neglected the work which she wanted done quickly and have done work for other people? If this work is not finished tonight, I shall not treat you as a daughter of mine in future.'

The Lady did not answer, but only wept, her tears falling 'tsubu, tsubu.'

The Chūnagon having said this went away.

The Lady was in the depths of shame that the Lord had heard all this, and had learnt that it was she who was called by the name which he had spoken so badly of. She wanted to die at once. She pushed away the sewing, and turning her back to the light, wept bitterly. The Shōshō also wept in sympathy for her, for he could understand her sorrow and shame.

'Come into bed for a little while,' he said. He persuaded her to lie down with him, and he comforted her as well as he could.

'It is she who is called the Lady Ochikubo,' he thought. 'I am sorry that it was my contemptuous words that have humiliated her. It is strange that the Chūnagon abuses her as much as her step-mother does. He must hate her very much. How can I make them see her worth?' and then it was that he firmly determined to avenge the Lady's wrongs on the Kita no Kata.

'What I have said will make her angry,' the Kita no Kata was thinking meanwhile, 'and being alone she will work more slowly, and will not be able to finish all those robes.' She therefore sent a servant, a pretty girl named Shōnagon, to help her.

'Which part shall I help you to sew?' Shōnagon asked the Lady. 'Why are you taking a rest? The Kita no Kata keeps on saying that you won't be able to finish them in time. You know that, don't you?'

'I feel ill,' answered the Lady. 'Please finish the rest of the pleating of the **hakama**.'

Shōnagon drew the **hakama** to her and began to sew.

'If you are feeling better, could you get up?' Shōnagon said soon afterwards, 'I do not know how to do these pleats.'

'Wait a moment. I will show you,' the Lady said, raising herself up a little and coming out on her knees.

The Shōshō looked out and saw by the light of the lamp that Shōnagon was very pretty; the maids of the house were all very pretty, he thought.

Shōnagon looked at the Lady and saw how the tears glistened on her cheeks. She must have felt a deep compassion for her. 'If I tell you what I think, you will say that I am a great flatterer,' she said out of her pity. 'But it would be a shame if I did not say anything; and you would never know my feelings. I should like to leave these people whom I have reluctantly served for so many years and enter your service, for I have seen for a long, long time that you are very kind-hearted. The people in the main building are very inquisitive and censorious, and so we have to be very careful. Therefore I have not been able to help you even in secret.'

'I am very glad to hear you speak so kindly,' the Lady said, 'for even those people who ought to be most kind to me show me no sympathy.'

'Yes, it is certainly very strange. It is perhaps natural that the Kita no Kata is cruel to you, but it is disgraceful that your sisters never visit you and do not treat you kindly,' and Shōnagon. 'It is a great pity that so beautiful a Lady as you should live here so forlorn. They are busy now preparing for the wedding of the Fourth Lady. It is what the Kita no Kata wants that is always done here.'

'That is good news. Who is to be her husband?'

'The Sakon no Shōshō; the son of the Sadaishō. He is very handsome. People at the Court praise him as one who will rise to great heights of power. He is also high in the favour of the Mikado. He is not yet married, and will be a good son-in-law. The Great Lord has always said that he would like to marry one of his daughters into that family. The Kita no Kata has been very busy trying to arrange the marriage, and finding to her great delight that the Fourth Lady's foster-mother had an acquaintance in the family, after a lot of talking and whispering, she got her to take a letter to the Shōshō.'

The Lady found it very amusing to hear all this while the Shōshō was so near. 'And then?' she asked. Her face now beamed with smiles; in the light of the lamp she was so beautiful that it filled one with adoration to look at her. 'What does the Shōshō say to this?' she asked.

'I do not know; but he has probably consented, and the people here are making all their preparations in secret for the marriage,' Shōnagon answered.

The Shōshō wanted to call out, 'It is a lie,' but on second thoughts decided to remain silent and lie where he was.

'If another son-in-law comes to live here, it will make it all the harder for you. If you get in touch with someone, it would be better for you to get married,' said Shōnagon.

'What! Such an ugly person as I cannot hope to do that, can I?'

'Oh, that is not so at all. Why do you say such things? The other ladies in this mansion who are so tenderly cared for are much——.' Shōnagon left her sentence unfinished and then went on, 'You know the Ben no Shōshō whose good looks are so famous, and who for this reason is nicknamed Katano no Shōshō.[1] Shōshō, my cousin, is in his service and I often go to visit her. I once saw her in the Lord's apartment when he was there. He learnt that I was from this house, and he was very attentive to me. His beauty is fascinating—absolutely incomparable. He told me that he had heard that my master had several daughters and asked me to tell him about them one by one beginning with the eldest. So I told him a little about each, and when I told him about you, he showed a great deal of interest and sympathy. "Such a one is my ideal," he said. "Will you not take a letter to her from me?" But I replied, "As her mother is dead she is very sad and lonely in spite of the fact that she has many sisters, and so she does not think of such things." "It is because she has no mother that I feel such tender sympathy towards her," he went on, "My ideal is one who is beautiful, responsive to affection, sympathetic and modest at the same time. To search for such a lady, I would go as far as China or Korea. Here, except for my sister, the Imperial Consort, is there any such lady who is of noble birth? Living in my house as my darling, she would be much happier than living such a hard life as she does now." In this way Katano no Shōshō spoke very intimately with me until far into the night. The next time I went to his mansion, he said, "How are you progressing with that matter? May I

---

[1] A character in an old story not now extant.

write her a letter?" However I replied, "'There has been no opportunity yet for me to speak to her about it, but when I can, I will ask her.'"

The Lady made no comment on Shōnagon's story.

Just then, however, a messenger came in from Shōnagon's room. 'I have something important to say to you,' he said to Shōnagon.

Shōnagon therefore went out to speak to him. 'A visitor has come and wishes to speak to you in your room,' the messenger told her.

'Wait a moment. I must tell the Lady,' said Shōnagon and returned to the room.

'I thought that I should be able to stay and help you,' said Shōnagon to the Lady. 'However, someone has come to see me on an important matter. There are a great many other things which I want to tell you of—of his brilliant and charming conversation. I will tell you everything he said later. But do not say anything to the Great Lady about my having gone back to my room. She would think it strange and would punish me. If I can, I will come back,' she said as she went out.

The Lord now pushed aside the screen. 'She speaks very charmingly, doesn't she?' he said. 'I was just thinking how fascinating she was when she began to praise the beauty of Katano no Shōshō. And then I took a violent dislike to her. And because of my presence, you could not re-echo her praises and had perforce to keep silent. If I had not been here, you would have accepted his offer.

If you but read the letter he sends you, you will be lost.
His methods are so wonderful that not one of his letters
ever fails to produce the effect he desires. He has had
affairs with other men's wives, even with consorts of the
Mikado, and the result is that he has never been promoted. He says he will take you as his "darling"; he
proposes to make more of you than of any of his other
ladies.' His tone was very cold and cruel, and the Lady
did not answer him, thinking that his manner of expression was very vulgar.

'Why do you not say something? Is it that you do
not wish to answer because I am abusing him whom you
esteem so much? Every woman in the Capital allows
herself to be led astray by Katano no Shōshō. How I
envy him his power!'

'I am not among that number,' she said in a low voice.

'He comes of a noble family and so later on you would
become an Imperial consort perhaps.'

She did not know anything about such things, and so
did not answer.

Her white hands engaged in her sewing looked very
beautiful indeed.

Akogi, thinking that Shōnagon was with her mistress,
had gone into her own room in order to console Tachihaki
who was not feeling very well. So when the Lady had
finished the under-robe, and wished to fold the Court-
robe, she said, 'Well, I shall have to call Akogi to get
up to help.'

'I will pull it,' answered the Shōshō.

'It would look very strange for you to do it.'

'No, let me do it. I am very clever at it,' said the Lord, getting up and putting the screen in front of the door, and then sitting down opposite her to pull the other end of the robe. He looked extremely foolish doing it for his actions were very clumsy; he was certainly going too far in his efforts to be kind to her. The Lady laughed as they folded the robe.

'It is really true that you are going to marry the Fourth Lady then, isn't it?' said the Lady. 'Why do you continue to pretend that you do not know anything about it, when all the arrangements have already been made between her parents and yours.'

'Nonsense! When you become the darling of Katano no Shōshō, then I will announce my marriage to the Fourth Lady,' the Lord said laughing. 'It is getting very late. Do come to bed.'

'I shall not take long to finish this sewing. You go to bed. I will just finish this.'

'I cannot let you stay up alone,' he said, and stayed up with her.

'She will have gone to bed without finishing the sewing,' thought the Kita no Kata. Therefore, when everything was quiet and everyone asleep, she went and peeped into the room at the place she had used before, being anxious to see if the Lady had gone to bed.

Shōnagon was not to be seen. The Kita no Kata could

not see well on account of the screen, but looking in from the other side, she saw the Lady with her back towards her, folding something which she had in her hands, and a man sitting opposite her pulling the other end of a robe. The Kita no Kata felt drowsy no longer; she gazed in amazement at the man. He was dressed in a fine, white robe with a glossy yellow silk under-robe, and a lady's skirt lay over his legs. He looked very handsome and charming in the bright light, more handsome than the Kurōdo no Shōshō whom till then she had prized as her ideal.

'I thought she had found a lover,' said the Great Lady to herself, shocked at this discovery, 'but I thought he would be some ordinary man. Really this is no ordinary man, and their love is no ordinary love when he sits with her like this and helps her with such feminine work. This is a bad state of affairs. If she improves her position, she will not be available for me to use as I wish.' She forgot all about the robes to be made, and stood there for a while, burning with malice and jealousy.

'This unaccustomed work has tired me rather,' the Lord said. 'And you also are sleepy. Go to bed and leave the sewing unfinished. And put the Kita no Kata into her usual state of bad temper.'

'But it makes me very sad when I see her angry,' said the Lady, going on with her sewing, to the Lord's disgust. So he blew out the light with his fan.

'How impatient you are! Let me put away the sewing

first, at least,' said the Lady, rather reprovingly.

'Oh, hang it over the screen,' he said, taking it and throwing it untidily over the screen. Then he took her in his arms and carried her to bed.

This kind of talk had made the Kita no Kata very angry. 'That man said "her usual bad temper",' she reflected as she lay in bed that night. 'He must have heard me speaking angrily to her, or else she must have told him.' She was filled with malice as she planned what she should do. 'I will tell the Great Lord about this,' she thought. 'No, I won't though. He looked very nice and he must be a noble, judging by the noble's robe which I saw there. If he is, he will surely wish to take her publicly. The position is dangerous. Instead of doing that, I will tell the Great Lord that it is Tachihaki who is her lover; that she has done such a thing because she has been left too free; and that she must be shut up closely somewhere. They will not be able to talk again of making me angry!' she thought, planning all kinds of things in her malice. 'When she is kept closely confined, she will forget this lover. My uncle, the Tenyaku no Suke,[1] who lives here, in spite of his poverty and his sixty years, is very dissolute. I will keep him near her all the time.' So she lay and planned all the night.

Meanwhile the Shōshō was talking fondly to the Lady,

[1] The Assistant-Director of the Bureau of Medicine of the Imperial Household Department.

and when dawn came, he went away. And the Lady then began sewing again busily.

When the Kita no Kata got up, she sent for the robes for she thought they could not have been finished yet, and that therefore she would be able to storm at the Lady. The robes were brought back, all folded up beautifully. This was a great surprise to her, and an unpleasant one, but she said nothing and only wondered how the sewing could have been finished so soon.

A letter arrived from the Shōshō. 'Tell me if your step-mother was angry because the robe was not finished,' he wrote. 'I should very much like to know. Well, I came away and forgot my flute. Would you please send it to me? I am going to a concert at the Court.'

She found the flute, a splendid one, wrapped it up and sent it to the Lord with this letter. 'Do not speak so cruelly of my step-mother becoming angry. People might learn of your speaking in this way. Do not think of her as always being so bad-tempered. Now she is in smiling good-humour. I send the flute with this. When I think that you could forget this, I think—'

> When thus you forget
> This your long, long cherished flute,
>   It cannot but cause
> The suspicion that your vows
> You as easily forget.

The Lord was very sorry to read this and answered—

> Full of fear, you think
> That constant I may not be,
> But I swear that like
> The immortal bamboo root,
> My love shall last for ever.

Meanwhile, just at the time when the Shōshō was sending this, the Kita no Kata was telling her husband what she had discovered. 'What I feared has come to pass,' she said to him. 'The Lady Ochikubo has done a very shameful and scandalous thing. And also, if it had been with some stranger, it would not be so dreadful. It is really outrageous.'

'What is the matter?' asked the Great Lord, surprised and thoroughly agitated.

'A man called Kotachihaki, in the service of the Kurōdo no Shōshō, has been, we have understood, Akogi's lover for several months. But now it appears that he has transferred his affections to the Lady Ochikubo. Foolishly enough, he let fall in front of the Kurōdo no Shōshō a letter which the Lady had sent him and which he was carrying in his bosom. The Kurōdo no Shōshō saw it and, being a very shrewd man, pressed Tachihaki to confess whose letter it was. Tachihaki was not able to hide anything and told him all the story. The Shōshō then came to me with a very horrified countenance and said, "You have got a fine new son-in-law, haven't you? What a shameful thing! What will people say? You must not allow him to remain here."'

The Chūnagon was very old, but it was with great force that he snapped his fingers at this. 'What an unspeakable thing she has done!' he said, when he had learned all the details. 'Living here, everyone looks on her as our daughter. This fellow is of the Sixth Court Rank, but he is not even a Kurōdo official. The fellow has no rank; he is only a **tachihaki**;[1] he is only twenty years old and as short in stature as a dwarf. How could he have done such a thing! I had thought of marrying her off to a Provincial Governor without explaining the circumstances of her birth. What a shame!'

'It is a great pity,' agreed the Kita no Kata. 'I suggest that you shut her up in a room before her scandalous conduct becomes known to everyone. Otherwise in her love she will run away with him. Later, you can do as you like with her.'

'Yes, that is a good plan. Drive her out of her room and shut her up in the store-room in the North Wing. Give her nothing to eat. Starve her to death,' he said, speaking with the randomness of one in his second childhood.

The Kita no Kata was delighted. She picked up her skirts, went to the Lower Room and confronted the Lady. 'What an unspeakable thing you have done!' she said. 'The Great Lord is very angry indeed at your disgracing our daughters like this. He said to me, "Do not let her live in the Lower Room any longer. Confine her strictly somewhere at once, where I can watch her. Drive her

---

[1] Bodyguard of the Crown Prince.

here at once." Come with me now then.'

The Lady was grieved, frightened, disgusted; she could do nothing but weep. She wondered what her father could have heard; any words would be foolishly inadequate to describe her state of mind.

Akogi came out; she also was extremely agitated. 'What is it that the Great Lord has heard that she has done?' Akogi asked.

'Do not interfere,' the Kita no Kata said to Akogi. 'The Great Lord has not told me all the facts; he has learnt them from someone outside. You think more about an evil woman like this than about the Lady in whose service you really are and who has been very kind to you. This person is not to stay any longer in this room and you are not to stay in this house any longer either,' and then turning to the Lady, she said, 'Come. The Great Lord has something to say to you.' She lifted the Lady to her feet by pulling her up by the shoulders of her robe. Akogi wept bitterly, and the Lady also, as if she were out of her senses. Kicking things to one side, the Kita no Kata, holding the Lady's sleeves in her hand, as if she were arresting a runaway thief, forced her to walk in front of her. The Lady was dressed in a soft aster-coloured damask robe, and over it the white robe which the Lord had left for her. Her hair had been recently dressed and looked very beautiful; how beautiful it was to see her hair hanging down her back and five inches of it trailing along the floor!

Akogi watched her being taken away and wondered

what would be done to the Lady. She was nearly fainting and felt like weeping and stamping her feet on the floor in her anger, but she forced herself to be calm and began to put back in their places the things which had been kicked about.

The Lady, almost out of her mind, was dragged in before the Great Lord.

'It has been very difficult. She would not have come if I had not dragged her here,' said the Kita no Kata.

'Shut her up quickly. I do not even want to look at her.'

She was pulled to her feet again and shut up in the store-room. The Great Lady's conduct was too cruel for a woman's; the Lady was half-dead with fright.

The room in which she was shut up was composed of two of the outside rooms and was used to store such smelly things as saké, vinegar and fish. It was shut by a swing door; it only contained one mat, near the door.

'This is what happens to people who want to have their own way,' said the Kita no Kata, roughly pushing her in. Then she shut and locked the door with her own hands and went away.

The smell of the many things which filled the room made the Lady feel very miserable; her disgust was so great that it dried up all her tears. She had not been told why she had been punished; she could only conjecture the reason, and that but vaguely. She wished eagerly, but in vain, that at least she could see Akogi. She pondered sadly over her sorrowful fate as she lay crying on the floor.

Meanwhile the Kita no Kata had gone to the Lower Room. 'Where is the comb-box? Akogi is interfering enough to have taken it away and hidden it,' she said, and not without some justification.

'Here it is,' was the answer.

'Nothing must be taken from this room until I open it,' said the Great Lady, for though she wished to take the things away from the room, she could not for shame do so. Now having securely fastened it, she thought that everything had been done as she wished, except for telling the Tenyaku no Suke; she would have to wait until no one else was near before she could do that.

Akogi, shut away from the Lady, was in despair. 'Why has this happened? I think it is better to leave this house,' she thought. But being anxious about the Lady, and wishing to know what had happened to her, she wrote a very humble appeal to the Third Lady. 'I have been condemned as guilty of some great crime about which I know nothing. And I have been told that I must leave this house. I am sorry that I must leave your service before my term of service expires. I should so much like to see you again, if only once. Please intercede for me to the Great Lady that I may be pardoned this once. It was only when I was very young that I served the Lady

Ochikubo and I have been out of her service so long that I had not the vaguest idea of what she was planning. How miserable I am! How sorrowful it will be for me to leave this house where I have been so happy, serving so kind a mistress!' So she appealed with cunning words for the Third Lady's help, and the Third Lady believed her and felt extremely sorry for her.

'Why are you punishing Akogi?' the Third Lady asked her mother. 'We are accustomed to her service and if she is not here, we shall be very inconvenienced.'

'That girl and Ochikubo have a strange devotion to each other. She is as bad as a thief; she has done all this in order to better the position of Ochikubo who herself has no such ambitions. Ochikubo has never shown any signs of wishing to meet a man.'

'But please pardon her this once. She has written me a most pathetic letter.'

'Well, do as you wish. But do not tell me that Akogi is such a good servant. It is very foolish of you to say that.'

The Third Lady could not but yield to her advice so, instead of summoning Akogi to her at once, she wrote to her. 'Wait patiently a little while,' the letter ran, 'I will do what I can for you later.'

Akogi continued to plan what she should do but could decide nothing, while the Lady, shut up in her room, was too agitated even to think. 'They have shut the Lady up without food,' Akogi was worrying, 'and the servants will never think of taking her any. It makes my heart ache when I recall the sight of the Kita no Kata dragging my beautiful Lady out of the room. Oh, how I wish that I could make myself a person of influence in a moment so that I could have my revenge on them!' Her heart beat wildly at the thought. 'What will the Shōshō think when he hears of this tonight?' she wondered and wept as bitterly as if she were lamenting someone's sudden death, until her maid, Tsuyu, was alarmed to see her.

Meanwhile, the Lady was still lying on the floor of the stinking store-room. 'If I die, I shall never be able to talk to the Shōshō again. We promised each other that we should be constant to each other for ever,' she thought sadly, and her sorrow increased as she reminded herself of how he had helped her with the folding of the robe on the previous night. 'What sin did I commit in a former life that I should be forced to suffer thus? Everyone says that it is usual for a step-mother to be cruel, but how unnatural it is that the Great Lord is so cruel to me!'

That night when the Shōshō heard what had happened he was horrified. 'What must she be feeling! It is all through me that this has happened,' he said, filled with grief. 'When no one is near, give her this message, "Words would be all inadequate to express the horror I felt when I came expecting to meet you and learned what had happened to you. How can I tell you of my grief?

How can I get to see you?"'

Akogi took off her long robe, pulled up her **hakama**
and stole round by the lower corridor. Everyone was
asleep; all was quiet.

She tapped softly on the door. 'Yaya,' she called
softly. There was no answer.

'Have you gone to sleep? This is Akogi.'

The Lady heard the faint sound of her voice and stole
noiselessly to the door. 'How did you manage to come
here?' she asked. 'How terrible this is! What has caused
them to treat me in this way?' she went on, hardly able
to speak for her tears.

Akogi was also crying bitterly. 'Since this morning,
I have come near this room several times, but I have had
no opportunity of speaking to you. How sad it is that
this has happened! How terribly cruel the Kita no Kata
is!' Akogi said, and then she went on to relate all that
she had heard that the Great Lady had said.

The Lady wept more and more bitterly.

'The Shōshō has come. When I told him of all this,
he could only weep and weep,' Akogi said and gave the
Lady his message. The Lady found it very pathetic.

'Please tell him that I am so upset that I can think of
nothing and can send him no reply. As for seeing him
again—

> As one already
> Dead I live, when about to
> Return to the Shades;

> I feel how small the chances
> Are that we shall meet once more.

I am nearly driven mad with the odour of all the filthy things in this room. It is only while I am living that I must suffer thus! How I wish I could die!' said the Lady; it would be foolishly inadequate to say only that she wept. How grieved Akogi also was may as easily be imagined. She returned to the Shōshō noiselessly so as not to awaken anyone.

When the Shōshō heard her message, his love and his sorrow increased and he wept sorely, covering his face with his sleeves.

'Take her another message,' he said, after a short while. '"My dear, I also wish that I could die.

> To-night when I learn
> To see you again is grown
> More difficult now;
> I feel that I cannot wait
> Till to-morrow to see you.[1]

However, do not understand from this, that I am really contemplating that."'

On her way to the store-room again, Akogi accidentally made a sound.

'What is that sound of footsteps from the direction of the store-room?' the Kita no Kata said as she awoke.

---

[1] He hints that he will kill himself to meet her in death.

'I shall have to return quickly,' Akogi said, giving the Lady the Shōshō's message amid her bitter tears.

'This is my reply,' answered the Lady.

> Once I doubted you
> And that your love was short-lived
> Did I once believe;
> But now do I sadly fear
> I may not have long to live.

Akogi could hardly wait to hear the end before running back. She explained to the Shōshō how the Kita no Kata had been awakened and that she had not had time to hear everything that the Lady had wished to say. How the Shōshō wished to be able to go into the Kita no Kata's room and beat her to death!

So all three passed the night in weeping.

'Tell me if an opportunity of rescuing her occurs,' the Shōshō said tenderly, as he went away next morning. 'How full of sadness she must be!'

'Now that the Great Lord has been told an infamous scandal about me, it is useless for me to remain here any longer,' thought Tachihaki, and so he left the mansion, riding on the back of the Lord's carriage.

Akogi was wondering what she should do about taking food to the Lady, for she could not help her mind dwelling continually on the Lady's sufferings. She put some boiled rice and red beans in a parcel so that no one could tell what was in it, but she could think of no method of getting it to the Lady. Just then the Third Son, the little boy with whom she was very friendly, came along.

'What do you think of the Lady being shut up in the store-room? Don't you feel very sorry for her?' Akogi asked him.

'How could I be otherwise than sorry?'

'Then will you give her this letter without anyone seeing you?'

'All right,' he answered, taking it and going to the store-room, although he knew that he was disobeying his mother's orders.

'Open this door,' he called out on finding the door of the store-room shut. 'Open this door quickly.'

'Why do you want it opened?' the Kita no Kata asked in an angry tone.

'I have left my shoes inside. I want them,' he replied and continued to call out loudly and beat on the door.

'He only wants to strut about in his shoes. Open the door for him at once,' the Chūnagon said, for this, his youngest son, was his special favourite.

'Let him wait a while until we have to open the door for some other purpose,' said the Kita no Kata, scolding him.

'I shall break down the door then,' the boy cried out loudly in his anger.

The Chūnagon therefore came out and opened the door himself. The boy entered and instead of looking for his shoes he bent down and gave the Lady the letter.

'That's very strange. They are not there,' the boy said as he came out without his shoes.

'You see what a silly thing you have done,' the Kita no Kata said, catching hold of him and cuffing him.

Meanwhile, the Lady was opening the letter by the light which came in through the cracks of the door. She found a long letter from Akogi with rice and red beans hidden inside, but she had no appetite and she laid it all on one side.

The Kita no Kata had not changed her attitude towards the Lady. 'She may have food once a day. We must not let her die of hunger, or she will not be able to do the sewing,' she said.

When no one was near, the Kita no Kata summoned the Tenyaku no Suke and told him everything that had happened and of how the Lady had been shut up in the store-room. 'I want you to understand the situation,' she concluded.

The Tenyaku no Suke was highly delighted; he smiled until his mouth reached round to his ears.

'Tonight you may go to her room,' she said.

The Tenyaku readily agreed to do that, and as other people came in, he left her.

Akogi received a letter from the Shōshō. 'How are things going on? Is the Lady still shut up in the store-room?' he wrote. 'I am very anxious to know when an opportunity occurs of seeing the Lady. If you can, give her the enclosed letter without fail. If I have an answer, it will relieve my feelings a great deal, for her misery weighs heavily upon my heart.'

The letter to the Lady was full of loving and tender expressions of his anxiety. 'When I remember your last letter, forlorn and hopeless,' he wrote, 'I become frantic with anxiety.

> How it pains my heart
> To hear you say that never
>   Shall we meet again.
> If we remain in this world,
> The day when we meet must come.

My darling, comfort yourself and be strong. I wish I were shut up with you.'

Tachihaki also wrote to Akogi. 'Thinking about this affair,' he wrote, 'has so worried me that I have had to take to my bed. The thought of how the Lady is suffering so distresses me that I feel like renouncing the world to become a priest, for it is through my fault that all this has happened.'

'I will do as you request,' Akogi's answer to the Lord ran, 'but how is it possible for you to meet the Lady? The door is still kept closed and will remain so. What can I do? How can I even give her your letter? However, I will let you know if an opportunity of seeing her occurs.'

She also wrote a letter in the same mournful tone to Tachihaki.

Book Two will tell
the details of the
rest of the story.

THE SECOND BOOK

AKOGI, anxious to give the Shōshō's letter to the Lady, went to the store-room with it in her hand, but to her grief she found the door still closed.

Meanwhile, the Shōshō and Tachihaki were plotting how to steal the Lady away. 'I feel bitterly sorry for her, because it is through me that all this has happened,' the Shōshō thought to himself. 'How can I steal her away and then have our revenge on the Kita no Kata by bringing disgrace upon her?' He dwelt long and deeply on this aspect of the matter for he was of a very unforgiving nature.

Next the servant, Shōnagon, who had spoken to the Lady about Katano no Shōshō came with a letter to her from him, and was shocked and grieved to find that the Lady had been shut away. 'What must she be feeling! How horrible it must be for her to be shut up in there!' she said to Akogi in a low voice and with many tears.

Akogi was still wondering how she could deliver the letter when night fell.

The Kita no Kata was very vexed because she could find no one to make a flute-bag for the Kurōdo no Shōshō. As it was needed urgently, she opened the door of the store-room and went in to the Lady. 'Sew this at once,' she said to the Lady who, not feeling well, was lying down. 'If you do not do it, I will shut you up in a shed. I have had you put here so that I can make you do this kind of work.'

The Lady, thinking that the Kita no Kata would certainly do as she threatened, arose and began to sew in spite of feeling half-dead with pain.

Akogi, seeing that the door had been opened, called the Third Son to her. 'I am very thankful to you for doing what you did for me,' she said to him. 'Now will you give this to the Lady while the Great Lady is not looking? Be sure that no one sees you.'

'All right,' he said, taking the letter, and holding it to his mouth, he went along to the store-room pretending that he was playing a flute as he walked, until he came to the side of the Lady. There he sat down and he slipped the letter under her robe.

The Lady went on with her sewing, wishing all the while to read the letter. At last the bag was finished and taken away and then with difficulty she read the letter and was filled with love and pity. Having no brush or ink, she wrote an answer with the point of a pin.

> Am I then to die
> As vanishes the dew-drop,
>   Without revealing
> To you the thoughts which long
> I have cherished in my heart.

'Those are my thoughts,' she wrote.

The Kita no Kata came in. 'This bag is well done. However the Great Lord has scolded me very much for opening the door,' she said to the Lady, shutting the door and preparing to lock it.

'Please, I wish to tell Akogi to bring the box from the other room,' the Lady said.

'Bring the Lady Ochikubo's comb-box here,' the Kita no Kata called out to Akogi, leaving the door shut.

Then when Akogi hurried along with the comb-box and handed it in to the Lady, she put the letter in Akogi's hand, and Akogi carried it away without it being seen by the Kita no Kata.

'Your letter was given to the Lady and this answer obtained from her with great difficulty, during the short time that the door was open, while the Lady was making a flute-bag,' Akogi wrote when she sent the Lady's answer to the Shōshō. He was deeply grieved.

The day was quickly drawing to its close, but to the Tenyaku no Suke, with his thoughts of what the night would bring, it seemed as if the time would never come.

He went to the room where Akogi was. 'No doubt Akogi will treat this old man with more respect in future,' he said to her with a leer.

'Why is that?' asked Akogi, finding him very horrible and repulsive.

'As the Lady Ochikubo has been given to me, you will

be in my service, won't you?'

This shocked and terrified her. Though she could hardly restrain her tears, she tried to hide her feelings and did not answer rudely, for she saw that a catastrophe menaced them.

'I am very glad to hear that, for I have never yet been in the service of a lord, and my life has been very uninteresting and tedious. Has the Great Lord arranged this, or the Kita no Kata?' she asked.

'The Great Lord has been very kind and the Great Lady even kinder,' he answered, very delighted.

Akogi thought that this was the gravest of news. She wondered what she could do, and how she could get the news to the Shōshō; her usual serenity of mind was gone.

'Well, when is the happy day?' she asked at last.

'Tonight.'

'Today is an Unlucky Day for her.[1] She will not consent.'

'That does not matter. She already has a lover, and so it will be dangerous to postpone it. I must hurry,' he said, going away and leaving Akogi sorely perplexed.

Taking advantage of the opportunity while the Kita no Kata was serving dinner to the Chūnagon, Akogi went to the store-room and knocked on the door.

'Who is that?' asked the Lady Ochikubo.

Akogi explained the grave situation which had arisen.

---

[1] Kinichi, a day when one should be most careful of one's purity.

'I have told him that it is your Unlucky Day. Oh, this is a terrible situation!' she said, and went away without waiting for any answer.

The Lady had heard this with feelings of great horror. She did not know what to do. What she had suffered in all her life till that moment seemed now but trifles compared with this. She could not see any way of escape; her grief was so great that she wished she could die immediately. She felt a great pain in her chest; she pressed her hands on it and lay face-downwards on the floor, weeping bitterly.

The Chūnagon was in the habit of retiring to bed early, so, as usual, soon after the lights had been brought in, he went to bed and the Kita no Kata went out to further the Tenyaku no Suke's affair. She unfastened the door of the store-room and looked in to find the Lady lying on the floor, weeping bitter tears.

'Are you in pain? Why are you weeping and moaning?' the Kita no Kata asked.

'I have a pain in the chest,' the Lady answered in a low whisper and with difficulty.

'That is bad. It is probably indigestion. Master Tenyaku is a doctor. Let him examine you.'

'No, it is only a cold,' the Lady answered, very agitated at this new development. 'I do not need a doctor.'

'But a pain in the chest is a dangerous thing,' and as the Kita no Kata was saying this, Tenyaku passed the door. She therefore called to him and he promptly entered. 'The

Lady is suffering from a pain in the chest. It is probably indigestion. However, examine her and give her some medicine for it. I will leave her in your hands,' the Kita no Kata concluded and went from the room.

'I am a doctor. I will soon cure you. From tonight, put yourself completely in my hands,' said the Tenyaku no Suke, beginning his examination. When his hands touched her, the Lady cried out in terror, but there was no one to stop him. The position was extremely dangerous for her; there was nothing else to do but to plead for delay with tears. 'Thank you very much for your kindness, but the pain is not too bad now,' she said.

'Why? I should wish that I might fall ill instead of you, if it were possible for you then to recover,' he said, embracing her.

The Kita no Kata, relying on the fact that Tenyaku was with the Lady, went to bed without locking the door as usual. Akogi then hurried to the store-room to see if he had gone into the room and it was with very mixed feelings of delight and fear that she saw that the door was partly open. She went in and found Tenyaku bending down over the Lady.

'I did not expect to find you here after my having told you that to-day was an Unlucky Day for the Lady,' Akogi said to him in a very angry tone.

'Why? You would be justified in being vexed if we were lying down together. However, the Great Lady has asked me to treat her for a pain in the chest,' he answered.

It was true, she could see, that he was still fully dressed.

The Lady meanwhile was crying bitterly in fear as well as with pain.

Akogi, fearing that all was lost unless she did something, wondered why it was that the Lady who had always had to suffer should now be subjected to this new series of torments.

'Will you not have a hot stone put on it?' Akogi asked the Lady. The Lady agreed.

'Now we are in your hands completely,' said Akogi to Tenyaku. 'Would you go and get some hot stones for the Lady? Everyone is now fast asleep, and if I ask for hot stones, they will refuse. You have here an opportunity of showing how great is your love for the Lady.'

'I have now only a few more years to live, but if she puts herself completely into my hands, I will do for her everything I can. If she wished me, I would try to move a mountain—and to bring a few hot stones is much easier than that. I could heat the stones with the warmth of my heart.'

'If you are going to do it, do it quickly,' urged Akogi.

'It seems too familiar for me to do this kind of thing for her, but I am quite willing. To show my love for the Lady, I will heat the stone,' he thought and went out.

'You have suffered tribulations for many years but this seems to be the most painful and the most difficult to escape. What can we do? What sins did you commit in a former life that you should be so punished; and in what body does the Kita no Kata think to be reborn when she treats you in this shameful manner?' exclaimed Akogi.

'I cannot think about anything,' the Lady answered. 'My only regret is that I have lived until now. I feel very ill. I hate the thought of that old man coming back here again. Shut the door and keep him out.'

'That will only make him angry. Keep him in a good humour. We have no one to rely on; to whom could we go in the morning, if we kept him out of the room tonight? The Shōshō is worried and upset by your situation, but he can do nothing to help you; it is impossible for him to get near you here. Pray from your heart to Buddha and the gods for help.'

Truly the Lady had no one on whom she could rely. There had never been any love between her and her sisters; there had only been enmity; she could not appeal to their sympathy. In her extremity she had no one who could help her; her only friends were her tears and Akogi.

'Stay here with me for the night,' the Lady pleaded, and they wept together.

Then the old man came back with the stone wrapped up. The Lady's grief and horror increased at the thought of his hands touching her to put the stone on, but the old man unloosed her robe and drew her near to him.

'Do not do that, my dear,' the Lady said to him in great grief and pain. 'When the pain is severest, I find it relieves the pain if I sit up and press my hands on it. Think of the future and tonight just go to sleep.'

'Yes, it is only for tonight.' agreed Akogi, 'And besides it is an Unlucky Day for her. So go to sleep.'

'Then lean against me,' said Tenyaku, believing what they said to be true. He lay down and the Lady leaned against him weeping. Akogi while she abhorred him was glad that through his presence she had been able to enter the room.

Very soon, he went to sleep and began to snore. The Lady contrasted him with the Shōshō and he seemed very ugly and disgusting to her eyes. Akogi was planning how they were to escape.

The old man woke up and the Lady pretended to be in great pain. 'I am truly sorry that you are in such great pain, especially on the night when I am with you for the first time,' he said, and soon went off to sleep again.

When the day dawned, they were both overjoyed. Akogi then woke up the old man. 'It is already broad day. Please go now. Let us keep this secret for some time. If you think of the future, you will see that it is best to do as the Lady wishes,' Akogi said to him.

'Yes, I agree with you,' answered the old man, and he forced open his sleepy, discharge-encrusted eyelids and went out, his back bent double with age.

Akogi opened the door and fled back to her own room so as not to be found in the store-room. In her room she found a letter from Tachihaki. 'I came here with difficulty to find, to my sorrow, that the door was shut and my visit in vain. You may be thinking that it is through lack of love that I have not come before. But seeing the sorrow of the Shōshō, I have not a moment of ease. Here is his letter. I must see you somehow or other tomorrow night.'

Akogi thought that she had at once a good opportunity of delivering the Shōshō's letter to the Lady and so hurried there, but she found when she arrived at the store-room that the door had already been locked by the Kita no Kata. Returning in deep disappointment, she met Tenyaku who handed her a letter for the Lady. She took it and ran to the Kita no Kata.

'This is a letter from Master Tenyaku. How shall I deliver it?' she asked.

'Oh, is it his letter asking after her health?' the Great Lady asked with a smile, opening the door of the store-room. 'That is very nice of them. How nice it is that they love each other so much!'

Akogi thought these remarks very humorous. She handed in the letter together with the one from the Shōshō.

The Lady read the one from the Shōshō. 'How are you?' he had written. 'As the days pass by without our meeting, my agony increases.

> That, full of deep sorrow
> For you in your misery,
>   My thoughts are with you,
>   My sleeves, wet with tears, do know—
>   It is they alone that do.

I am besides myself with anxiety. What can we do?'

She read the letter with grief. 'Your sorrow, great as it is, is but due to pity; how much greater then is my sorrow!'

she wrote in answer.[1]

> In my sore distress,
> My tears flow without ceasing,
> Sad that I still live.
> It seems that I am drifting
> Along a river of tears.

As it seemed to her disgusting to have to read then the old man's letter, she wrote in the margin of it that Akogi was to answer it. Then she handed it with the answer to the Shōshō to Akogi, who took them both and went away.

'Oh, how very, very sorry I am for you!' the Tenyaku no Suke had written. 'I am afraid that I brought you bad luck and caused you to be ill last night. My dear, my dear, make me happy this very night. Living with you, my life will be prolonged and I shall be restored to youth. My dear, my dear!

> Although an old tree
> People may think me to be,
> Yet assuredly
> Will I send forth new blossoms
> For you to see and admire.

Again and again I entreat you, do not reject me.'

Akogi thought it disgusting to have to answer this, but she wrote a reply. 'The Lady is suffering so much that she cannot answer you herself.

---

[1] As the Lady had now her comb-box she could write an answer.

When can an old tree,
The hour of whose withering
Is now near at hand,
When can such a tree send forth
Delightful blossoms anew?'

She was rather afraid that he would be angry on reading this reply, but instead he smiled with pleasure.

Akogi then wrote to Tachihaki. 'Last night I also should have liked to have seen you and eased my heart just by telling you of the most distressing thing which has happened. But it was impossible. This morning's letter was with difficulty delivered. A very serious situation has developed. When I see you I shall be able to explain.'

To Akogi's delight, the Kita no Kata, feeling quite certain that the Tenyaku no Suke would watch over the Lady, left the door of the store-room unlockd. However, as night came on, she was sorely perplexed as to what was to be done; she wondered how the door could be fastened from within so that it could not be opened.

Meanwhile, the old man came to her. 'How is the Lady feeling now?' he said.

'She is still in great pain,' Akogi answered.

He wondered what it could be that was the matter with her, and heaved as great a sigh as if he himself were feeling the pain, but his sympathetic expression only made him look the more foolish.

Akogi learnt with great delight that the Kita no Kata wished to take the Third Lady to see the procession of the special festival on the following day as the Kurōdo no Shōshō was to take part in it. Her heart beat wildly with joy at the thought that she and the Lady would then be left alone in the house. She thought that it would only be necessary for the old man to be kept out of the room for that one night, so she looked around for something that could be used to wedge the door. Having found something that would do for that purpose, she hid it under her arm. Then in the confusion attendant on the bringing in of the lights, she went to the store-room and put the wedge between the door and the frame, in such a way that it could not be seen. The Lady inside the room had also been thinking what she could do to keep Tenyaku out and had put a big cedar chest behind the door. With trembling hands, she held it there and prayed to Buddha and the gods that the door should remain fast.

The Kita no Kata gave the key of the room to Tenyaku. 'Go in when everyone is asleep,' she said.

Then when everything was quiet, Tenyaku went with the key to open the door. The Lady inside was terrified as she waited for what was to happen. He turned the key and tried to open the door; it was so hard to open that he staggered back. Akogi, standing some distance away, listened; to her delight, he did not find the wedge, although he felt about to discover what was holding the door.

'Strange! Very strange!' he said. 'Have you fastened it from inside? It can only have been done to distress me.

You have been given to me, so you cannot evade me for ever, can you?' But there was no answer. He pulled the door and pushed it, but on account of the things holding it both inside and outside he could not even shake it. Expecting every moment that the door would be opened to him, until the night was far advanced he sat on the boards of the verandah waiting, until his whole body was cramped for it was a cold, winter night. For some days he had been troubled with his stomach and in addition he was not very warmly dressed; now therefore, the coldness of the floor began to make his bowels rumble—'koho, koho.'

'How unfortunate! It is too cold here for me,' the old man said, and his bowels went on rumbling 'koho, koho' and then more violently—'hichi, hichi.' Dreading what was about to happen, he felt his way out, holding his hands to his rear, but in spite of his urgent desire to get away from there quickly, he locked the door and took out the key. Akogi was very disappointed to see him take away the key but overjoyed that the door had not been opened.

She then went up to the door. 'He has gone away in need of having his clothes cleaned,' she explained to the Lady, 'so he will not be coming back. You can go to sleep in peace. Tachihaki must have arrived at my room by now, and I will ask him to take your letter to the Shōshō.'

'Why have you not come before?' Tachihaki asked her when she arrived at her own room. 'What is the situation now? Is she still shut up in the store-room? The situation seems to be becoming graver. The Lord is in great distress about it. He said to me, "Would it not be possible to steal her away by night? Go and make arrangements for us to do so." '

'Things have become much more serious. The door is opened once a day only, so that food may be served. Worse still, the Kita no Kata intends to give the Lady in marriage to her uncle, in spite of his great age. She gave him the key and told him to go to her room tonight,' said Akogi, going on to explain how the door had been fastened from inside and outside. Tachihaki, though he felt very sad at this piece of news, could not help laughing uproariously when he was told of how the old man had stood outside and tried to get in, and in what condition the old man's clothes had been when he went away. 'Since the Lady heard of the intention of the Kita no Kata,' Akogi went on, bursting into tears, 'she has been suffering from a terrible pain in the chest.'

'The Lord intends to steal her away,' said Tachihaki, 'and then get his own back on the Kita no Kata.'

'I am certain that the Great Lady will be going to the festival to-morrow. Tell the Lord to come then and take her away.'

'That will be a good opportunity. I wish it were morning now.' Thus they conversed, impatiently waiting for the dawn.

Meanwhile the Tenyaku no Suke had found his **hakama** very filthy but before he had done more than roughly wash it, he felt so helplessly sleepy that neither his desire for love nor his sense of decency prevented him from going immediately to bed.

When morning came, Tachihaki hurried away to the Lord. 'What did she say?' the Shōshō eagerly asked him.

Tachihaki told him what Akogi had said. The thought of Tenyaku filled the Lord with disgust and with envy; and the misery of the Lady excited in him overwhelming compassion. 'I shall be going away from this house for some time,' he then said to Tachihaki. 'I am going to the house at Nijō. Go there then and open the lattices and clean the house. The Shōshō's heart beat wildly with joy at the thought that the Lady would be with him at his house in Nijō in the course of the day.

Akogi was very agitated but she tried to hide her joy as she went about preparing for the Lady's escape.

Towards noon, the Third Lady and the others, calling noisily to each other, came out and entered two carriages.

'Oh, someone may go in during my absence. It is too dangerous to leave the door open,' the Kita no Kata called out, her voice rising above the noise of the others. She sent to Tenyaku for the key and, to Akogi's great disappointment, carried it away with her.

The Chūnagon also went out to see his son-in-law in the procession.

As soon as they had started with a great deal of noise, Akogi sent to inform the Shōshō.

Joyfully impatient, the Shōshō came in his carriage, but
not his usual one, with reddish-brown curtains behind the
bamboo blinds, accompanied by many men. Tachihaki on
horseback rode on ahead. The Chūnagon's men had gone
in three parties, with the Chūnagon, with the Kita no Kata
and with the Kurōdo no Shōshō. So there was no one
about at the mansion.

The carriage stopped at the gate while Tachihaki went
in by the back-gate. 'The Lord's carriage is here. Where
shall I have it brought in?' he asked Akogi.

'Straight to the north side,' she answered.

As it was being brought in, one of the Chūnagon's men
appeared. 'What carriage is this? Everyone has gone
out,' he challenged them.

'But this is for the servants,' answered Tachihaki, leading
in the carriage and taking no further notice of the man.

All the servants who had not gone to see the procession
were in their own rooms. No one was visible.

'Please get down quickly,' said Akogi. The Lord hurriedly descended from the carriage. He found the door of the
room locked. He was grieved that she should have been
shut up in such a place. He tried to enter by wrenching
off the lock but he could not even move it. He called to
Tachihaki to come and together they forced off the edge
of the door-frame so that the sliding doors could be pulled
out. When that was done, Tachihaki went out. The Lord
was sad indeed to see the piteous plight of the Lady; he
took her in his arms and carried her to the carriage. 'Get
in too, Akogi,' he said.

Akogi did not wish the Kita no Kata to remain under the delusion that the Tenyaku no Suke had been successful in his love affair, so she left rolled together the two letters she had delivered to the Lady in a place where the Kita no Kata was sure to find them. Then she picked up the comb-box and in happy mood sprang into the carriage. All were now jubilant. The carriage flew out through the gates, a crowd of the Lord's men surrounded it and eventually they arrived safely at the Nijō house. There they were free from care; there was no one there to disturb their peace. He took her from the carriage and they went to bed. They related to each other the events of the past few days, now with laughter and now with tears. The filthy incident of the Tenyaku no Suke was the cause of a great deal of laughter.

'What a failure as a lover! How vexed the Kita no Kata will be to hear the story!' commented the Lord. They put aside all reserve as they lay and talked together.

Tachihaki and Akogi were also in bed. There was now nothing to cause them uneasiness, they told each other.

When evening came, Akogi prepared food and Tachihaki busied himself with the duties of a steward.

When the Chūnagon returned from seeing the procession, as soon as he alighted from his carriage, he saw that the door-frame had been broken and the door of the store-room had been forced. Everyone was astonished to see this, and more so to find that the room was empty. Dismayed, they wondered what had happened while they had been absent. Soon the whole mansion was in an uproar.

'Was no servant left in the house to prevent anyone going straight to this hiding-place and breaking open the door and pulling down the frame?' the Chūnagon said in furious anger. 'Who was in charge during our absence?'

The Kita no Kata was mortified beyond words to find that the Lady Ochikubo had escaped. She went to look for Akogi, but Akogi too had disappeared. She opened the door of the Lower Room and found that the curtain and screen that had been there had gone also.

'It is that thief Akogi; she has done this, taking advantage of our absence,' the Kita no Kata called out. Then she went on angrily to the Third Lady, 'I had thought of dismissing her a short while ago, but you said that she was a good servant. And this is the evil way she serves you. You were kind-hearted enough to keep her in your service and she is ungrateful and does not return your kindness.'

The Chūnagon had now found one of the men who had been left in charge of the house.

'I do not know anything about it,' the man replied to the Chūnagon's questions. 'Only, a very splendid basket-work carriage with double blinds came in directly after everyone had left and later departed hurriedly.'

'That is who did it. A woman could not have broken down the door in this way. It must have been a man. Who could it have been that came thus into my house in broad daylight and did such things?' The Chūnagon was extremely angry but there was nothing he could do.

The Kita no Kata read the letters left behind by Akogi and was further angered to find that what she had planned to happen between the Lady and Tenyaku had not come to pass. She called him in to her and explained how the Lady had disappeared. 'Putting her in your charge was useless. She has run away like this. Didn't you become intimate with her? According to these letters which were left behind, you did not.'

'You talk unreasonably,' protested Tenyaku. 'On the night when she was suffering so badly from a pain in the chest, she would not allow me to get near her. Akogi was there and said that that day was her Unlucky Day and begged me not to do anything that night. And the Lady said the same. She was in such great pain that all I could do was to lie as near to her as I could. The next night I decided to make her give way to me, but when I went there, I found the door fastened against me from the inside. I could not open it and I stood outside on the boards till midnight and caught a cold. My abdomen began to roll 'koho, koho.' I took no notice of it for the first few times but when I made a last effort to open the door, a filthy thing happened. I was able to think of nothing else but what had happened and went back to my room, and by the time I had cleaned myself it was already dawn. It was not my fault.'

Full of anger, she reprimanded him but yet could hardly keep from laughing. How much more ludicrous did it appear to the young ladies who were listening to this conversation; they nearly died of laughing!

'Well, all right, all right, you may go, I cannot tell you how I hate that girl. I ought to have put her in charge of someone else,' the Kita no Kata said.

'You are very unjust,' protested Tenyaku getting angry. 'Oh, how anxious, how anxious I was to realise my desires! It was because I am growing old that I did such a foolish thing and spoiled my clothes. It could not be helped. No one could have tried harder than I did to open that door.' He then went away, leaving all the people roaring with laughter.

'It was all due to her being so ill-treated,' the Third Son said. 'Why was she shut up in that store-room and married to such a foolish old man? How sad she must have been! My sisters and my brothers may have to meet her in the future. That will be very embarrassing for us,' he argued in quite a grown-up manner.

'Wherever she goes, she will never be fortunate,' replied the Kita no Kata. 'What would she be able to do to my children if ever they did meet?' There were three sons; the eldest was in Echizen as Governor of that Province; the second was a priest; and the third was this young boy.

At last the people of the house realised that all this noise and talking was of no use, so they all went to bed.

At the house in Nijō, as the Shōshō lay in bed, he spoke to Akogi as she brought in the lights. 'Tell me fully all about the events of the last few days. The Lady here will say nothing about it,' he said.

Akogi told him fully of the Great Lady's cruelty and the Shōshō was very sad to hear the full story of the sorrowful experiences which the Lady had undergone.

'We have too few servants here,' the Shōshō then said, 'and it is not very convenient. Find some please, Akogi. I had thought of bringing some from my father's house, but it would not be interesting to have here the servants I am accustomed to there. And you must act as upperservant, for you are quite mature in mind even though you are young in years.'

The two lovers spent the night in happy conversation and perfect tranquility and remained in bed till noon next day, when the Shōshō went to visit his father, leaving the Lady in Tachihaki's care. 'Remain near the Lady; I will return soon,' he said to Tachihaki.

Akogi wrote a letter to her aunt. 'I have been very busy,' she wrote, 'and have not been able to write to you lately. Today or tomorrow, could you find me some good olderservants and maids? If you have any good servants, would you lend me one or two? The reasons I will give later when I see you. Come to see me sometime.'

At his father's house, the woman who had told the Shōshō of the proposal to marry the Chūnagon's Fourth Lady came in to see him. 'Excuse me,' she said. 'About the matter of which we were talking the other day, the people wish the marriage to take place before the end of the year

and wish you to send your letter to the lady as soon as possible. They urge that you do so quickly.'

'They seem to be acting in this matter in a manner quite
contrary to the ordinary,' said the Lord's mother, the Kita
no Kata of the Taishō. 'However, I think it would be good
to consent to what they urge on you; it would be rude to
refuse flatly. It is disgraceful that you have remained single
to your present age.'

'If that is what you think, then I had better take her
quickly. If they want me to send a letter, I will send one
at once. But the present style is to arrange the marriage
without this sending of letters,' the Shōshō said smiling as
he left the room. He went to his own room and sent to
Nijō the furniture he was in the habit of using, with this
letter to the Lady, 'How are you now?' he wrote. 'I am
very anxious about you. I have come to my father's house,
but I shall be returning when I have been to the Imperial
Palace.

> If in a fine robe
> I should attempt to wrap up
> My joy at having you
> In my own house, the sleeves would
> Be torn away at the seams.

My anxiety about you is greater nowadays.'

'As for me—' the Lady answered,

> The sleeves of my robe
> Are in rags through the soaking
> Of tears which I shed

In that sad time of sorrow;.
In what can I wrap up my joy?

This made the Shōshō feel very sad. Meanwhile at the
Nijō house, Tachihaki was attending to the Lady with
tender care.

Akogi received an answer from the wife of the Governor
of Izumi. 'As I felt anxious about you, having had no news
of you for some time,' the letter read, 'I sent yesterday to
inquire. The messenger was told that you had run away
after behaving scandalously. He had to run away to escape
being beaten. I was therefore very anxious about you and
am very glad to learn that you are safe and happy. I will
find servants for you as you ask. We have no suitable ones
here at present, but a cousin of my husband who is living
with us might suit you.'

At nightfall, the Shōshō returned to Nijō. He explained
to the Lady what had been arranged with regard to the
Fourth Lady. 'I shall find someone to impersonate me
to visit her,' he concluded.

'How dreadful!' exclaimed the Lady. 'If you do not
want her, let the matter drop. How great a sorrow it will
bring upon her, and what an evil man she will think you!'

'I am only doing it to have my revenge on the Kita no
Kata.'

'Forget her and what she has done, as soon as you can.
Have you any reason for injuring the Fourth Lady?'

'You are too tender-hearted. You do not remember

how they ill-treated you.   You are too gentle.'
Speaking in this way, they went to bed.

The woman who had spoken to the Shōshō returned to
the Chūnagon with the news of the Lord's consent to the
proposal of marriage.   The Kita no Kata was very pleased
and began to make great disturbance as she ordered preparations for the marriage.   As these preparations pro-
gressed, she realised more and more how convenient it had
been when the Lady Ochikubo was with them, for if she
had been there, all the sewing could have been left in her
hands.   'Oh, Buddha, if she be alive, bring her back!'
she exclaimed.   To the vexation of the Kita no Kata, the
Kurōdo no Shōshō began to make continual complaints
about the clumsy making of his clothes.   She would move
heaven and earth to try to find a girl to replace the Lady
Ochikubo.

'We must take him as son-in-law at once now that he has
consented or he may change his mind,' said the Chūnagon,
restlessly hurrying on the preparations.   The marriage was
arranged for the Fifth Day of the Twelfth Month and they
hastened their preparations from the end of the Eleventh
Month.

'Who is the new son-in-law?' the Kurōdo no Shōshō
asked the Kita no Kata.

'The son of the Sadaishō, the Sakon no Shōshō,' she
answered.

'He is a fine man.   It will be very enjoyable having him

for a fellow son-in-law,' he said, highly delighted.

The Kita no Kata was in high spirits too now that her daughter was to marry the Sakon no Shōshō, but he had consented only because he had a secret plot to bring disgrace on the Kita no Kata in revenge.

Thus ten days elapsed since the Lady's arrival at the Nijō house. Now there were more than ten new servants; Everything in the house was spick-and-span, and the atmossphere was congenial. Hyōgo, the cousin of the Governor of Izumi, had been offered for service by her parents at the request of Akogi. Akogi herself was the upper-servant and had been renamed Emon. Though she was small and young, she went about her work cheerfully, and naturally the Shōshō and the Lady valued her more than anyone else.

'Is what I have heard true,' the Kita no Kata of the Taishō, the Shōshō's mother, said to him, 'that you are keeping a lady at the house at Nijō? If it is, why did you agree to the proposal of the Chūnagon?'

'I had thought of telling you, but I was only thinking of keeping her some time, until the arrival of my real wife,' he answered. 'However, I have heard that this Chūnagon of whom we are speaking is one of those who quite approve of having more than one wife. Are men to have only one wife then? I am expecting that the two ladies will amuse each other by being very amicable and chatting together friendlily.'

'Oh, what things to say! To keep many ladies is to

suffer many troubles. And it is bad for your health. Do not think of doing so. If you are fond of the lady you are keeping at Nijō, do not think of marrying anyone else. I will write to the Lady of Nijō sometime soon.'

Not long afterwards, she sent a splendid present to the Lady of Nijō and they exchanged letters.

'The Lady of Nijō does things very splendidly,' the Kita no Kata of the Taishō said to her son. 'She writes a very nice hand indeed. Whose daughter is she? You ought to decide to be constant to her. I have daughters myself, so I can feel for others. I shall be ashamed of you if you trifle with the daughters of others.'

The Shōshō laughed. 'I shall never desert the Lady of Nijō, but I am fond of the other also,' he said.

'What do you say? How hateful you are! I cannot understand what is in your mind,' she answered and smiled; she was very good-natured as well as beautiful.

Thus the end of the month came.

'The day after tomorrow is the day arranged, you remember,' the Shōshō's mother reminded him. 'Although I know you are fond of the Lady of Nijō, I must remind you of your promise.'

'That is all right. I am going,' he answered, smiling to himself as he thought of his secret plan.

Now his mother's uncle was the Jibu no Kyō.[1] He was disliked by all people on account of his eccentricity and stupidity, and was almost ostracised. His eldest son was

---

[1] The Minister of the Department of Civil Administration.

the Hyōbu no Shōyu.[2] The Shōshō went to see him. 'Is the Shōyu in?' he asked the father.

'He is probably in his room. He does not go out as he is afraid of people laughing at him. Please favour him with your friendship, and accustom him to being among people. I was also like him when I was younger, but I found that if one endured being laughed at for a short time, one could very soon become accustomed to working at Court.'

'How could I forsake him?' the Shōshō answered with a smile.

He then went to the son's room and found him still in bed. His stupid ways caused the Shōshō to smile.

'Yaya. Get up. I have come to tell you something,' he said.

The Shōyu stretched himself out at full length with his arms above his head, and then arose, as if with difficulty, and went to wash his hands.

'Why don't you come to see us?' the Shōshō asked him.

'I am afraid of people laughing at me,' the Shōyu answered.

'That may be so. But that is only when you go among strangers. And why is it that you are not married yet? It is very miserable living alone.'

'It is not miserable living alone until someone arranges a marriage for me.'

'Still, even if it is not miserable, are you going to remain

---

[2] The Assistant Vice-Minister of the War Department. (The original pronunciation of this title was undoubtedly Shō, but by analogy with the title of the Vice-Minister, Taiyu, the pronunciation Shōyu became the ordinary one.)

single for ever?'

'I am waiting for someone to arrange a marriage for me.'

'I will arrange one for you. I have a very suitable lady in mind.'

At this, in spite of his assurance that he did not find single life miserable, he smiled, and when he did so, with his snow-white face and turned-up nose and small head set on a very long neck, one would have expected him to jump to his feet and begin neighing, 'hi-hi', he was so like a horse. One had to laugh when one looked at him.

'That is very delightful. Whose daughter is she?' the Shōyu asked.

'The fourth daughter of the Minamoto Chūnagon. They wanted me to marry her. But I have a lady I cannot part from, and so I think of passing this lady on to you. The day for the marriage is the day after tomorrow. Get ready by that time.'

'She will not be expecting me and so she will laugh at me.'

The Shōshō thought it very humourous that he should blame anyone for laughing at him but he managed to keep his countenance. 'She will not be so cruel as to do that,' he said. 'Say to her parents, "Since last autumn I have been visiting your daughter in secret. Hearing that the Shōshō was going to marry her, as I am a kinsman of his, I explained the situation to him and asked him why he was taking my place with the lady. He answered that I had good reason to speak so, that he would give up the idea of marrying her, and that it was no doubt in ignorance of my secret relations with her that her parents had chosen another as her husband, but that such an arrangement was foolish. He therefore urged me to make my relations with her public and take his place tonight." If you say this, they will have to consent. How could she laugh? If you continue to visit her, she will come to love you.'

The Shōyu nodded his agreement.

'All right then. Go and visit her tomorrow night.' the Shōshō said, and went away.

Remorse struck him as it crossed his mind how the Fourth Lady would feel, but he had already made up his mind to revenge himself on her mother.

At the Nijō house, the Shōshō found the Lady bent over a wooden brazier, smoothing out the ashes as she looked out at the falling snow. She made a very attractive picture. He sat down on the other side of the brazier, and she wrote this poem in the ashes—

> If ere I came here,
> My life had been extinguished,
> Then my love for you, . . .

He read it and was deeply touched. Then he finished the poem—

> Being thus concealed, would in
> Blaze of passion burn me up.

Then he wrote this poem—

> So great is my joy
> To find the fire still blazing
> Beneath the ashes,

That I clasp it to my breast
And carry it to my bed.

Saying this, he took her in his arms and carried her to
bed. The Lady smiled and said, 'How dangerous to clasp
to your breast the fire!'

At the Chūnagon's mansion, all were busy preparing,
for the wedding day had arrived.

The Shōshō sent a message to remind the Hyōbu no
Shōyu. 'Tonight is the night of which I told you. Go
about eight o'clock,' he said.

The Shōyu answered that he would.

He had told his father about it and the foolish old man
had said that it was a not unsuitable match. 'What you
have been encouraged to do by people who are kind to you
cannot have bad results. Be punctual!' the father said. He
caused his son's clothes to be got ready, and the Shōyu
went off in the evening in his best robes.

In formal dress, the people of the Chūnagon's mansion
were awaiting him, and when they heard that he had
arrived, they ushered him in. They did not see in the
dim light that it was this simpleton, but he appeared to
their eyes very noble and slender.

'How slender and charming he looked when he went
into the Lady's room!' the servants said loudly, thinking
it was the Shōshō so universally admired.

The Kita no Kata, overhearing these remarks, smiled
with great pleasure. 'What a fine son-in-law I have! How

fortunate I am!' she said to everyone. 'I have a paragon
of a son-in-law. He will soon be made a Minister.'

And everyone agreed that was certain to come to pass.

The Fourth Lady also, not detecting that it was this
fool, went to bed with him. And, at dawn, he left the
house.

Next morning, the Shōshō was amusing himself by imagining how things had gone the previous night and found
it highly humorous. 'The Chūnagon took a son-in-law
last night,' he told the Lady.

'Who is he?'

'The Hyōbu no Shōyu, the son of the Jibu no Kyō, my
uncle. He is a very nice-looking man with a handsome
nose.'

'That is usually considered one of his characteristic
defects,' the Lady said with a smile.

'What! It is his distinctively attractive feature, as you
will see when he calls on us soon,' he said and went to the
servant's room to have a letter sent to the Hyōbu no Shōyu.
'How are you?' he wrote. 'Have you sent a letter to the
Lady yet? If you have not yet done so, send this poem
with it. I think it is very good.

> Lovers feel their love
> Intenser grown on the morn
>   Of their first meeting,
> So have I always been told;
> But these are not my feelings.

I remember the "entwining creeper."[1]

When this letter arrived, the Shōyu was vainly labouring to compose a poem suitable for sending on such an occasion. He thought that the one sent him by the Shōshō most appropriate for the purpose, and quickly copied it out and despatched it to the Fourth Lady.

Then he wrote to the Shōshō. 'I was very successful last night,' he wrote. 'And was very delighted that no one laughed at me. I will tell you about it all in detail when I see you.' I had not already sent a letter to the Lady and so I was pleased to get your poem and have sent it to her.'

This pleased the Shōshō very much, yet though he had determined to revenge himself on the Kita no Kata, he made up his mind that the Fourth Lady should be more favoured afterwards in compensation for her present shame. The Lady of Nijō was still in rather a melancholy mood, and out of compassion he said nothing more to her of the Chūnagon's new son-in-law, but not being able to keep this laughable incident to himself, he told Tachihaki. They laughed together heartily over it.

'That was very well done,' said Tachihaki in his delight.

At the Chūnagon's mansion, the Fourth Lady was await-

---

[1] Referring to the poem—

> The autumn hagi
> Is troubled by the creeper
>   That entwines around it;
> So seems your love to me now,
> For I do not love you more.

ing the usual letter and when it arrived, she took it and
opened it at once. However, when she found what kind
of a letter it was, she sat paralysed with shame and was
unable to rise. When the Kita no Kata took the letter to
see what the hand-writing was like, the Fourth Lady was
ready to die with shame; she felt now a greater shame than
the Lady Ochikubo had felt on being asked who 'this
Ochikubo' was. The Kita no Kata looked at the letter
and with some misgiving compared the handwriting with
that of the letter which had been sent before by the Sakon
no Shōshō. She was astounded to find that the writing
was not the same.

The Chūnagon also snatched at the letter to read it, but
his eyesight was too weak. 'This dandy's affectation is to
write in very pale ink, is it not? Read it to me,' he said.

The Kita no Kata took the letter from him and remembering the words of the poem which the Kurōdo no Shōshō
had sent on the morning following his first meeting with
the Third Lady, she said, 'It says, "I feel that the day will
never come to an end."'[1]

The Great Lord laughed. 'He is a true dandy; he knows
how to write letters. Write a good answer at once,' he said
and went out.

The Fourth Lady's pain was almost physical in its vio-

---

[1] Referring to some such sentiments as the following—

Although well I know
That this day also will be
Followed by a night,
Yet do I feel that the day
Will never come to an end.

lence; she went and lay down on her bed.

The Kita no Kata talked the matter over with the Third Lady. 'Why has he written in this way?' she asked very sorrowfully.

'But would he have written in this way, if he had taken a dislike to the Fourth Lady?' asked the Third Lady. 'Such expressions as "My love has intenser grown to-day" have become hackneyed and commonplace by long use. Has he therefore chosen this odd method of expressing his love? Still, it seems rather strange.'

'You may be right. A dandy often thinks he can do what other men would not venture to do,' the Kita no Kata agreed, and told the Fourth Lady to write her answer at once.

But the Fourth Lady, with her mother and sisters around her thus speaking pityingly and suspiciously, could not find the strength to rise from her bed.

'I will write it then,' said the Kita no Kata, and wrote this poem as the answer—

> 'Those who are too old
> To know the delight of love
> Cannot see why differs
> The morning after first meeting
> From any other morning.

The Lady herself is too indignant to write anything.'

She rewarded the messenger and asked him to carry the answer to the Shōyu. The Fourth Lady lay in bed all day, and then, just as night fell, the Shōyu arrived, very early.

'I told you,' commented the Kita no Kata as she went out joyfully to meet him. 'Had he disliked the Lady, he would not have come so early as this. He used those odd expressions purposely.'

The Fourth Lady was filled with shame but could do nothing else but meet him. She found his manner of speaking so slow and stupid that when she recalled what the Kurōdo no Shōshō had told her of the Sakon no Shōshō she thought that there was something suspicious about him. 'It is I and not he that should have said, "I do not love you more,"[1] she thought.

Next morning while it was still dark, he went away.

Magnificent preparations were now made for the Third Night. Proper arrangements were made for the entertainment of the new son-in-law's attendants. Even the Kurōdo no Shōshō came and busied himself helping with the preparations. The Great Lord himself went out to welcome him when he arrived for the Shōshō was a lord favoured by the Emperor infinitely more than any other lord was.

'Please come in this way,' the Great Lord said, and the guest came in and sat down without the exchange of any civilities. Now in the bright light it could be seen that he had a very thin neck, a white face, as white as if it had been powdered, and a turned-up nose.

The people gazed at him in amazement, and when they recognized the Hyōhu no Shōyu, they could not restrain

---

[1] The reference is to the 'entwining creeper' mentioned in the Shōyu's letter.

themselves from bursting into loud laughter. The Kurōdo no Shōshō was a man who always laughed very heartily at everything; he now positively roared with laughter.

'It is "Omoshiro no Koma," isn't it?' he said and went out, laughing and striking at things with his fan. At the Court this was what the Hyōbu no Shōyu was called and when people saw him coming they laughed and said, 'Here's the White-faced Colt; he has got loose again.'

'What a thing to happen!' the Kurōdo no Shōshō tried to say but could not for his laughter, when he had returned to his own room.

The Chūnagon was speechless with amazement. He was furious with anger for he could see that he was the victim of a plot. Still, on account of the large number of people present, he had to restrain his wrathful indignation. 'This is a surprise! We were not expecting you. This is very strange,' he exclaimed.

The Shōyu then began in his stupid manner to make his explanations in accordance with the instructions of the Shōshō, but the Chūnagon, feeling that it was useless to stay and listen to him any longer, got up and left the room, without offering him even a cup of saké. The Shōyu's attendants, meanwhile, went on noisily eating and drinking in the room to which they had been shown, in complete ignorance of what was happening. The Shōyu, miserable at thus being left alone, at last went into the Fourth Lady's room by the door which he had used on the former occasions.

When the Kita no Kata heard what had happened, she

was overwhelmed with amazement and could not even utter a word. The Chūnagon was filled with bitter resentment that such a disgrace should have fallen on him in his old age and went to his own room. The Fourth Lady was already lying within the screen and when the Shōyu came in and lay down she could not escape from him.

The servants felt very sorry for the Fourth Lady. The woman who had acted as go-between could not be blamed for what had occurred as having done this purposely out of enmity, for she was the Lady's foster-mother. All the people passed the night in lamentation, while the Shōyu next morning remained in bed as if he were never going to get up, as if he thought that it was the usual custom to stay at the house for the whole of the Fourth Day.[1]

'There are plenty of men in the world,' the Kurōdo no Shōshō said to his wife. 'Why then did you bring this White-faced Colt here? This is absolutely beyond words. It will be extremely disgusting for me to be a fellow son-in-law to him and meet him here. How could this stupid fool they call the "Court Horse" who is almost ostracised by everyone have got in here? It must be you who planned it,' he added with a laugh of derision.

The Third Lady answered only that she knew nothing at all about it. She was very sorry for her sister; she thought to herself that the cruel expressions in the letter the Shōyu had sent had been due to his stupidity and

---

[1] On the Fourth Morning, the bridegroom remained till broad daylight before returning—on the previous two mornings he returned while it was yet dark.

eccentricity; she was filled with great pity for her sister. One can well imagine the feelings of the Kita no Kata.

It was half past eleven and the Shōyu had not been served with washing water nor with gruel. A large number of servants had been carefully chosen for the Fourth Lady's service but they did not go to serve him. 'Who wishes to be in such a fool's service?' they said to each other.

The Shōyu himself was lying idly in bed. The Fourth Lady watched him; how ugly he was, with his upturned nose, the nostrils of which seemed large enough for a man to go up; she was disgusted. She got up slowly and left the room as if she had business to do.

The Kita no Kata was waiting for her; she had much to say to the Lady. 'If you had not been so self-willed as not to confess at the beginning about yourself and the Shōyu,' she said, 'we could have kept the affair secret, but now that everything has been announced publicly with so much ado, it would bring disgrace both on us and on his family. Tell me who it was that acted as go-between. Tell me,' her mother urged her.

The Fourth Lady's heart was filled with bitter sorrow; she could but weep piteously. She had not known who it was who was visiting her, but it was no use protesting when her mother thus cunningly insinuated that she had known all the time who he was.

'What will the Kurōdo no Shōshō think of me? A woman's lot is truly a sorrowful one,' the Fourth Lady moaned, but her tears had no effect on her mother.

The Shōyu still slept on as though he would never wake.

'I am sorry for him though,' the Chūnagon said. 'Serve him the washing water and food. If he were to forsake the Lady now, it would add a worse disgrace to our shame. Is it not her Fate? It will not make things as they were before to cry and weep loudly now.'

'But how can I remain perfectly tranquil while such a fool takes my dearest daughter?' cried the Kita no Kata in great agitation.

'Do not speak so badly of him. How much worse than it is now would it be if he were to forsake her!'

'Yes, if he did forsake her, I might think that was true. But at this moment, I feel that it would be a good thing if he were to cease coming,' was the Kita no Kata's reply.

At two o'clock in the afternoon, the Shōyu, very embarrassed that no one had come in to see him, went away.

In the evening, he returned. The Fourth Lady wept and would not go in to him until the Chūnagon, very angry, compelled her to do so. 'If you dislike him so much, why did you allow him to come to visit you secretly in the first place?' he said to her. 'Now that the marriage has been publicly announced, is it to bring a double disgrace on your parents and brothers that you act in this manner?' He remained with her and continued to urge her, until at last she went in to him, feeling very forlorn and weeping bitterly.

The Shōyu thought it very strange that she should weep, but he said nothing to her and they went to bed.

Thus the affair continued with the Fourth Lady extremely unhappy and reluctant, and the Kita no Kata doing her best to put an end to their relations which only continued because of the Chūnagon's wishes.

However, very often the Shōyu came and returned without the Fourth Lady receiving him.

Then a most unfortunate thing happened; the Fourth Lady began to feel some distress in the mornings.

'Oh, dear! You must not have a child. The Kurōdo no Shōshō and his wife have not yet had a child in spite of all their longings for one. And now you are going to have one by this fool,' the Kita no Kata exclaimed.

The Fourth Lady agreed; but more than anything else, she wished to die.

Meanwhile, the Kurōdo no Shōshō was finding his worst fears realised. 'How is the White-faced Colt?' the young nobles at the Court began to say to him. 'You must bring him to the White Horse Ceremony.'[1] or 'Which of his sons-in-law does the Chūnagon favour more, you or the White-faced Colt?' And then they would all laugh. This was very annoying to the Kurōdo no Shōshō who had always stood on his dignity. Also from the first, his love for the Third Lady had been but half-hearted and it had only been because of the cordiality of his welcome and the great hospitality shown him at the Chūnagon's mansion that he had continued his relations with her. His visits

---

[1] Aouma no Sechie, held on the Seventh Day of the First Month, when the Emperor inspected twenty-one white horses from his stables.

now began to be shorter and less frequent, and the Third
Lady grew more and more melancholy.

Daily the Lady of Nijō was growing more and more
beautiful and the Lord's endeavours for her pleasure were
boundless. 'Employ as many servants as you wish,' he
said. 'Where there are many maids, the whole househould
is comfortable and happy.' So one servant brought another
until there were over twenty employed. As the Shōshō and
the Lady were both generous and kind, the work was done
cheerfully. Everything was arranged in a very up-to-date
style—when the servants went to the main building in the
morning, they changed their robes, and again when they
came out in the evening. And the head of the whole staff
of servants was Emon.

Tachihaki had told his wife about the affair of the
White-faced Colt.

'Now my prayer for revenge on the Kita no Kata has
been answered,' Emon thought, her heart filled with a great
joy; but aloud she said, 'Oh, how sorry I am to hear that!
What must the Kita no Kata have felt! Some are sure
to be punished for that.'

The end of the year was now approaching. Many rolls
of fine cloth, damask and yarn, and red, violet and blue
dyes were sent from the mansion of the Taishō, the Lord's
father, with a letter. 'The Shōshō's robes should be made
at once,' he wrote. 'We are too busy with our own work

to make them here.'

As we have already learnt, the Lady of Nijō was very skilful in making clothes, and she went on with this task very busily.

A countryman of some means, having been appointed Uma no Jō[1] through the influence of the Shōshō, presented him with fifty rolls of silk which he ordered to be shared among the servants. Emon did the sharing and did it with perfect impartiality.

The house at Nijō belonged to the Lord's mother. She had two daughters, the elder of whom was an Imperial consort. Her eldest son was the Shōshō; the second was a Chamberlain, who was interested in nothing else but music; and the third was a young boy who, however, was already allowed entry to the Court.[2] From his infancy, the Shōshō had been the favourite son of his father, the centre of everyone's admiration and the favourite of the Emperor. He had therefore been allowed perfect freedom. When his name was mentioned, his father smiled always in pleasure. And all the servants down to the lowest, and even the ox-drivers, served him with all their heart.

Thus the New Year arrived. The Shōshō's New Year robe had been made very beautifully, the dyeing and everything else all splendidly done. He himself thought it magnificent, and so put it on and went to see his mother.

---

[1] A minor position in the Imperial Stables.
[2] That is, to study Court etiquette.

'How beautiful!' exclaimed the Kita no Kata of the Taishō when she saw it. 'How clever she is at making robes! When your sister needs a robe for some important ceremony at the Court, I will ask her to make it. The sewing is as nice as one could wish for.'

At the time of the General Appointments, the Shōshō was appointed Chūjō[1] and given Third Court Rank. Therefore, of course, his reputation among people in general increased still further.

About this time, the Kurodo no Shōshō offered marriage to the Chūjō's sister, the second daughter of the Taishō.
'He is a very estimable man. If you are intending to marry her to an ordinary noble,[2] it would be well to accept his offer. He has many merits,' the Chūjō advised his mother. The Kurodo no Shōshō was the one of her sons-in-law whom the Kita no Kata of the Chūnagon prized highest; it was to please him that she had treated the Lady Ochikubo so cruelly. Now the Chūjō in revenge gave this advice to his mother in order that the Kurodo no Shōshō should break off his relations with the Third Lady.

This suggestion of the Chūjō's was approved by his mother who herself thought that the Kurodō no Shōshō would prove a fine son-in-law. She therefore allowed her daughter to answer his letters.

From this time then, the Kurodo no Shōshō, being con-

---

[1] Lieutenant General (of the Bodyguard of the Left).
[2] That is, not intending to make her an Imperial consort.

fident of his success here, began to treat the Third Lady with more and more disdain. He found fault with the robes made at the Chūnagon's mansion which formerly he had praised. He would take advantage of any faults in their making to speak angrily. 'What is the matter here?' he would say, refusing to wear robes he had once been so willing to wear. 'Where has that girl gone who used to make clothes so well?'

'She ran away with one of the men,' the Third Lady answered.

'Which of the men here could it have been? I am sure she ran away on her own. Are there any men here whom she would be likely to run away with?'

'Perhaps you are right. It seems that nothing in this house gives satisfaction to you nowadays. I am sorry that it is so.'

'Oh, yes, there is. There is the White-faced Colt. I am very jealous that you have that incomparably graceful noble here.'

The Kurōdo no Shōshō's visits had become infrequent, and he came always only to torment her in this way and leave her full of jealousy and sadness.

The Kita no Kata missed Ochikubo very much; her hatred for the Lady was still increasing and she racked her brains to find her and have revenge on her. She had thought how fortunate she was in having obtained such a good son-in-law in the Kurōdo no Shōshō but now it seemed that this son-in-law in whom she had felt such pride was deserting the Third Lady for another. And she had also made herself a laughing-stock by her elaborate preparations for the Fourth Lady's marriage, only to obtain as a son-in-law the White-faced Colt. The Kita no Kata lamented so deeply that her health was feared for.

The last day of the First Month was a Lucky Day, and as on this day pilgrimages to temples brought many blessings, the Third and Fourth Ladies went with their mother in one carriage to make an incognito pilgrimage to the temple at Kiyomizu. By chance, the Chūjō of the Third Rank and his Kita no Kata[1] were also going there at the same time. The Chūnagon's carriage was in front with no runners for they were incognito. But the Chūjō's party had a great number of runners for both the Chūjō and his Kita no Kata were there, and they dashed animatedly along, scattering the ordinary pilgrims from their path. The people in the Chūnagon's party were most annoyed to find themselves chased so hotly, and the people in the Chūjō's party could see by the light of the torches that there were so many people in the first carriage that it was only with great difficulty that the ox could pull the carriage up the hill. Continually the ox had to stop and rest, and the second carriage had to stop also and wait till it moved on again, to the great anger of the runners belonging to the second party.

'Whose carriage is that?' the Chūjō demanded of one of his men.

---

[1] Referring to the Lady Ochikubo.

'It is the Kita no Kata of the Chūnagon making a pilgrimage incognito to the Temple,' was the answer.

'How blessed to me this pilgrimage to meet her on the way!' he thought in delight. 'Tell the attendants to hurry along with that carriage or pull in to the side of the road to let us pass, my men,' he ordered.

'Your ox seems to be tired,' the attendants therefore called out. 'It is not able to go quickly enough. It would be better to pull to one side and let our carriage pass.'

'If the ox is weak, let the White-faced Colt pull it,' the Chūjō said. His voice was sweet and refined, but the people in the other carriage heard him distinctly enough and were very humiliated, wondering in their vexation who it was who could have said that.

The carriage was not pulled to one side so the Chūjō's men began to throw stones at it and shout, 'Why can't you pull the carriage to one side?'

The Chūnagon's men were also angry. 'You act as if you were in the service of the Taishō,' they shouted back. 'This is the carriage of a Chūnagon. If you want to attack us, attack us now.'

'We are not afraid of you even though you are in the service of a Chūnagon.' they answered, and stones descended on the Chūnagon's carriage like a shower of rain. They forced the carriage further and further over to the side of the road to make way for their own carriage. The Chūnagon's men, realising that a contest was impracticable as they were inferior, even in number, made no reply even when they were pushed so far to the side of the road that one of the wheels of their carriage went down into the ditch.

'What a humiliating result!' exclaimed those who had been arguing with the Chūjō's attendants.

The people in their carriage were much annoyed; the old Kita no Kata more than anyone else. 'Who is it that is making a pilgrimage?' she asked her men.

'It is the Chūjō of the Third Rank, the son of the Sadaishō,' one answered. 'He is one of the first men of today; we were not wise to challenge his attendants as we did.'

'I wonder why he acts in such a hostile manner and puts us to shame like this. No doubt it was he who brought disgrace on us with the affair of the Hyōbu no Shōyu. If he had but said "No" in a straightforward manner, we should have given up the idea of marrying the Fourth Lady to him. And now he acts towards us worse than a stranger would, like an enemy. What a cruel man he is!' the old Kita no Kata said, wringing her hands.

The ditch was very deep and it was difficult to lift the wheel out of it. There was a great deal of noise and confusion and, to their great annoyance, one of the wheels was broken. Then they put their shoulders to the wheel and lifted it out. They tied the broken wheel with a piece of rope so that the carriage would not be likely to overturn, and then went on slowly up the hill.

The Chūjō's carriage had meanwhile gone on to the Temple and it seemed an infinitely long time before the other carriage came staggering slowly along.

'Has that strongly-built wheel of yours got broken then?' one of the Chūjō's men called out, and they all laughed in derision.

Now as it was a Lucky Day there were large crowds of people at the Temple and as it was impossible for the other carriage to come up to the steps, the Chūnagon's men thought it better to go round to the back of the Temple for the people to descend there.

The Chūjō then called Tachihaki to him. 'Go and find out where those people are alighting,' he said. 'I want to forestall them and take possession of their room before they get there.'

Tachihaki therefore ran round to the back of the Temple and found that the old Kita no Kata had called to her a priest whom she knew and was relating the events of the journey, how they had started out early but had come into collision with a Chūjō of the Third Rank and that they had had their wheel broken and had been delayed. 'Have you reserved a room for us?' she went on. 'We are very tired and should like to alight at once.'

'How annoying that must have been!' exclaimed the priest. 'A room has been reserved for you, as you ordered. No doubt that rascal of a Chūjō will be wanting a room and will be taking one by force, for all the rooms are reserved. What an annoying evening this is going to be!'

'Then we must alight quickly or our room will be stolen while it is empty,' the old Kita no Kata said and hastened to alight, sending one of the Temple servants in front to find out where the room was. Tachihaki followed him to discover the whereabouts of the room, and then ran back to the Chūjō to report what he had learnt and to suggest that they took possession of the room first.

Tachihaki helped them to alight, a screen being carried to conceal the Lady from the gaze of the people. The Chūjō did not leave her side; in all things his care for her was boundless.

The Kita no Kata of the Chūnagon and her party were hastening to arrive at the room before the Chūjō alighted while the Chūjō and the Lady entered in a most ceremonial manner, their shoes sounding 'soyo-soyo, hara-hara.' Tachihaki preceded them, clearing the crowds from their way. To their great vexation, the members of the Chūnagon's party were forced to stand aside for the passing of the Chūjō and the Lady; they stood among the crowd looking most embarrassed.

Seeing them standing thus, the Lord laughed loudly. 'You are always behind, aren't you? After all your efforts to get in front of us, you get left behind,' he said.

All the members of the Chūnagon's party were extremely vexed, and not being able to proceed quickly, they were a long time reaching the room reserved for them. Here an acolyte had been left but the Chūjō's party arriving there first, he had naturally thought that they were the people for whom the room was reserved and had gone out as the Chūjō had entered.

Then the Lord called Tachihaki to him and whispered to him so that the Lady should not hear that he should laugh at the other party when they arrived, and assure them that the room had been reserved for the Chūjō.

Therefore, when the Chūnagon's party were about to enter the room, a man said to them, 'You have evidently made some mistake. The Chūjō is in this room.' The other party stood dumbfounded and all the people laughed. 'This is very strange,' the man went on. 'Did you make certain before you alighted that a room was reserved for you, and that this was your room? You cannot get a room so easily as this. I regret that you are in such a difficulty, but I suggest that you try to find one in the Retreat Apartments near the Niō Hall. There is always plenty of room there.' Tachihaki with an innocent look had instructed this rash young man to say this, to avoid revealing his own presence.

Laughed at in this manner, the old Kita no Kata and her daughters felt very humiliated. To return at once would have been to leave their pilgrimage uncompleted; to say only that they were desolated would be a foolish understatement of their feelings. They stood there for a little while but realising that it was of no use standing there in the middle of the crowds of people, they left. If they had outnumbered the other party, they would have contested the Chūjō's right to the room, but it was useless to fight. It can easily be imagined with what feelings of distress they went outside. They fled back to their carriage broken-hearted.

'One who just bore us a grudge would not have acted in this way,' said the old Kita no Kata. 'He must have some deep malice against the Great Lord. What has caused him to act in this way?' So they lamented together and the Fourth Lady more than all, for the White-faced Colt had been mentioned.

They sent for the Chief Priest and told him what had happened. 'This has brought a great shame on us. Have you another room?' asked the old Kita no Kata.

'Where can I find another room?' the Chief Priest replied. 'Other nobles have also forced their way into reserved rooms. It is a great pity that you were later than the Chūjō in alighting. But there is now nothing you can do. You can only stay the night in your carriage. If he were just an ordinary noble, I would try to persuade him to give the room up to you, but he is the first man nowadays. Even the Dajōdaijin[1] dare not make a sound in his presence. His younger sister also is in great favour with the Emperor. He regards himself as the greatest favourite with the Emperor. One must be careful not to offend him,' the priest added and went away.

Nothing more could be done. As they had reserved a room, they had thought that they would not be long in the carriage, and so six of them had come in the one carriage; now they found it too small to move in. Their sufferings were greater than those of the Lady Ochikubo shut up in the store-room.

At last dawn came. They hurried to make their depar-

---

[1] The President of the Supreme Council of State.

ture before the cruel Lord came out, but as their wheel was being tied up, the Chūjō came out and entered his carriage.

Fearing further annoyances, they decided to follow after his carriage on the return journey and waited for him to leave.

The Chūjō thought that it was necessary to punish the old Kita no Kata heavily that she might remember her humiliation, so he called a page to him. 'Go near the shafts of that carriage,' he ordered the boy, 'and say, "Have you had enough?"'

The page went near and spoke as he had been instructed.

'Who asks that?' asked the old Kita no Kata.

'The people of that carriage,' the boy answered.

'Well,' whispered the Great Lady to the others in the carriage, 'he did all that on purpose out of malice then,' and wondering what would happen next, she answered, 'Not yet.'

The boy returned to the Lord with this message. 'The foolish woman returns a spiteful answer,' the Chūjō said to the Lady with a smile, 'She does not know that you are here.' Then he sent this message to the old Kita no Kata, 'If you have not had enough, you will have more soon.'

The Kita no Kata was about to make a reply but the Third Lady whispered to her, 'Do not answer him. This disgusts me.'

So, as there was no answer from the carriage, the ox-driver went back to tell the Chūjō who then made his departure.

'I am very sorry you did that,' said the Lady of Nijō
to the Chūjō. 'The Great Lord will be told of this and
of how cruelly you have behaved. Do not send such
messages again.'

'The Chūnagon is not in the carriage, is he?'

'No, but his daughters are and so it is just the same
as if he were present.'

'You will be able to show your affection for him later
in compensation for this. I shall continue to carry out
what I have decided to do.'

When the old Kita no Kata returned, she went to relate
the incidents of the journey to the Chūnagon. 'Has the
son of the Taishō, the Chūjō, any ill-will against you?'
she first asked him.

'No, he behaves with great care and courtesy to me at
Court,' the Chūnagon replied.

'That is very strange,' she commented and told him all
that had happened. 'I have never seen such spiteful conduct. What he said just before he left was most provoking.
I must have my revenge on him in some way,' she went
on, writhing in agony.

'I am an old man now and my memory is fading. On
the other hand, it is expected that the Chūjō will soon be
promoted to the rank of Minister. It is therefore not in
my power to have revenge on him. He must have had
reasons for provoking you and for putting my family to

especial shame,' the Chūnagon said sadly, snapping his fingers.

Thus the Sixth Month came. By the inducings and urgings of the Chūjō, his parents consented to the marriage of the Kurōdo no Shōshō to their second daughter. The news of this almost broke the hearts of the people of the Chūnagon's family. 'The Chūjō did what he did[1] to get the Kurōdo no Shōshō away from us and bring this about. I wish I could become a ghost and haunt him,' said the Chūnagon, wringing his hands in his agony.

The Lady of Nijō was very sorry for them in their loss of the son-in-law whom they had prized so much. As she was so clever in sewing, she had been asked to make the robes for wearing on the Third Night of the marriage. She busied herself dyeing the silk and making the robes, and as she did it, she thought of former days.

> The one for whom now
> I sew these robes, formerly
> I used to sew for,
> And now as I sew, I think
> Of how I fled that house.

When the robes, all splendidly made, were sent back, the delight of the Chūjō's mother was boundless. And the Chūjō himself thought that they were made as well as one could hope for.

---

[1] Referring to the affair of the Hyōbu no Shōyu.

When the Chūjō met the Kurōdo no Shōshō for the
first time, he said, 'My sister was very timid about meeting
you, having heard that you were the lover of a very terrible
woman, but we succeeded in persuading her, for we wished
to become more closely connected with you. However, if
you do not find my sister as good a companion as you
expect, do not treat her as you did your former mate.'

'What a thing to fear!' answered the Kurōdo no
Shōshō. 'Listen to me. Since you consented to my
marrying your sister, I have not even written to that other
one. My reliance on you is infinite.' It was true that he
had completely given up visiting the Third Lady. He was
more than delighted by his welcome and hospitality at the
mansion of the Taishō and also by the beauty of his new
wife and so he never thought of renewing his relations
with the Third Lady. And because of her sorrow and her
burning indignation at his desertion, the old Kita no Kata
completely lost her appetite.

Hearing that many pretty maids were being taken into
the service of the Chūjō and that there they were very
kindly treated, Shōnagon, the servant from the Chūnagon's
mansion, came on the recommendation of the Lady Ben[1]
to the Nijō house, not knowing that the Lady Ochikubo
was mistress there.

Looking at her through the curtains, the Lady recognised
her and sent Emon out to her. 'I thought it was a stranger!'
she made Emon say to her. 'I have not forgotten your

---

[1] A fellow-servant from the Chunagon's mansion.

great kindness to me in the old days. It has always weighed heavy on my heart that I could not inform you of where I was, but I have had to be very cautious. I am very glad to see you now. Come inside at once.'

Shōnagon was startled at this address, dropped down the fan with which she was covering her face, and full of excitement crawled nearer to Emon on her knees. 'What is that? Who sent that message?' she asked.

'You can easily guess that from my being here,' answered Emon. 'It was from her who was formerly called the Lady Ochikubo. I also am very glad to see you. Not being able to see a single person whom I knew of old has made me very lonely here.'

'I am glad also. She is our own Lady. I could never forget her; she has always remained most dear to me. It must be that Buddha has shown me the way here.'

So, full of delight, she went into her presence of the Lady, and when she saw her, it brought back to her memory the time when the Lady had lived in the Lower Room. Now she found her looking more maturely beautiful and refined; she was evidently extremely happy in her new home.

In the room with them were more than ten young and pretty attendants clad in summer robes of hemp which rustled 'soyo-soyo.' They all looked most attractive as they sat and worked and chatted. 'Who is this who is received by the Lady so soon after her arrival here? We were not,' said one, expressing the envy of them all.

'Yes. She must be an important person,' the Lady answered, smiling.

'The Lady is far happier here than her sisters are under the care of their father and mother,' thought Shōnagon, 'and it is because of the charm of her manner.' When the others were within hearing, she spoke of her good fortune at being taken into the Lady of Nijō's service; and when no one else was there, she gave the Lady details of life in the Chūnagon's mansion. When she told her of Tenyaku's reply to the old Kita no Kata, Emon laughed very much. 'And the Great Lady was also made sorely ashamed and angry about the son-in-law she took afterwards, but it seems as if it must have been her Fate; soon the Fourth Lady found that she was pregnant, and the Kita no Kata had to resign herself to the continuation of the relations with the Hyōbu no Shōyu, though very much against her will.'

'That is strange about the Fourth Lady's husband', said the Lady. 'According to what the Chūjō says, he is a fine handsome man with a splendid nose.'

'He told you that as a joke,' Shōnagon replied. 'His nose is uglier than all his other features. The nostrils of his turned-up nose are so large that one could build the East and West Wings of a mansion in the right and left, and the Main Building as well.

'What an awful thing!' exclaimed the young Kita no Kata. 'How terrible for them to have such a son-in-law!'

Just then the Chūjō returned from the Court, very

drunk, his handsome face ruddy. 'I was summoned for a Concert. Many lords pressed me to drink one after another and I had a difficult time! I played the flute and was given this robe as a reward by the Emperor,' the Lord explained, taking a heavily-scented pale-red robe and putting it on the Lady. 'That is for you to wear,' he said.

'What is this a reward for?' the Lady inquired with a smile.

The Lord then noticed Shōnagon. 'Is not this one of the attendants I saw at the Chūnagon's mansion?' he asked.

'Yes, she is,' answered the Lady.

'Why has she come here? How very much I should like to hear the rest of the story of the handsome Katano no Shōshō!' the Chūjō said.

Shōnagon did not know that he had been present when she had spoken to the Lady in the Lower Room, and so did not know what he was alluding to. She therefore remained silent.

'This is very miserable. Let us go to bed,' the Chūjō then said, and he and the Lady went within the curtains.

'How charming and handsome he is!' thought Shōnagon. 'I am sure he loves her dearly. Most fortunate are those who have as charming a character as she has!'

Now the Udaijin[1] had an only daughter whom he had wished to become an Imperial consort but, thinking of what might happen to her after his death, he had decided

---

[1] The Minister of the Right.

to marry her, if possible, to the Chūjō of the Third Rank, whom he knew from close observation to be sound and reliable and one who would look after his daughter carefully. 'He has not yet taken a noble lady for his wife, although I hear that he keeps a lover at Nijō,' the Minister thought. 'I have observed him carefully for a long time and I believe that he will make an ideal husband for her. And he will be promoted to very high rank in the near future.' He therefore sent by a friend a message suggesting this marriage to the Chūjō's foster-mother.[1]

She told the Chūjō what had been suggested and urged him strongly to accept this very good offer.

'Yes, perhaps it would be a good offer—if I were single. Hint to him that I am living with one I love,' the Chūjō answered and left her.

However, his foster-mother did not give this answer to the Minister of the Right for she thought that it would be easy to persuade the Chūjō to consent, as it was evident that the Lady of Nijō had no parents and had only the Lord on whom to rely. Further she thought that it would be a much better arrangement for the Lord if he married someone whose parents could help him to success. So she sent instead this message, 'We are very pleased with the proposal. On the next Lucky Day, I will bring his letter to the Lady.'

The Minister, thinking that everything was satisfactorily arranged, busied himself with the preparations. He decided

---

[1] Tachihaki's mother.

that the marriage should take place in the Fourth Month; magnificent furniture was made; young maid-servants were sought for; and all other necessary preparations completed.

Emon heard of this from one of the household of the Chūjō's father. 'Does the Lady of Nijō know that the Chūjō is to marry the Udaijin's daughter?' she was asked.

Emon was very agitated to hear this. 'I have never heard anything about it. Is it certain?'

'Yes, it is quite certain. The marriage is fixed for the Fourth Month, and they are busy making preparations for it.'

Emon told the Lady this piece of news and asked her if she had heard anything of it. The Lady was greatly distressed and wondered if it could be true. 'I have heard nothing of it. Who told you about it?' she asked.

'The news is reliable for it comes from one of the Taishō's household who even told me the month in which the marriage is to take place.'

'His mother must have urged him to do this,' the Lady thought, 'and if she pressed him to do so, he could not refuse.' She told no one her thoughts but full of anxiety waited for the Lord to give her this cruel piece of news. However he said nothing.

She tried to hide her misery but he noticed how melancholy she seemed to be. 'Is something troubling you?' he said to her. 'You seem as if something is wrong. You know I am not like most men; I do not continually say,

"I love you," "I will never desert you," "I long for you";
still my sole object is to shield you from all anxiety. That
has been my object since the beginning of our love. It
pains me to see you so sorrowful. At the very beginning,
when I went to see you in spite of the heavy rain and was
laughed at as a white-legged robber, was I cold then? Tell
me what is wrong.'

'Can there be anything the matter?' the Lady said.

'I do not know; but you are looking so melancholy.
Something must have caused you to feel such constraint
towards me.'

The Lady answered with this poem—

> Hearts that feel constraint
> Are covered with many leaves
>   Like the **hamayū**
> Which grows so free on the coast
> Of distant Mikumano.

'It pains me to hear you speak thus,' he replied. 'It is
as I feared; you have some trouble.

> Unlike **hamayū**
> Which grow so free on the coast
>   Of Mikumano
> With its numerous leaves,
> I have but one—you alone.

You may have heard something about me which has caused
you sorrow. Tell me what it is.'

However, the Lady remained silent; what she had heard
might not be true, she thought.

Next morning, Emon spoke to Tachihaki of the rumoured marriage. 'Was it to save me anxiety that you told me nothing of all this? But such a thing could not be kept secret for ever, could it?'

'I have heard nothing about it,' Tachihaki answered.

'But strangers have heard of it and have condoled with the Lady's servants. How can you be ignorant of it?'

'It is very strange. I will see what the Lord is intending to do,' Tachihaki said and went out to find the Chūjō.

The Chūjō had returned to Nijō to find the Lady looking out into the Spring garden. Seeing a beautiful branch of plum-blossom, he broke it off and gave it to her, saying, 'Look at these incomparable flowers, and with them delight and soothe your heart.'

The Lady returned the flowers with this poem—

> Though I have not been
> By any sorrow taught this—
> It is sad to think
> That the affections of man
> Fade as quickly as blossoms.

The Chūjō, though he thought the poem very pretty, was grieved for he could see that she must have been told that he was fickle of heart. 'You seem still to doubt my love,' he said in an anguished tone. 'But I have not been inconstant in the slightest degree. You will see that my heart is not fickle.

> These few plum-blossoms
> In spite of sad cold weather

Have kept their beauty,
But may soon be scattered by
The blast of your jealousy.

From this poem, you may know my thoughts.'

The Lady answered with this poem—

'If you should leave me
Like a plum-blossom tempted
By a breeze to stray,
Sad in my loneliness
Then should I be left behind.

That is my only cause for sadness.'

He wondered what it was that she had been told which could cause her to be so heart-broken.

While he was thus pondering, his foster-mother came to speak to him. 'When I took your favourable reply to the house of the Minister of the Right,' she said, 'they told me that they would not raise objections to your paying frequent visit to the Lady of Nijō after your marriage to the Minister's daughter, as the Lady of Nijō is not of noble birth. The Minister has informed your father that the marriage is arranged for the Fourth Month and that he is busying himself with all preparations. Please prepare for it yourself.'

'What is that?' exclaimed the Chūjō with a very embarrassing smile. 'Are these things carried out by force against the will of the bridegroom? It perhaps shows my poor character—but I do not wish people to be so kind as to arrange such matters for me. Do not do such things for me, please. This is too much. How do you know that the Lady Ochikubo is not noble? She is not so ill-born that you should disregard her in this way.'

'How unreasonable you are!' exclaimed his foster-mother. 'The Minister has been making all the preparations in great expectation. Consider the matter carefully. How can you reject the proposal which such a noble lord urges on you? Can you refuse flatly? It is the custom nowadays to marry someone whose parents can help one with their favour. Even if you are already keeping a lady, you can still keep her and yet send a letter to the Minister's daughter. The Lady of Nijō is the daughter of a noble, it is true, but she used to be called the Lady Ochikubo and regarded as of inferior rank. It is strange to me that you should make so much of such a woman. One cannot be permanently happy unless one has the loving care not only of a wife but also of her parents.'

The Chūjō reddened at this speech. 'Perhaps it is because my ideas are old-fashioned that I do not like those things which are considered polite and up-to-date. I do not wish for success. I do not want the favour of my wife's parents. I shall not give up the Lady of Nijō whether her name was Ochikubo or Agarikubo.[1] What can I do then? People speak evilly of me. It is natural when, as I am sorry to say, even you do so. However, the Lady of Nijō will grow more affectionate to you, even if now she does not seem to like you.' Then he got up

---

[1] Upper Room.

and went out; there seemed to be no probability that he would consent to the proposals.

Tachihaki had been listening impatiently to all this. 'Why did you say such things?' he said to his mother, snapping his fingers. 'You are the Lord's foster-mother, but you must be more deferential to him. He and the Lady now feel that they could never part, and then you try to persuade him to accept the Minister's proposal and marry this other lady. Your sole object is to make things better for yourself. Oh, how sad! Could a woman of any moral character entertain such infamous ideas? And why did you mention that word "Ochikubo"? Alas, old age has made you feeble-minded! If the Lady of Nijō hears of what you have said about her, what will she think of you? Do not mention such a thing again. I am sorry and ashamed when I think of what the Lord must be feeling. Are you so desirous of having the favour of the family of the Minister of the Right that you should attempt such a thing? Even if you have not their favour, you have me, your son, Korenari, and I can look after you without anyone else's help. A person as greedy as you is a great sinner. If you mention the matter once again, I, Korenari, will become a priest. I feel very sorry about it. Is it not a disgraceful thing to come between happy lovers?'

'You go on talking like that only to prevent me from saying a word,' retorted his mother. 'Who is talking about the Lady leaving here or his deserting her immediately?'

'Well, doesn't it amount to the same thing if you bring

about this marriage?'

'Oh, stop your talking! What evil have I done in suggesting the marriage? Why do you express your amazement and horror so violently? It is mainly on account of your love for your own wife that you do not wish this new marriage to come about,' went on his mother, though it was only for the sake of talking; she loved him very much and would not act against his wish.

'All right! All right!' said Tachihaki, with a laugh. 'It seems you are still thinking to persuade him. Well then, Korenari becomes a priest. You are committing a great sin. And when a son learns of his mother's sins, can he remain tranquil without renouncing the world? Next time you speak of this marriage,' he went on, taking a razor and getting up to go, 'I will shave my head.'

He was her only son and her feelings were hurt by his words. 'It is terrible to hear such words from your own mouth,' she said. 'But my determination can break your razor.'

Tachihaki only smiled in answer.

However, his mother realised that it was useless to try to obtain the Chūjō's consent to the marriage and in view also of what her son had said, she decided to tell the Minister of the Right that it was of no use continuing with his proposal.

As the Chūjō realised that it was only because the Lady had heard of this proposal that she had not been in her usual serene spirits, he went to Nijō. 'I am very glad to be able to say that I have found the reason for your having been so melancholy lately,' he said to her.

'What do you mean?' she asked.

'It was the proposal from the Minister of the Right, wasn't it?'

'Now, it was not,' she said, smiling.

'You make me vexed,' he said. 'Now I have you, I would refuse even the Emperor's daughter. I have told you that from the beginning I have been anxious to avoid even the appearance of being unfaithful to you, for I have heard that a woman's greatest sorrow is when her place in her husband's affections is taken by another. So I have tried to avoid any such sorrow for you. Whatever you may be told, be assured that there is no cause for your suspicion.'

'However, even if I try to believe that, perhaps "the bank is crumbling away underneath."'[1]

'If I said that I loved you, you might doubt whether it was true, but when I say only that I will try to be faithful to you and not bring sorrow to you, how can my resolution be otherwise?'

'Do not be so doubtful of the Lord's constancy,' said Tachihaki to Emon, when he told her what had really happened. 'His constancy is beyond any doubt.'

---

[1] Quoting from the poem—

> A fickle man is
> Like a bank which is crumbling
> Away underneath;
> Although he says he loves you,
> You cannot put trust in him.

The Chujo's foster-mother did not mention her plan again after having thus been roughly spoken to by her son. She told the people at the mansion of the Minister of the Right that the Chūjō was already visiting a Lady, and so with deep regret they gave up their plan.

Thus the Chūjō and the Lady of Nijō lived peacefully and happily in harmony and mutual love. Then the Lady became pregnant and was all the more kindly treated.

The Fourth Month came, and the Kita no Kata of the Taishō decided to go to see the procession of the Kamo Shrine with her daughters and the princess, her grandchild.

'You should let the Lady of Nijō go to see this,' she said to the Chūjō. 'Young people like to see these things. I have often regretted that until now I have not been to visit her, and I should like to take this opportunity of meeting her.'

The Chūjo was delighted with this suggestion. 'I do not know why,' he answered, 'but she does not seem to be so interested in these things as other people are. However, I will ask her to go.'

He went to the Nijō house at once and told her what his mother had proposed.

'I know from my feeling unwell nowadays that I am going to have a child, and I think it would be most inconvenient for them to have me with them,' she said sadly.

'Who will see you? There will only be my mother

and the Second Lady, and you should look on them as being as near to you as I am,' he answered, and begged her to go so strongly that at last she consented to do as he wished.

Meanwhile, a letter arrived from the Lord's mother. 'Please go with us,' it read. 'I wish to share with you the pleasure of seeing delightful things.'

When the Lady of Nijō read this, it brought back to her mind how she had been left all alone when the others had gone on pilgrimage to Ishiyama, and she was overcome with melancholy.

Along the main road at Ichijō, a magnificent grandstand roofed with cypress bark had been built. In front, white sand had been laid, and in the sand trees had been planted. It was furnished as if they were going to reside there permanently.

They set off at dawn, Emon and Shōnagon feeling as if they were in Paradise; once they had been accustomed to bitter and spiteful words being used to those who showed the slightest sympathy to the Lady Ochikubo; now they thought themselves extremely fortunate in being in her service and being so kindly treated.

The Chūjō's foster-mother also came with them, and to show her good feelings towards the Lady of Nijō, she went about saying, 'Who is the Lady with Korenari's Lord?' The younger servants all laughed at her.

'Why should you think that I should not be kind to

you?' the Kita no Kata of the Taisho said to the Lady of Nijō, making her sit next to her and her second daughter. 'Nothing can bring peace and love between kinsfolk except continual contact.' She watched the Lady and found her charming, not inferior to the Second Lady or to her grand-daughter, the princess. The Lady of Nijō was wearing a dark-red damask lined robe over a red and blue damask robe with an inner robe of gauze in the same colours of a darker shade. With her shyness and her beauty, she was very charming indeed.

The young princess was certainly not like ordinary folk. She was very noble and though only twelve years of age, her beauty was striking. The Second Lady, in her youthful way, was very much taken with the beauty of the Lady of Nijō and talked to her in a very friendly and intimate manner.

When the procession was over, they went to the carriages which had been brought up to the stand. The Chūjō was about to take the Lady back to Nijō, when his mother interrupted him. 'It has been too noisy here to say all I wish to say to you,' she said to the Lady. 'Do not leave us. Come with me so that we can spend a day or two in quiet conversation. Why are you in such a hurry to take her back, Chūjō? Do as I ask. The Chūjō has a very wicked heart. Do not love him too much!' And the Kita no Kata smiled and kept the Lady close beside her.

The carriage was brought near; the princess and the Second Lady entered the fore part and the Lady and the Lord's mother the rear. Everyone else went back in the other carriages and with the Chūjō returned to the Taishō's mansion.

Here the Western Wing of the Main Building was hastily prepared and the Chūjō and the Lady of Nijō installed there. Her attendants were placed at the end of the West Wing near the Chūjō's apartments. The Lady was very kindly treated. As she was the wife of his dearly loved son, the Taishō exerted himself to be kind to her, and even to her servants.

The Lady stayed there four or five days, and then returned to Nijō, promising to come back again for another visit after the birth of the child.

After this meeting with her kinsfolk, she was now even more kindly cared for by them. She was now sure of the Chūjō's constant love. He was extremely careful to do all he could to make her happy.

'Now I should like to tell my father where I am,' she therefore said to the Chūjō. 'He is getting old and one cannot tell whether he will die unexpectedly in the middle of the night or at early dawn. I am very unhappy when I think that perhaps I shall not see him before he dies.'

'I understand how you feel,' was the Chūjō's invariable answer to this plea, 'but do not think about it at present, and do not tell him where you are for a while. After you have told your father where you are, we shall unfortunately not be able to revenge ourselves on the old Kita no Kata, and I wish to punish her a little further. Also, I should like to be promoted to a little higher rank before I present myself before him. The Chūnagon is not going to die immediately.'

So they continued to live their hidden life until, before they were aware, the New Year had arrived. On the Thirteenth Day of the First Month, the Lady of Nijō gave birth to a son, with no complications at all. The Chūjō was very happy. Being anxious about having only young attendants in charge of the Lady, he sent for his own foster-mother. 'Let everything be done as you did for my own mother,' the Lord said to her as he put the Lady in her charge, and she began her duties by bathing the child.

Now that she was able to see the Lady of Nijō in a more familiar atmosphere, she could see that it was quite natural that the Chūjō would not desert her for another.

All the kinsfolk of the Chūjō vied with one another in giving congratulatory dinner-parties in honour of the birth.[1] We will not describe them in detail but their magnificence may be imagined by the fact that only silver dishes were used. There was much noise of music and merrymaking.

'How I should like to tell the old Kita no Kata about all this!' thought Emon in the midst of all this happiness of the Lady of Nijō.

The child's foster-mother was Shōnagon who also had had a child at about the same time, so the child was nursed with very tender love.

At the General Appointments, the Chūjō was promoted

[1] On the third, fifth, seventh, fiftieth and hundredth days after the birth.

two steps at once to the rank of Chūnagon.[1] The Kurōdo no Shōshō was appointed Saishō[2] and Chūjō. The Taishō received the appointment of Minister of the Left in addition to the position he was holding. 'At exactly the same time as he is born, his father and I receive great honours. He is a prodigy,' the new Minister of the Left said.

The new Chūnagon, the child's father, received the additional appointment of Saemon no Kami[3] and his reputation among people increased the more.

At the mansion of the old Chūnagon; the Kita no Kata and the Third Lady were sorely grieved at this rapid promotion of the Third Lady's former husband, the new Chūjō, so that they often wept in regret at having failed to keep him in the family, and were filled with vain envy of his greatness.

The Saemon no Kami, as he grew greater and greater in reputation and rank, took every opportunity to revenge himself on the old Chūnagon's family. However, it is not necessary to describe all these incidents, for they were no different from those which have already been told.

In the autumn of the following year, another son was born to the Lady of Nijō.

'Oh, another beautiful son!' the Kita no Kata of the Minister of the Left said. 'We'll take charge of this one.' She therefore went to the Nijō house accompanied by the

---

[1] The intermediate rank was that of Sangi.
[2] The Chinese term for Sangi, Counsellor.
[3] Commander of the Gate Guards of the Left.

murse and brought back the boy with her.

Tachihaki had been appointed Saemon no Jō[1] which allowed him entry to Court. Thus everything was happening happily just as they wished, except that the Lady was still very sorry that she was not able to reveal where she was to her father.

The old Chūnagon, partly on account for his great age and partly because he often lost himself in melancholy reverie, did not go out among people any longer and remained shut up indoors.

The Lady Ochikubo had inherited from her mother a very beautiful house in Sanjō and the title deeds had been given her by her mother.

'Now that she is no longer in this world,' said the old Chūnagon to his wife, 'I will take possession of the house.'

'That will be quite all right,' the old Kita no Kata answered. 'Even if she is still living, she will have no use for such a grand house. It is quite large enough for us and our children.'

So two years' revenue from their estates was spent in repairing the house; even the boundary walls were rebuilt. Not one piece of the old wood was used in the repairs; everything was done carefully and splendidly.

'This year, the festival of the Kamo Shrine will be unusually splendid,' someone said to the Saemon no Kami,

---

[1] Lieutenant of the Gate Guards of the Left.

so he decided to take the whole household to see it, as there was little to amuse them in the mansion.

'Have a new carriage made. Let the servants have new robes, and let them look very nice,' the Saemon no Kami said, and they all busied themselves in the preparations.

On the day of the festival a notice-board was erected in the main street at Ichijō so that no one else could take that position. They therefore did not need to leave the house so early.

There were five carriages for the twenty older servants and two carriages for four young maids and four under-servants. As the Saemon no Kami was with them, there were many men of the Fourth and Fifth Rank as runners. In addition there were the Lord's younger brothers, the one formerly a Chamberlain but now a Shōshō, and the younger, mentioned before as a boy but who was now Hyōe no Suke.[1] 'We will go and see the procession with you,' they had said, and they had therefore come in their own carriages with their own attendants. Altogether there were more than twenty carriages.

When at last the party arrived at the place where the notice-board had been erected, they saw that on the opposite side of the road, there were standing two carriages, an old one of palm-leaf, and the other a basket-work carriage.

'Have my brothers' carriages placed just opposite ours, that is, on the opposite side of the street, for I want to have them near us,' the Saemon no Kami commanded.

---

[1] Colonel of the Military Guards.

'Have those carriages pulled on a little so that these carriages can be put there,' one of his men called out to the servants of the carriages on the opposite side of the street. However, they refused to move.

The Lord therefore asked his men to find out whose carriages they were, and discovered that they belonged to the old Chūnagon. 'I do not care whether they belong to a Chūnagon or a Dainagon,' the Lord said. 'Why have they been placed here? They must have seen the notice-board. There is plenty of room further along the street. Tell them to pull along a little.'

The attendants went across and took hold of the carriages. The servants of the other carriages remonstrated. 'What are you doing? What hot-tempered fellows you are! Your swaggering lord is of the same rank as ours, a Chūnagon. Does he want the whole street of Ichijō for himself? That is unreasonable,' they protested.

'Even the ex-Emperor, the Crown Prince and the Sai-in[1] give way in awe before our Lord,' a violent-tempered one of them retorted.

'Your lord may be of the same rank as ours,' another added, 'but they cannot be mentioned in the same breath.'

As his brothers' carriages had not yet been brought into position, the Lord called for the Saemon no Jō.[2] 'See that those carriages are taken a little distance away,' he ordered.

---

[1] The Imperial Princess in charge of the Kamo Shrine.
[2] Tachihaki, Korenari.

The Saemon no Jō and his men therefore took hold of the carriages and dragged them away. The number of attendants on the other side was small, and they could make no resistance. There were a few runners but they said, 'It is useless. We cannot fight against them. We could kick the Dajōdaijin's behind, but we cannot lay a finger on this Lord's ox-driver.'

They took the carriages and placed them inside someone's front gate and left them there. The people inside peeped out. 'What a mishap! What shall we do now?' they said.

(Though the Lord was the Commander of the Gate Guards and might seem fierce in the eyes of the world, he was very loving and gentle).

The silly old man Tenyaku no Suke was inside. 'I will ask them to make room for us,' he said and alighted hurriedly from the carriage. 'Do not act so cruelly in this matter. If we had put our carriages where you had put your notice-board, you would have been justified in becoming angry with us. Why do you do this when the carriages were placed on the opposite side of the road? You should think of the consequences before you do such a thing. We shall have our own back on you,' the foolish old man threatened.

The Saemon no Kurōdo[1] was very glad when he saw that it was the Tenyaku no Suke whom he had long been wishing to meet again.

The Saemon no Kami also recognised Tenyaku.

---

[1] Tachihaki, Korenari.

'Korenari,' he called out, 'Why do you allow that fellow to talk like that?'

Korenari understood. He winked to the servants who were ready for any violence and they rushed on the old man.

'You tell us to think of the consequences, old man. What are you going to do to the Lord?' one asked and knocked off the old man's hat with his long fan. And when everyone saw his thin queue and his bald and shining head, they shook with laughter. The old man covered his head with his sleeve and tried to retreat to his carriage, but the men closed on him and each gave him a kick, saying, 'What will be the consequences of that?' to their hearts' content.

'I am dying,' cried the old man, but he had hardly breath to say it from the cruel way in which they were treating him.

'Stop that. Stop that,' shouted the Lord, but he did not intend that they should. After knocking him down and trampling on him, they hung him partly in the carriage and dragged it still further away. The attendants belonging to it would not come near out of fear, for they had grown wiser by experience. They stood not far away, but behaved as if they were strangers. When the carriage had been left in the middle of the road up a lane, they slowly returned to the carriage and lifted up the shafts. It had all been a very shameful spectacle.

All the people in the carriage, even the old Kita no Kata, decided that they must return home without waiting to see the procession. They hurriedly brought up the oxen and then one of the straps that held the carriage on the axle and which had been weakened in the contest broke with a 'futsu, futsu.' Then the carriage fell off the wheels into the middle of the road with a thud.

The people of humble position all around saw it and laughed until they shook. The servants who had been knocked over, their feet in the air, when the carriage fell, could not replace the carriage quickly. 'To-day has been the most Unlucky Day for us. We have come to the depths of shame,' one of them said, snapping his fingers in his excitement and grief.

The feelings of the people in the carriage can only be left to the imagination. All were weeping; and the old Kita no Kata wept more than all, for she was sitting in the rear end of the carriage while her daughters were in front, and so she had had further to fall. With difficulty she crawled back into the carriage again for her elbow was dislocated and wept and sobbed, 'oi-oi.'

'What is this tribulation a retribution for?' she said as she wept.

'Do not make such a noise,' her daughters urged her unfeelingly.

At last the runners returned and, seeing the fallen carriage, in great distress began to put it back on the shafts.

'What a disgrace those people have had!' all the people around said. The people inside felt grievously ashamed to hear such comments and could not even speak to one another, they could only look at each other. Then with great difficulty the carriage was put together again and then very slowly, for the old Kita no Kata was doubtful about the safety of the carriage, they returned home. At last they arrived at the mansion and when they drew up, the Great Lady alighted, leaning on the shoulders of the attendants.

The Chūnagon was amazed to see her thus return after so short an absence and with eyes swollen with tears. 'What's the matter? What's the matter?' he inquired.

She told him all that had happened. 'That was a very great disgrace for you to meet,' he said. 'It makes me feel like renouncing the world to become a priest.' But his love for his wife and his children would have been too great for him to have done that.

Everyone heard of this affair and laughed about it very much. It came to the ears of the Minister of the Left. 'Is this true?' he said to his son. 'Did you do this? It is said that you treated ladies in a carriage in this cruel way. And that at that time the attendants of the Lady of Nijō acted in a very violent manner. What is the meaning of it?'

'I did nothing that could be called cruel,' answered the Saemon no Kami. 'They put their carriages where my notice-boards had been erected. Our servants asked them why they had placed them there when there was plenty of room elsewhere. This led to words on both sides, and in the confusion the strap of the carriage was broken. As for a man being hit, he spoke very rudely to us and, in his indignation, one of our men knocked off his hat and the rest pulled him down. My brothers, the Shōshō and the Hyōe no Suke, saw it all. Nothing at all was done that could lead people to say such things.'

'Do not invite the criticism of the public. I have learnt that by experience,' his father answered.

The Lady of Nijō was greatly grieved about the affair.

'Do not be so pained about such a trifling incident,' said Emon. 'You would be justified in grieving if the Great Lord had been in the carriage. Did it not serve Tenyaku right to be knocked down? Was it not punishment for what he did?'

'You are too wicked. You can leave my service and go into that of the Lord. Then you will be able to say what spiteful things you like.'

'Then I will go into the Lord's service,' replied Emon. 'He lets me do as I like, and I shall prize him more than you do.'

The old Kita no Kata suffered terribly from the illness caused by this mishap and did not recover until after prayers had been said for her recovery by all her children assembled together.

THE THIRD BOOK

THIS succession of misfortunes induced the old Kita no Kata to hurry along the reconstruction of the house at Sanjō so that she could move into it in the Sixth Month, for she believed that it was owing to the unlucky position of the old mansion that these mishaps had occurred.

Emon heard of this and came to tell the Saemon no Kami as he lay in bed. 'The mansion at Sanjō has been splendidly reconstructed by the Chūnagon, and the family will be moving into it very soon,' said Emon. 'The Lady's mother told her many, many times to make that mansion her home all her life as the Lady's grandfather had been very happy when he lived there in grand style, and that the house was very dear to her for that reason. In spite of this, they are about to take possession of it under our very eyes. How can we prevent them?'

'Has the Lady the deeds?' asked the Lord.

'Yes, certainly she has.'

'I am very glad that you have told me of this. Find out for me the exact date on which they are going to move.'

'What are you going to do?' the Lady asked him in a rather angry tone. 'It is your fault, Emon. You are always inciting the Lord to mischief.'

'Why are you scolding me? I am not acting unjustly towards anyone. If I were, you would be justified in reproving me,' said Emon.

'Do not tell her anything more of this,' the Saemon no Kami said to Emon. 'She is quite eccentric; she takes pity on people who do harm to her.'

'She feels herself abused,' the Lord added smiling.

'How can I tell? said Emon, but she understood the Lord's plan.

The month passed away.

'When are you moving?' Emon asked one of the old Chūnagon's household in a casual manner, and thus learnt that the date was fixed for the Nineteenth Day of that month. She reported this to the Saemon no Kami.

'We will move in there on that day,' the Lord then said. 'Search for a few more maids. Are there any more suitable ones in the Chūnagon's mansion? If there are, persuade them to come into my service without telling them the reason why you wish them to come. In that way we shall further annoy these people.'

'Very well,' answered Emon. It was obvious that she was well pleased with the plan. So they walked about plotting, and the Saemon no Kami told her to tell no one at all and to keep it a secret especially from the Lady.

'Someone has found a fine new mansion for us,' the Saemon no Kami told the Lady. 'I wish to move in there on the Nineteenth Day of this month. Have robes prepared. I wish to take this opportunity to have this house repaired, and therefore I wish to move out so soon.

Please make haste with the preparations.' He gave her silk and dyes, and she, not knowing anything of what he planned, busied herself with the preparations for the removal.

Emon took every opportunity of inviting pretty attendants from the old Chūnagon's mansion. The best of all the maids there was considered to be Jijū, a very pretty girl in the service of the old Kita no Kata. Emon had also decided to persuade Suke, Taiyu and Maroya in the service of the Third Lady as being very suitable girls. She took every opportunity of sending them messages telling of her happiness in her present situation, of how powerful her master was and of how kind he was to those who were in his service. These girls, being very young, had been so disgusted at the foolishness and lack of determination of their own master that when Emon's welcome messages were beginning to arrive they were thinking of leaving his service as quickly as they could. They guessed that the greatest noble of the time to whom Emon referred was the Saemon no Kami; they therefore all accepted Emon's offer, made their preparations and left the Chūnagon's house under pretence of returning home. They never dreamed that they were entering the service of the Lady Ochikubo, nor that they were all going to the same place, for each had kept the matter secret from the others.

Emon sent a carriage for each and received each one separately as she arrived. They were infinitely charmed at the numbers of people there and by the splendid decorations of the mansion. When they met each other, they looked at one another and thought it very humorous that the carriages had set them all down at the same place. Then, just as they had been told by Emon, they saw about twenty pretty and young attendants in white silk robes with purple skirts and red under-robes, and five or six others in crimson under-robes with damask robes and lilac skirts. They came out in a body and looked at the newcomers who were not happy to be thus stared at.

As the Lady was suffering rather from the heat and could not receive them, the Saemon no Kami said, 'I will see them instead then,' and went out to them.

The newcomers felt exceedingly bashful and would not raise their heads to look at him. However, they looked round at each other, and when they did steal a glance at him in his red under-robe, white unglazed-robe and silk gauze over-robe, they found that he was as charming and handsome as they had expected from report.

He looked them over carefully. 'They are not bad. As they are introduced by Emon, even though they have faults, I ought not to say anything,' he said, and the Lady said with a smile, 'You trust her implicitly.'

'It is because you do not understand how busy I have been that you can say that they have faults,' replied Emon, 'I have been so busy attending on the Lady that I have not had time to look over their toilets.'

The newcomers were most surprised that Akogi should

give him such an answer. 'How wonderful that she should be so much in favour with the Lord!' they thought.

Then Emon pretended to have seen them for the first time. 'How wonderful!' she exclaimed. 'I think we have seen each other before.'

'Yes, we also think that we have met before and we are very glad to see you again,' they answered.

'I think it is extremely sad that we have become such strangers to each other, not having been able to meet each other during the last few years,' said Emon.

As they were thus talking over things of the past, an attendant came in, carrying on her back a very pretty fair-complexioned child about three years old. 'The Lady wishes to see you, Emon,' she said; and they saw then that it was Shōnagon.

'How it brings back the old days to hear your sweet voice again!' the newcomers said; but we will not write down all that was said in their joy at meeting each other, for it would be very tedious indeed to read. The newcomers were exceedingly glad to find with what kindness their old friends had prepared for their respective transfers.

Thus came the eve of the day on which the old Chūnagon was to move to the new mansion. The Saemon no Kami heard that the ladies' things and the servants' things were being carried over to the new house, and that blinds were being put up and the place furnished. He therefore summoned to him his dependants, Tajima no Kami,[1] Shimotsuke no Kami,[1] the Emon no Suke[2] who was also

---

[1] Governors of these provinces.   [2] Colonel of the Gate Guards.

his Mandokoro no Bettō,[1] and many servants. He told them how the mansion at Sanjō had come into his possession, and went on, 'I had thought of putting the place in repair and removing there, but now I hear that the Gen Chūnagon, for what reason I do not know, has had the mansion reconstructed and moving in there. I have been waiting to hear some explanation from him but he has said nothing, and now I hear that he is removing there tomorrow. Go and say to them, "Why are you doing this? Why are you moving to this place without letting us know. We ought to have been told of your intention." Do not allow them to take anything to the house. I intend to move there myself tomorrow. Fix a guard on the house and take servants there.'

They all went at once to Sanjō to carry out his orders. They found the mansion very finely appointed, with sand laid around, and the bamboo blinds hung up.

The Chūnagon's men were amazed to see such a large number of men arrive. 'Where are you from?' they asked.

'We are retainers and servants of the Saemon no Kami,' was the answer they received. 'He has sent us here to ask why you have taken possession of this mansion without notifying him, as he is the owner. We have been ordered not to allow you to move here.' They then entered the grounds. 'Fix the guard-house here. Put that here and do this like that.' They changed everything just as they wanted.

---

[1] Chief Steward.

Some of the men, furiously angry, ran back to tell the old Chūnagon what had happened. 'The servants and retainers of the Saemon no Kami came and prevented us going near the house. They said that he would move into the house tomorrow, and they fixed the place for the Steward's Office and the Guard House and changed everything just as they wanted it.'

The Chūnagon in his senile fashion was extremely agitated. 'What a terrible thing!' he exclaimed. 'I have not got the deeds, but the house belongs to my child. If it is not mine, whose is it? If my child were still alive, I should think this was her doing. I wonder why he is doing this. It is of no use fighting to gain possession. I will go and see the Lord's father, the Minister of the Left.' Feeling ready to die with annoyance, he went there, not stopping even to put on his ceremonial robes.

'I have come to ask the Minister something,' he said when he arrived at the Minister's mansion.

The Minister came out to him. 'What is it?' he asked.

'There is a house at Sanjō that I have owned many years which I have recently had reconstructed. I was going to move there tomorrow and was having everything carried there. However, many people calling themselves retainers of the Saemon no Kami came and said that the house was the property of their lord, asked why I had not notified him of what I was doing, and told me that he was moving into the house himself tomorrow. They will not allow my men to approach the house. Their conduct in interrupting the work like this astounds me. I am certain that the house can belong to no one but me. What is the meaning of all this? Has your son the deeds?' All this he said in a most pitiful manner.

'I do not know anything at all about it,' the Minister replied. 'I can therefore give you no answer. From what you have said, it seems that the Saemon no Kami is in the wrong. Still, he may have some explanation. I will ask him to explain the circumstances, and then I will give you a definite answer. As this is the first I have heard of it, how can I give you any other answer now?'

He said this in such a half-hearted manner that the Chūnagon saw that it was useless to say anything further and went away, feeling very downcast at the manner in which his appeal had been received. 'What is there to do?' he thought. 'I have devoted myself to the reconstruction of this house only to be laughed at.' To say only that he was grieved would be a foolishly mild expression.

When the Saemon no Kami came back from the Court, his father told him what the Chūnagon had said. 'Is all this that he said true? What is the meaning of it?' he asked.

'It is all true,' the Lord answered. 'I have been thinking of going to live there and sent some of my men to make some repairs. They found that the Chūnagon was about to move in there. I was amazed to hear that and sent some of my retainers to inquire into the truth of the matter.'

'The Chūnagon said that it was outrageous for anyone to take possession of the house, for it could belong to no one but him. How long has it been in your possession? Have you the deeds? From whom did you obtain them?'

'The house belongs to the Lady of Nijō. It once belonged to her mother's father, an Imperial Prince. The Chūnagon is completely domineered over in his dotage by his wife and had allowed the Lady of Nijō to be very cruelly treated. In revenge for that, I am going to prevent him taking possession of the house. I have the deeds, of course. It was very foolish of him to do all those repairs when he had not the deeds, thinking that the house could belong to no one but himself.

'Then there is nothing more to be said. Show him the deeds at once. He was certainly grieved about the matter.'

'Yes, I will show him the deeds.' He returned to Nijō and ordered some of his retainers to act as fore-runners on the morrow and decided which of the maids should ride in the Idashiguruma.[1]

The Chūnagon spent a night of lamentation and early next morning sent his eldest son, the Governor of the Province of Echizen, to the Minister. 'My father wished to come himself,' the Echizen no Kami said to the Minister, 'but he has not been feeling well since he returned from here yesterday. What is the answer to his appeal?'

The Minister in reply told him what the Saemon no Kami had said. 'If you wish for a more detailed answer, I can only refer you to the Saemon no Kami himself. It is impossible for me to decide on the rights and wrongs

---

[1] A decorated carriage, the **dashi** seen on modern festivals.

of the case as I do not know enough about the circumstances. It seems to me that it was extraordinarily foolish
of your father to take possession of the house when he
had not the deeds.'

On receiving this answer, the Echizen no Kami left the
house and went to the mansion of the Saemon no Kami.
He found him dressed informally, sitting in front of a
bamboo screen. The Echizen no Kami took his seat before
him in a modest humble manner. The Lady of Nijō, who
was sitting hidden behind the screen, thought it very pitiful
to see her brother sitting so submissively before the Lord.
And Emon whispered to Shōnagon with a smile, 'When
was it that we were so nervous and humble before him?'

The Echizen no Kami related to the Lord what he had
heard from the Minister. 'Is it really true that you have
the deeds?' he went on. 'I should like to have details
about them. Of course, if we had known that you had
the deeds, neither my father nor I would have made any
protest against your taking possession of the house. But
we have been reconstructing this house for two years. It
is a great pity that you have kept silent so long before
interrupting our removal.'

'I have had the deeds some years,' replied the Lord.
'And as I knew the holder of the deeds is the only person
entitled to possession of the house, I did not think that
it was necessary to tell everyone that I was the owner. It
was not until I learnt of what you were doing that I
informed you that I was the owner. However, have you
the deeds?' he went on in a very mocking manner, while

he fondled the fair-complexioned, pretty, three-year-old child who was sitting on his knee.

The Echizen no Kami felt sad and indignant at the manner in which the Lord was discussing this matter, to him so important, but he restrained his feelings. 'We have lost the deeds of the property,' he explained, 'and have been trying to find them, but up to the moment we have been unsuccessful. I suppose you have bought them from someone who stole them. If that is not so, there can be no one but us with right to the possession of the house.'

'I have not bought the deeds from anyone who stole them and sold them to me. If we look at the matter rationally, we shall see that the one who has the right to the possession of the house can be no one else but myself. You must give up your pretensions. I will tell the whole story to the Chūnagon in detail as soon as it is convenient to me to do so, and at that time I will show him the deeds.' When he had said this, the Lord left the room with the child in his arms, and the Echizen no Kami, seeing that further speech was useless, left the house feeling very downcast.

The Lady who had been listening most attentively to all this, then said to the Lord in a sorrow-stricken voice, 'I see that the place to which you are intending to move is Sanjō. When they learn that I am here, they will feel all the more indignant at your interference with their plans to move to the house they have spent so long in repairing. To cause grievous pain to one's own parent is the most terrible of all sins. It grieves me that I am not living with him to serve and cherish him. How sad it makes me to think how sorely this recent interference of yours will have afflicted him! It is all Emon's fault.' She looked sad.

'Would anyone in the world allow his own house to be seized by another, even by his own father? You can compensate your father by more fervent attentions afterwards for your present sin of causing him sorrow. Even if you do not move into the new house, I shall do so with all the servants. It would make me look foolish not to go now after saying what I have said. If you wish to present the house to him, you can do so after you have made known to him your presence here.'

To this she made no answer, for she knew that further speech was useless.

The Echizen no Kami returned home. 'It is of no use,' he said to his father. 'We can but relinquish the house to them, thinking only that it is a great disgrace to us to have had to do so. I spoke to him seriously, for this is an important matter to us, but he regarded it as a trivial affair and sat caressing the pretty child he was nursing and took hardly any notice of what I said to him, and at last left the room. The Sadaijin had said also, "I myself know nothing about this matter. The Saemon no Kami has the deeds, and the one who has the deeds is in the strongest position." It is useless to do anything further. Why did you not find where the deeds were? At the Saemon no Kami's house, they were all busy noisily making preparations with regard to carriages and servants for the moving.'

The old Chūnagon felt that this news was dreadful; in his bewilderment he did not know what to do. 'When the Lady Ochikubo's mother died,' he said, 'she gave her the deeds of that house. And I never thought of asking her for them. Then she left this house. And what happened then? Evidently she sold them to someone from whom the Saemon no Kami bought them. How people will laugh at us for this! Even if we appeal to the Imperial Court, we should not be able to find one lord who would judge impartially between us and them, for everything is done there just as they wish it to be done. The saddest thing is that we have spent so much in the reconstruction of the house. The times are not sympathetic to me. I am unlucky in all things. It is really dreadful.' In his distress, he could only sit and look up at the sky.

At the mansion of the Saemon no Kami, a new robe was given to each of the servants in preparation for moving into the new house. The newcomers were especially pleased at this for it was not usual for such presents to be made to those who had come into service so recently.

The people who had been sent by the old Chūnagon to bring back their possessions from the new mansion at Sanjō returned and reported, 'They will not even let us into the house.'

The old Kita no Kata beat her hands together in her

mortification. 'What cause of enmity has the Saemon no Kami against us that he should be so offensive to us?' she asked, full of distress.

The Echizen no Kami went to see the Saemon no Kami again. 'It is useless to dispute the matter with you now,' he said. 'However, we should like to take back our furniture.'

'Take it away quickly then,' the Lord answered. Still, though the Saemon no Kami made this gentle answer, his men would not allow the others to enter the mansion at Sanjō. It was impossible for the old Chūnagon's men to oppose them, and indignant that such a mishap had befallen them, they gathered together in one place and heaped curses on the Saemon no Kami.

About eight o'clock next morning, the Saemon no Kami and his whole household removed to the new mansion at Sanjō in a grand ceremonious procession of ten carriages. They alighted there to find that the main building was completely furnished; there were screens and curtains and all the floors were matted. As the Lord looked round he felt sorry when he thought of the mortification which the Chūnagon's family must be suffering; but what he had done had to be done as revenge against the old Kita no Kata.

The Lady, also, imagining the feelings of her father, found no pleasure in the possession of the new mansion and was filled with longing thoughts.

'Do not lose any of their things. I shall certainly send everything back safely to them,' the Lord said to his servants.

While the Saemon no Kami's household was so full of joy, the Chūnagon's servant, who had been sent to see if the others had occupied the mansion yet, returned with a report of the splendid manner in which they had made the removal. The whole family, thinking that now there was nothing more which they could do, came together and lamented.

At Sanjō, meanwhile, all was merry, and in Emon's opinion, the Lord had done just as she had hoped that he would.

The next morning, the Echizen no Kami arrived at the Sanjō house. 'I wish to take back the things we brought,' he said to the Lord.

'They must not be taken away for a day or two. Come for them the day after tomorrow. But are you quite sure that the things are here?' was all the answer he obtained.

Seeing that no particular attention was paid to anything he said, the Echizen no Kami was infinitely disturbed in mind.

For three days the merrymaking was carried on in a very splendid and up-to-date manner, and on the morning of the fourth day, the Echizen no Kami came again. 'Let me have the furniture today at least,' he pleaded. 'It is very inconvenient for there are here even such things as the ladies' comb-boxes.' It was very pleasing to the Saemon no Kami to see how humble he had become. However, he returned the furniture to him, checking it over with an inventory.

'Have you still that mirror-box with the old lid?' the Lord said to Emon. 'I will send it back with the rest of the things. The old Kita no Kata valued that box very much.'

Emon was delighted at the thought. 'I have it still,' she answered, and went to fetch it. Everyone who had not seen it before laughed. 'What an awful thing!' they exclaimed, astonished at its poor appearance.

'We ought to send a note with it,' said the Lord, 'if only because it is the proper thing to do.'

'I do not know what to write,' the Lady said. 'Now when they have so many things to worry them, I do not wish to add to their troubles by making myself known to them at this moment.'

'However, do so,' urged the Lord.

The Lady therefore wrote on the back of the box this poem—

> Through the livelong day,
> Did this mirror once reflect
>   Sorrowful events;
> It brings back the memory
> Now of my dear step-mother.

The Lord wrapped the box in two sheets of coloured

paper¹ and fixed it to a spray of leaves. 'Give this to the Echizen no Kami,' he said, handing it to Emon.

Then he called in the Echizen no Kami. 'I know that you think that my actions have been very strange,' he said, 'but I had heard that you were moving to this house, so I had to do as I did. I will personally ask your father to pardon my offences in this, and will show him the deeds of the house. Would you ask him to come here tomorrow as I have some things which I wish to speak to him about? You all no doubt think me a very disagreeable person, but later on you will find me a friend.' All this he said in such a friendly tone that the Echizen no Kami was amazed. 'Be sure to ask your father to come, and come with him yourself,' the Saemon no Kami went on.

The Echizen no Kami then left the room and as he passed a door on his way out, a servant stopped him, saying, 'Please come here.' He thought this very strange but went nearer to the door, when a beautiful sleeve and a hand holding a parcel were put out, and a voice said, 'Please give this to the Kita no Kata. Once she prized it dearly and we have kept it safety for her. And now that we are returning the other furniture, the Lady has remembered this and has told us to return it at the same time.'

'From whom shall I say that the message comes?' asked the Echizen no Kami, very surprised.

'She will know without your having to tell her,' was

---

¹ The colour varied with the seasons.

the answer. 'Is not my voice one you knew of old?'[1]

'It must be Akogi,' he thought. 'She must be in the service of the Saemon no Kami.' But aloud he said, 'I have been away from the Capital so long that I have completely forgotten the things of old. So how can I remember your voice? When I come to this house next time, I should like to meet you as an old friend.'

'Well, here is another of your old acquaintances,' said another maid appearing. It was Shōnagon. The Echizen no Kami wondered how it was that they had all collected there. Then another voice called from inside, 'As the old poem says, "You are surrounded with flowers,"[2] and so my being here will not astonish you.' It was Jijū who had formerly been in the Second Lady's service. The Echizen no Kami had favoured her, and they had been lovers. He was speechless with surprise at thus hearing there the voices of so many of those who had formerly been in the service of his father.

'How is the Third Lord?' asked Emon appearing. 'Has he performed his coming of age yet?'

---

[1] The words Emon misuses are from the poem—

> At the Capital
> Where I used to live of old,
>   All is changed save
> The call of the cuckoo which
> Remains as it was of old.

[2] Quoting from—

> You are surrounded
> With lovers, like flowers in
>   A flower basket;
> Not counted with such, I shall
> Before long be forgotten,

The Echizen no Kami replied with details of how his brother was. 'This Spring he was promoted Daibu,'[1] he concluded.

'Please bring him with you when you come tomorrow. We have many things to tell him about.'

The Echizen no Kami agreed to do so and hurried away from the house, for he was anxious to see what was in the parcel. On his way home, thinking over what he had seen of the household of the Saemon no Kami, he wondered if the lady of the house were not the Lady Ochikubo. Akogi was there and seemed to be in high position. When he thought how unexpectedly he had found so many of the people from his own home collected there, he was sure that it could be no one but the Lady Ochikubo whom they were serving, and he was very glad, for as yet he did not know how badly the Lady had been treated by the old Kita no Kata while he was absent in Echizen.

When he returned home, he told the old Chūnagon what had happened, and he handed the parcel to the old Kita no Kata. She wondered what it could be and opened it to find to her great astonishment the mirror-box which she had given to the Lady Ochikubo. She was most disturbed, wondering why it had been sent back to her, and more so when she found the poem written on the back of the box. When she saw that it was in the Lady Ochikubo's handwriting, her eyes and mouth opened wide

---

[1] Lord of Fourth or Fifth Rank, without office.

with amazement. It is impossible to try to describe the spiteful anger she felt when she realised that it was this once despised person who had caused all the shameful disgraces which had befallen her during the past few years. Her screams of anger made the whole house shake.

As for the old Chūnagon, when he discovered that it was his own child who had done all this, his feeling of anger melted away. 'Why did I neglect that one of all my children who was born to become so fortunate?' he exclaimed. 'That house really belongs to her for it was given to her by her mother, and so she had every reason to do as she did.'

These words fanned the old Kita no Kata's anger till she became completely frantic. 'They can take the house, but the trees and plants are ours. We must get them back from her. I should like to get the trees back as the price of their taking possession.'

'What do you mean? Are you going to treat them as strangers?' asked the Echizen no Kami. 'We have no one of influence in the family. On the contrary we have such a one as "Omoshiro no Koma" whom to our great shame everyone who sees ridicules. The Saemon no Kami though he is still only a young lord, is unrivalled in the Imperial favour. How delightful and how advantageous it will be to have him as a kinsman!'

'Taking possession of the house at Sanjō is nothing in comparison with the ill-treatment the Lady Ochikubo received while she was living here. It was horrible,' the Daibu said.

'What! What ill treatment?' asked the Echizen no Kami.

'The way she was treated was terrible,' the Daibu answered, and related to his brother one incident after another of this cruelty. 'Would not Akogi have told the Saemon no Kami of all this?' he went on. 'When I meet them, I shall be very ashamed.'

'How dreadful!' exclaimed the Echizen no Kami, snapping his fingers. 'Being absent in Echizen, I knew nothing of all this. That was disgraceful conduct. The Saemon no Kami has kept all this in mind and has had his revenge on us by disgracing us as he has done. How he must despise us! Would it not be better not to become more friendly with him?' The Echizen no Kami was very distressed at the shame of these disclosures.

'Hold your tongue! It cannot be undone now,' the old Kita no Kata said. 'Say nothing more about all this. I did it because I hated her so.' It was useless to try to persuade her of the evil of her conduct.

'Shōnagon and Jijū were also there,' the Echizen no Kami added.

'Why have we not gone also?' the young servants who overheard this said in their envy. 'We ought to have left these foolish people. Let us go even now. The Lady is extremely kind and will allow us to enter her service.'

The Third and Fourth Ladies were also displeased at the news; the Third Lady hated the idea of becoming intimate with one whose family had robbed her of her husband, the Kurōdo no Shōshō; and the Fourth Lady also thought that it would be more mortifying for her than for anyone else to meet the other family, for it was the Lord who had plotted against her and had brought such sorrow upon her by sending to her 'Omoshiro no Koma'. Her daughter by him was now three years old and was a very pretty little girl; she did not take after her father in the least. In her sorrow, the Fourth Lady had often thought of becoming a nun, but her love for this child was too strong a tie to cut loose from. The Shōyu had long ceased to come to visit her, for she loathed him and had never encouraged him with affection.

The old Chūnagon who had been so grieved because everyone despised him for his stupidity was quite elated, for he thought that now all his difficulties were at an end. He wanted to go to pay a visit to Sanjō at once, but was persuaded to postpone it till the following day as it was already dusk. The old Kita no Kata was sorely agitated for she saw that now the Chūnagon would make more of the Lady Ochikubo than of her own children. The Third and Fourth Ladies could now see why, at Kiyomizu, the Lord had called out, 'Have you had enough?' How many insults he had heaped on them to whom he had at last to introduce himself as a son-in-law of the house! It was no doubt because of his invitation that so many of their maids had left to enter the Lady of Sanjō's service. He had brought shame on them because of his deep indignation at their mother's treatment of the Lady Ochikubo.

'How mortifying this is!' exclaimed the old Kita no
Kita. 'How I should like to do something to avenge all
these wrongs which we have suffered at his hands!'

However, her daughters restrained her. 'Do not think
of doing such things now,' they urged her. 'You have
sons-in-law to consider. It was because of his great indignation at the Tenyaku no Suke's conduct that he allowed
him to be beaten as he did; it was all done according to
his will.' So they talked on through the night.

The next morning, a letter arrived from the Saemon no
Kami. 'Did the Echizen no Kami give you my message
yesterday?' the old Chūnagon read. 'If you are at leisure,
please call on me today as I have something to tell you.'

The Chūnagon answered the letter. 'I received the
message by the Echizen no Kami,' he wrote, 'and would
have gone to you at once but for the lateness of the hour.
I will visit you at once now.'

As the Echizen no Kami was also invited, he rode in
the rear half of the same carriage as his father. When
the Chūnagon was announced at Sanjō, the Saemon no
Kami ordered them to be shown in. The interview took
place in a drawing room in the main building in which
the Lady of Sanjō sat hidden by a screen. The Lord
ordered everyone else to go to the north side of the house.

'I must apologise for taking possession of this house in
the way I did,' the Saemon no Kami said to his visitors.
'But there is one here who, unknown to you, has been
very anxious about your welfare, and who has been press-

ing me for a long time to explain the whole situation to you. You did quite right in having this house repaired in order to take possession of it, but if you look at the deeds, it will be quite evident to you that this other person has more right to the house than you have. And as you began to move in here without any warning to us although we lived so near to you, we decided to move here ourselves, as it appeared to us that you were treating us with intentional rudeness, and we did not wish to be treated so contemptuously and as inferiors. This other person opposed my plan of moving here, saying, "It is outrageous for you to seize the house that someone else has repaired and which he likes so much. Make him a present of the deeds." She was so grieved about it that I have decided to present you with the deeds so that you can safely take possession of her house. I have asked you to come here so that I could tell you so.'

'You have done very well,' answered the old Chūnagon. 'Since my daughter disappeared so strangely a few years ago, we have heard nothing of her, and I believed that she was no longer in this world. If I, Tadayori,[1] were young, I might have thought that some day I might meet her somewhere again in my travels, but being so old when she deserted me, when I could not tell whether I should die today or tomorrow, I could but sadly lament that I should see her no more in this world. I knew that if she were alive, she would be the rightful owner of this house,

---

[1] Here for the first time the Chūnagon's personal name is given as Tadayori.

but as things were, I thought I could take possession of it. I therefore had the house repaired before it became too dilapidated. I had not heard that she was living in your care. It may sound foolish to say that I had hoped for this delightful match for her. Did she not trust Tadayori that she did not tell me of this before? Or was she so ashamed of the kinship with me that she desired to keep it secret? In either case, I feel ashamed. How can I receive the deeds from you? I would like to give them back to you again. It had seemed to me strange that I had remained alive till now, but now I see that it is that I might see my daughter's face again. My heart is full to over-flowing when I think of it,' he concluded in abashed confusion.

The Saemon no Kami was moved in spite of himself. 'At the very beginning, in her grief she said, "I must let him know where I am for one cannot tell whether he will pass away tonight or at tomorrow's dawn," but I, Michiyori,[1] would not allow her to do so for the time being, for I had other plans. For when I had visited her constantly when she was living in the West Wing[2] of your house, I had seen that she was treated even by you as inferior to the other children. And I know that the Kita no Kata treated her shamefully and used her cruelly and as if she were even lower than the servants. I therefore said to the Lady, "It will not make them happy to know that you are

---

[1] Here for the first time the Saemon no Kami's personal name is given as Michiyori.
[2] The Lower Room.

still alive. Tell them where you are living when you have risen some way in the world and when you can help your father." We believed that the thought of her being dead would not grieve you overmuch, seeing that you had had her shut up in that store-room and had allowed the Tenyaku no Suke to do as he did. I, Michiyori, always intended to avenge these wrongs which she suffered on the Kita no Kata, though we had no special cause of bitterness towards you. On the occasion of the Procession of the Kamo Shrine, our servants behaved outrageously, although they had been told that the carriages belonged to you. Although I called on them to stop, it was in reality I who incited them to behave as they did. I know how indignant all your family were against me, and how well I deserve this. However, the Lady Ochikubo is always lamenting that she has not the same opportunities as your other children of living with you and carrying out her daily duties as your daughter. This has caused me to think how wonderful are the ties between parent and child and has caused me to decide to serve you devotedly for the future. Also, our little children are growing up and we wish to have them admired by their grandparents.' Thus, with all detail, he explained everything which had happened from the beginning.

The old Chūnagon was ashamed to hear all this, and he felt infinite sorrow to think that their past actions had been due to the Saemon no Kami's deep indignation at the cruelty of the Kita no Kata. He therefore made answer very haltingly. 'I did not intend to treat her as inferior to the other children,' he said, 'but those whose mother was still alive always demanded to be served first. So she must often have suffered great humiliations, I regret to say. You had good reason for your indignation, and I have no excuse to offer you. Tenyaku is an abominable creature. I ought never have allowed him to do as he did. I had her shut up in the store-room because I had been told that she had behaved disgracefully. Now, more than anything else, I would like to see the children. Where are they? I should like to see them at once.'

The Saemon no Kami pushed aside the screen. 'Here is the Lady,' he said to the Chūnagon. 'Come out and meet your father,' he said to her.

The Lady was very shy. She crept out slowly on her knees. Her father gazed at her. She had grown very beautiful. She wore a splendid white damask robe with a silk under-robe dyed purple. He looked at her and saw how superior she was to those other daughters whom he had cherished so fondly, and he felt a great shame and humiliation to think that he should have shut up in that store-room such a lovely lady.

'It is with infinite relief and pleasure that I see you again,' the Chūnagon said, 'for owing to your indignation against us for our ill-treatment of you, you have kept us ignorant of your whereabouts till today.'

'Nothing was further from my thoughts than to bear malice against you,' answered the Lady. 'It was the Lord who told me to keep my dwelling secret. He was indignant, for he had come to visit me while I was being treated cruelly. I am exceedingly sorry that you have suffered so much because of the spiteful things he has done but without any real malice towards you yourself.'

'When these things happened,' the Chūnagon said with a laugh, 'I wondered what caused him to bring such shame upon us, but now I know that he did it to avenge the ill-treatment of my daughter, and I am very glad.'

The Lady was very sorry for her father. 'Although you bear us no malice, we are nevertheless extremely sorry for having done what we did.'

The Saemon no Kami then entered with a beautiful baby-boy in his arms. 'Look at him!' he said. 'Has he not a beautiful disposition? Not a person in the world, not even the most spiteful, not even your Kita no Kata, could feel hatred towards him.'

'You speak too freely,' the Lady reproached him.

The Chūnagon gazed at the child; to his grandfatherly eyes, he seemed very dear. A smile came naturally to his face. 'Come to me. Come to me,' he said. The child was not frightened by this old man whom he was seeing for the first time; he put his arms around the old man's neck and allowed himself to be hugged. 'Even the most devilish person in the world would do no harm to him,' said the old Chūnagon. 'He is very, very big. How old is he?'

'Three,' answered the father.

'Have you any other children?' asked the Chūnagon.

'His younger brother is being brought up at my father's house. We have also a daughter whom you will be able to see some other time; it is an Unlucky Day for her to be seen today.'

Then dinner was served to all. All the attendants, even the ox-drivers, were entertained magnificently, even if not formally. Before the interview with the old Lord, the Lord had called to him Emon and Shōnagon. 'Take the Echizen no Kami into your common room and entertain him,' he had ordered them.

They did so; at first the Echizen no Kami had refused to go with them out of shame, but, at last, persuading himself of his own innocence of having done any harm to the Lady Ochikubo, he went with them. The room was rather large and beautifully matted. Assembled there on leaving the presence of the Lord and Lady, were twenty well-chosen maids, each as beautiful as the next.

The Echizen no Kami was of an amorous disposition and was very happy to find himself there with all these pretty girls. With wide-open eyes he gazed around him in joy and could not say a word. There were five or six whom he knew who had been persuaded to come there from his father's house.

'The Lord has told us to make the Echizen no Kami drunk,' Emon said to the maids. 'It will be a great disgrace if he returns home without a red face. Offer him Saké, young ladies.'

One after another, they pressed wine on him, and he was soon quite drunk. 'Help me, Lady Emon,' he cried, 'you are torturing me cruelly!' He tried to run away but the pretty young ladies were sitting all around him and prevented him, and they kept persuading him to drink until, overcome at last, he fell to the floor and slept.

Meanwhile, the old Chūnagon and the Saemon no Kami were also drunk, having exchanged cups many times, and they were talking of many things.

'We have said that we shall do our utmost to serve you,' said the Lord. 'So it would make us very happy, if you tell us in what we can help you.'

The Chūnagon's joy was unbounded.

As it was by this time growing dark and time for the guests to return home, the Chūnagon was presented with a dresscase, containing a robe in the one section, and in the other a Court-robe and a priceless jewelled belt. To the Echizen no Kami was given a lady's robe and a damask under-robe.

'Although I had felt it to be a source of sorrow that I was still alive,' the Chūnagon said as he left, rather drunk, 'now I feel it a joy.'

Their attendants were not many; those of the Fifth Rank were given a robe, those of the Sixth a **hakama**, and the lower servants a roll of silk. All the attendants were amazed, wondering how it was that such a change had come over the relations between the Chūnagon and the Saemon no Kami.

When the Chūnagon returned home he told the Kita no Kata all that the Saemon no Kami had said from beginning to end. 'When he asked me,' he said, 'whether

I had really intended to marry the Lady Ochikubo to the Tenyaku no Suke, I was filled with shame and felt my face turn red. Their child is infinitely beautiful. From the appearance of them all, the Lady seems to be very happy indeed.'

It would be foolishly inadequate to say only that the Great Lady was filled with hatred and malice. 'Oh, how I hate to hear you speak like that!' she exclaimed. 'Did you think she was so wonderful formerly? Was it not you who suggested shutting her up in the store-room? It was not I. It was because you allowed me always to act at my discretion that I allowed Tenyaku to have access to her. Now that she has become the darling of a great man, why is it that you are trying to shift the blame from yourself on to others? Also remember that such over-prosperity never lasts long.'

The Echizen no Kami, very drunk, lay and talked of the wonderful experiences of the day. 'Thirty girls surrounded me closely and pressed me to drink,' he said. 'There was a girl from the service of the Third Lady and another from the service of the Fourth Lady, and Maroya and others who used to be in service here. I thought they all looked very beautiful in their fine new clothes.'

The Third and Fourth Ladies, lying in bed close by, could hear all this. 'These are the sorrows of life,' said the Third Lady. 'Who, having seen her when she lived in the Lower Room or when she was shut up in the store-room, would have thought that she would so far surpass us and have so many maids to wait on her? How ashamed our father and mother must be at the contrast! What are we to do? Oh, how I wish I could become a nun!'

The Third Lady wept and the Fourth Lady also. 'How ashamed I feel!' exclaimed the Fourth Lady. 'Our mother has brought us up so tenderly, not knowing to what sorrowful destiny we were born. What must people say when they compare us with her! When all these disgraces were falling on us, I wished to become a nun but I did not as at that time I was expecting a child, and when my child was born, my mother-love prevented me until such time as my child should have attained years of discretion. And thus I have remained here till now.'

The two thus spoke together with tears, and the Fourth Lady recited this poem—

> I have lived to find
> Myself in such sorrow and
> Sad circumstances,
> As those I rejoiced to see
> Others suffer under once.

The Third Lady replied—

> How true and how sad
> That the fortune of life is
> Like the shifting bed
> Of the Asuka River—
> Now deepening, now made shallow.

Thus they talked till dawn.

The next morning, the Chūnagon looked over his presents. 'This robe is not suitable for an old man like me to wear, the colour even is too gay,' he said. 'And this belt is a priceless one. I do not deserve such a valuable present. I ought to return it.'

Just then it was told him that a letter had arrived from the Saemon no Kami, and all hurried out to receive it. 'How sad I was yesterday to find that night was approaching!' the Lord wrote. 'As you were in a hurry to leave, I was not able to tell you of all that has happened of late years. If you do not come often to visit us in future, I shall be very offended. How was it that you forgot to take these deeds with you? Move into the new house at once or we shall think that you are still angry with us, and that will cause us infinite sorrow.'

A letter also came for the Fourth Lady from the Lady of Sanjō. 'Although I have wished to know how you are and tell you of my present life, circumstances have prevented me from doing so until now. Have you not foregotten me?

> Though true it may be
> That you do not say that me
> You have forgotten,
> True it is your love for me
> Is much less than mine for you.

That is what I think. Say to your mother and my sisters, "Now all that remains is the happiness of seeing each other again."'

The other four sisters and brothers had come together

and read the letter in turn. 'I wish she had written to me also,' the other sisters said. How strange to hear this wish from those who never thought of visiting the Lady when she was living in the Lower Room!

The Chūnagon answered the Saemon no Kami's letter at once. 'I had thought of remaining at your house for the night last night, but it was in an Unlucky Direction for me. It will lengthen my life and make me very happy to know that I can continually go to your mansion. Well, I told you yesterday that I felt that I could not accept the deeds from you. That you still continue to force them on me makes me think that you are still angry with me. As for the belt also, it is quite unsuitable for an old man like me, truly a "roll of brocade on a dark night," and I should like to return it but that you might think that I despise your kindnesses. I will therefore keep it for some time.'

The Fourth Lady also answered her letter. 'For years we have not known where to find the cedar tree that stands at your gate.[1] How delighted we are to learn it now! Yet we are sad that you should say we do not love you.[2]

---

[1] Referring to the poem—

> My little house stands
> At the foot of Mt. Miwa;
> 　When you come to me,
> You will recognise it for
> A cedar stands at the gate.

[2] Referring indirectly to the poem—

> Though I do not live
> Under far distant skies,
> 　You act as though you
> Do not know I am dwelling
> Not far away from you still.

That love is greater
Which is felt with mad longing
For the loved one,
Who having deserted me
Has fled I know not whither.'

After this happy reunion, the magnanimous Lord and Lady did all in their power to please the Chūnagon and his sons and daughters; the old man visited their mansion more often than was really proper; the Echizen no Kami and the Daibu, his younger brother, repressing their shame because of the Lady's former ill-treatment, went also, for the Saemon no Kami was the most influential noble of the day. The Lady of Sanjō was very glad at this and planned to bring rapid promotion to them, especially to the Daibu whom, because of his sympathy with her in former times, she looked on as one of her own children.

'Well, now I should like to see the Kita no Kata and my sisters,' the Lady of Sanjō said to the Echizen no Kami. 'I should like them to come here. Since the time when I lost my mother in my infancy, I have regarded the Great Lady as my real mother, for I lived so long under her care. I have long wished to repay her for her kindness to me, but for years she treated me with coldness and enmity. Please give my love to her and the other Ladies.'

When the Echizen no Kami returned home, he gave this message to the Kita no Kata. 'She thinks infinitely kindly of me,' he concluded.

The old Kita no Kata had become more reasonable as she realised the benefits her family were now receiving through the favour of the Saemon no Kami. 'Perhaps it is true that those are her real sentiments,' she thought. 'If she bore me any malice for my ill-treatment of her, she would have avenged herself on my children. It was the Lord who wished for revenge. It was assuredly he who was with her, helping her with her sewing, that night when I saw them together.' Gradually, therefore, she became willing to correspond with the Lady.

About the same time, the Saemon no Kami was talking to the Lady, 'Alas! The Chūnagon is getting to be very old,' he said. 'It is said by all that blessed are they who serve their aged parents with all fidelity. To celebrate the attainment of a parent's sixtieth or seventieth birthday, there are festivals of dance and music, the presentation of young herbs and a banquet at the New Year,[1] and the ceremony called **hakō**, when Buddhist pictures are drawn and sutras written for the intention of the repose of their souls. Which of these beautiful customs shall we follow? Some cause to be said for themselves while they are still living the requiem which should be said forty-nine days after their death. That does not seem appropriate for a person to do on behalf of one's father in his lifetime. However, say which of these ceremonies you would like to be held, and it shall be held.'

The Lady was very pleased with his suggestion. 'Dances

---

[1] On the Seventh Day of the First Month.

and music are interesting and amusing, but of no benefit
for the salvation of the soul in the next life. To have a
Forty-nine Day Requiem said is abominable. The hakō
ceremony seems to me the most beautiful from the point
of view of this world and most efficacious from the point
of view of the next. I should like to have that ceremony
held.'

'The idea is good, and I am quite of your opinion with
regard to its merits. Therefore let it be held this year.
Your father looks as though we cannot rely on having
him with us for long.'

Next day from dawn, they busied themselves with
arrangements for the ceremony. They decided to hold it
in the Eighth Month; artists were commissioned to draw
Buddhist pictures, and image-makers to make images. The
Lord and the Lady eagerly joined in the preparations.
Silk cloth and thread, gold and silver were ordered from
the provinces. There was nothing left undone that they
wished to be done.

Just at that time, the condition of the Mikado's health
became serious, and he abdicated in favour of the Crown
Prince, the eldest son of the Saemon no Kami's younger
sister who now became Empress Dowager, and her second
son was appointed Crown Prince. The Saemon no Kami
was promoted Dainagon,[1] his brother-in-law, the Kurōdo
no Shōshō, formerly the husband of the Third Lady,

---

[1] Great Counsellor.

became a Chūnagon; the new Dainagon's younger brother
became a Saishō.[1]   Only the Dainagon's kinsmen were
promoted on this occasion, and all power came into his
hands.   The old Chūnagon, his father-in-law, was highly
delighted and felt a great honour to himself.

Throughout the Seventh Month, the new Dainagon,
though extremely busy with Court affairs, used what leisure
he had to further the arrangements for the **hakō**, now definitely fixed for the Twenty-first Day of the Eighth Month.
At first he had thought of holding the ceremony at his
own house, but as the Lady's step-mother and her sisters
would not be easily persuaded to come there, he thought,
he decided to hold it at the mansion of the Chūnagon.
The house was put into good repair, white sand was laid
around it, and new blinds and mats were ordered.   The
Uchūben, the husband of the Second Lady, and the
Echizen no Kami had been appointed Stewards to the
new Dainagon, in addition to their own offices, and so
were put in charge of all the preparations.   All the ordinary everyday furniture was put away.   The Dainagon's
lodging was arranged on the North Side, and the old
Kita no Kata and her daughters moved into the room at
the western end of the plastered store-room.   As the
ceremony was to begin early the next morning, the people
moved to the residence of the Chūnagon by night.   The
space being restricted, not all of the Dainagon's attendants
were allowed to go and stay overnight at the residence.

---

[1] Counsellor.

The Lord and the Lady went in a procession of seven carriages. This was the first time she had seen the old Kita no Kata and the Ladies since her escape from their house. She wore a damask under-robe of deep red and a robe of greenish-yellow lined wi h blue. Her robes were so beautiful, so magnificent in every detail and in colour, that the contrast with her former shabby garments, given as a reward for her sewing, must have struck many there. While she was superintending the arrangements, she talked of former times with the Third and Fourth Ladies. She had looked strikingly beautiful even when formerly she was called Ochikubō, and now, her beauty having matured, she looked indeed a Kita no Kata. The robes of the Third and Fourth Ladies looked almost shabby by the side of hers. However, thought the Great Lady, nothing could be done about that and she began to converse with the Lady.

'You were but a child when you were put into my care,' she said, 'and I have regarded you ever since as one of my own children. I am rather hasty-tempered and speak my mind frankly without regard to what others think. I am infinitely sorry that you have had a bad impression of me through that.'

The Lady was at heart very amused at this. 'But has there been any unpleasantness then?' she said. 'I cannot think of any. My sole desire now is to find some way of showing my devotion to you. That is my one hope.'

'It is very nice of you to say that. We are all glad to

have you in your present position of eminence, for there are obscure persons in my family.

From dawn next day, all were busy with the preparations. Many officials of high rank came with, of course, an uncountable number of the Fourth and Fifth Rank.

'How can this old Chūnagon who has been in his dotage for so many years have got his daughter married to such an influential noble? He is certainly a lucky man,' they said one to another in their amazement. And the old Chūnagon looking at his just over twenty years old Dainagon son-in-law, going to and fro in splendid attire, busy with the arrangements, was filled with pride and joy, and shed senile tears of happiness. The Lord's brother, the Saishō-Chūjō, was there also with the Chūnagon, the former husband of the Third Lady, both very elegantly dressed.

At the sight of the Chūnagon, the Third Lady was overcome with sorrowful memories of former times. She gazed at him and saw how charming he looked and how splendidly he was dressed, and the sight pained her.

'If he had not deserted me,' she thought, 'it would have made me happy, but he would not now be a Chūnagon; and then he would not have been able to walk about like this with a Dainagon. But how happy I should be, even though he were not so high in rank!' In secret she wept because of the sorrows of her heart, and in secret she recited to herself this poem—

> Will he remember
> The happy days that are past,

Now we meet again?
I thought; but he is heartless,
And only I too easily hurt.

The ceremony commenced. Many religious teachers
and priests of the highest rank had assembled, and it had
been arranged that they should read nine of the most holy
books of the Scriptures—the seven books of the Sutra of
the Lotus with the Sutra of Immortality and the Sutra of
Amida. One book was to be read each day and one
image of Buddha dedicated, for nine sutras had been
written and nine images made. Everything was infinitely
splendid. Four of the sutras were written on varicoloured
paper dusted with gold and silver, and each was mounted
on a rod of black aromatic agilawood and provided with
a case. The other five were written on dark-blue paper
and dusted with gold; their rods were ornamented with
crystals and their separate cases had pictures on the lids
illustrating the most important passage of the sutra each
enclosed. It was worth while attending just to see the
sutras and images. A dark-coloured robe was presented
to each lecturer at each morning and evening session, for
the Dainagon wished nothing to be done in unworthy
style.

As the days passed, the fame of the ceremony spread,
and many more people, both high and low, came on the
later days. On the fifth day, the most important day as
then the Book of Deva was read, offerings were sent by
nobles and others, so that the house was filled with
attendants with offerings, until there was little room left

for more.   Just as the offerings of rosaries and surplices had been prepared and were about to be offered, a letter arrived for the Dainagon from the Minister of the Left, his father.

'I had intended to come to the ceremony today,' the letter read, 'but my beri-beri has become worse and I find it too painful to sit in formal style.   I send this trivial thing simply as a token of my devotion; please make an offering of it to Buddha.'   With the letter there was a golden orange in an emerald dish in a green bag attached to a spray of pine.

There was also a letter for the Lady from his wife, the Kita no Kata of the Minister of the Left.   'I have heard that you are holding an important celebration,' she wrote, 'but I was not able to show my eagerness to help you in the preparations, for you did not tell me of it beforehand. I present this practical offering that Buddha may be well-pleased because of its modesty.'   With it was a robe of Chinese silk gauze of light and dark reddish brown and a spray of **ominaeshi** flowers with half a pound of red silk-yarn for rosary strings.

While the Lady of Sanjō was writing an answer to this, a letter arrived from the wife of the Chūnagon, her husband's second sister.   'Was it because you did not wish us to share in your blessings that you did not tell us of the holy ceremony which you are performing?' said the letter.   With it was a carved open lotus on its stem, coloured bluish with large silver dew-drops.

Also the Lady Miya, Vice-Directress of the Maids of Honour, arrived with a letter from the Empress-Dowager. As the messenger of the Empress, she was suitably entertained to dinner in a special room where she would not be intruded upon by the rest of the people. The Echizen no Kami and his brother, the former Daibu who had been promoted Saemon no Suke[1] through the Lord's influence, were deputed to wait on her.

The Empress-Dowager's letter read, 'I will not write much today as you must be in a whirl. This is offered for the intention of closer relations with Buddha.' The offering was a gold rosary box with a rosary of the kernels of the sacred fig-tree. When all the people there, her sisters as well as others, saw how all the kinsmen of her husband competed with each other to show their devotion to the old Lord, they could see how highly fortunate she was.

The Dainagon promptly wrote his answer to the Empress-Dowager. 'I am most grateful to Your Majesty for the letter You have honoured us with,' he wrote, 'In accordance with Your Majesty's Will, I will personally offer Your present at the altar. When the ceremony is over, I will wait on Your Majesty to report all the details.' The lady-messenger was given a damask robe, a **hakama,** a reddish-brown Chinese robe lined with yellow silk and a pair of gauze skirts.

The ceremony began, and the lords and ladies there offered their gifts one after another, most of them silver

---

[1] Colonel of the Gate Guards of the Left.

and gold carvings of lotus flowers. The Chunagon's offering was a silver writing-brush, of the colour of burnt bamboo and covered with a gauze frame. An uncountable number of such things as surplices were offered and piled on one side. Lengths of split sappan wood, dyed a dark colour, were bundled together and offered.[1]

This day was the most splendid of all the days of the ceremony, and when people saw the offerings of the lords and ladies, they said, 'How fortunate the old Chūnagon is in his old age!'

'One ought to pray to the gods and Buddha only to have a beautiful daughter,' others replied.

Thus the nine days passed in the solemn performance of the ceremony.

Every morning of these nine days, the Third Lady wondered, 'Will he come to me today?' and the next day the same question, 'Will he come today?' but the Chūnagon never did. But his soul must have felt the reproach of her heart, for when he was leaving at the conclusion of the ceremonies, he stopped and called to her younger brother, the Saemon no Suke. 'Why are you not friendly to me?' he asked.

'How can I be?' the Saemon no Suke answered.

'Have you forgotten former days? How is she?'

'Who?'

---

[1] To remind the worshippers of Gyōki's statement that it was while he was a hewer of wood and a drawer of water that he came to understand this sutra.

'Is it necessary for me to say?   The Third Lady.'

'I do not know.   She is probably here, if you wish to know.'

'Then give her this poem—

> Your house I have found
> Without change since former times,
>   So also I find
> There has been no change at all
> In my affection for you.

and quote to her "Yo no naka wa."[1]   So saying, the Chūnagon left the mansion.

The Saemon no Suke thought it wrong for him to leave without at least waiting for an answer, and he realised that the Chūnagon could have no tenderness left for the Third Lady.   He went in and told her what had been said, and how the Chūnagon had gone away immediately.

'He should have stayed a little while with me.   If he had had no intention of doing that, why did he ask after me?   How sad it makes me feel!'   She thought it useless to send any answer to him, and so did not write.

The Dainagon, having given a grand banquet to celebrate the end of their period of fasting, was about to leave with his family.

---

[1] Quoting from the poem—

> This world is for us
> A journey to goal unknown;
>   We have no home;
> Each day at the journey's end
> We choose a place to rest at.

'Stay a few days more,' urged the old Chūnagon.

'It is inconvenient for the children to stay here as the house is so small,' the Lord replied. 'It would be better to take them home and come here again some time without them.'

'It is not necessary for me to make any comment on the grandeur and solemnity of the ceremony,' the old Chūnagon said. 'It was a great honour, and it will prolong my days that all your kinsmen from the Empress-Dowager down, and the Minister of the Left, have honoured me in this manner. One volume of the Scriptures and one picture of Buddha would have been enough for an old man like me. And yet you have done it in such a magnificent manner!' he concluded and wept for joy. The Dainagon and the Lady both remained silent, both very glad that what they had done had been successful in its aim of pleasing the old Chūnagon. 'I have been keeping this as my most precious possession,' the old Chūnagon went on, 'with the object of leaving it to someone. When the Chūnagon[1] used to come here formerly, he asked me to give it to him, but I refused. It seems as if I knew the time would come when I should want it to give to you. Let the little boy take it.' He handed a beautiful flute in a brocade bag to the child, who took it with a smile as if he knew it was intended for him. The Dainagon, his father, thought it a very beautiful flute, in sound as well as in appearance.

So late in the evening they returned to Sanjō. 'How

---

[1] Formerly the Kurōdo no Shōshō.

delighted the Chūnagon was! What shall we do to amuse him next time?' the Dainagon said to the Lady.

It was some little time after this that the Minister of the Left said to his son, the Dainagon, 'As I grow older, I find that the work of Taishō[1] is too much for me. It needs a young energetic man.' Therefore he resigned this additional post to the Dainagon. This could be done at their will; there was no one who could object to anything they did; the Lord's prosperity and influence was boundless.

The old Chūnagon's happiness was increased all the more by this new promotion of the Lord. Though he was not seriously ill, he had begun to feel rather poorly and kept his bed. The Kita no Kata of the new Taishō[2] was grieved at this. She prayed that her father might not die yet, so that they might have another such opportunity of showing their devotion to him as the last which had delighted him so much.

'If he had many more years to live,' the Taishō was also thinking, when he heard that the old Chūnagon was seventy years old that year, 'and plenty more opportunities of pleasure, I would have no need for hurry. Even though I may be accused of over-hastiness, I will hold a celebration of his seventieth birthday. I will realise what I have long wished to do. It would not be right to give

[1] The General of the Bodyguard (of the Left).
[2] The Lady Ochikubo.

him only one cause of joy, when I have given him so many causes of sorrow. However much one does for one's parents when they are dead, no one praises it and is happy because of it. What I do this time, I will do to the limit of my power.'

Thus he decided to celebrate the old Chūnagon's seventieth anniversary and set about the preparations. The governor of every province, eager to oblige the Dainagon and Taishō, willingly obeyed his order and sent the things which he had asked as presents. In this way, enough for the entertainment of the guests was collected.

Emon no Jō[1] had been promoted earlier to the Fifth Rank and had been appointed Governor of Mikawa. Emon had received permission to accompany her husband to his post, and the Lady had given her many articles for her journey, including a silver bowl and even a travelling robe, all the things prepared with loving care. Now, when the Taishō sent asking the Mikawa no Kami for a little silk for the ceremony, he at once sent one hundred rolls of silk, and his wife sent the Lady twenty rolls of silk, dyed with madder.

Children were engaged for the dancing. Articles of furniture were made, and much gold was used in their decoration.

'Why are you exerting yourself to do all this for the Chūnagon?' the Minister of the Left said to his son, the Taishō. 'Still,' he went on, 'the old man has not much longer to live. Do what you can to entertain him while

---

[1] Tachihaki, Korenari.

ho io otill alive. I will help his sons to gain promotion
as much as I can.'

Out of his love for the Taishō, he therefore assisted
in the preparations as far as he could.

The ceremony was held on the Eleventh Day of the
Eleventh Month, this time at the Taishō's mansion at
Sanjō. It seems useless to describe the celebrations in
detail; everything was done in grand style, and in a
manner well worthy of the Taishō.

Many new screens with pictures were made, but we
will not described them except, as an example, a six-leaf
screen at the end of the row.

For the First Month there was written this poem—

> Yoshino yama
> At daybreak today was seen
> To be covered with haze;
> It may be perhaps because
> Spring has come during the night.'

The picture for the Second Month was of a man looking at the falling cherry-blossoms, and the accompanying
poem read—

> O cherry blossoms!
> From this present year forget
> To fall from the tree,
> And remain as a model
> A thousand generations.

The picture for the Third Month represented a man
breaking off a branch of peach blossoms on the Third

Day of the Third Month.

> This peach tree bears fruit
> But once in three thousand years;
> I break off a spray
> To put in my hair, so that
> My fortune may be like yours.

The poem for the Fourth Month was—

> I had been waiting
> Long to hear the cuckoo's call;
> At last its faint note
> Startled me as if I had been
> Awakened from a dream.

For the Fifth Month was pictured a house with a bundle of iris blades hanging down under the eaves, and a cuckoo in flight.

> No doubt the cuckoo
> Sings so very loud today
> That he may tell us
> That the houses are adorned
> With the festival iris.

For the Sixth Month there was a picture of a Purification Ceremony.

> The depths of the stream
> Of my purification
> Are so clear—it seems
> A mirror in which I see
> The vision of your future.

For the Seventh Month, the picture of a house decorated for the Festival of the Weaver.

No cloud in the sky;
His beloved, the Weaver,
To meet, the Herd now
Is rowing his boat across
The calm River of Heaven.

The picture for the Eighth Month represented servants digging up flowers at Sagano for transplantation.

Ominaeshi!
They have come to Sagano
In such large numbers
To take you, it would be well
To be taken willingly.

For the Ninth Month, a picture of a house with a garden of white chrysanthemums.

Well might people think,
Seeing these white chrysanthemums,
Blooming by the fence,
That snow it was which had
Thus fallen out of season.

The picture for the Tenth Month was of a man looking up into a maple tree from which beautiful autumn leaves were falling.

These few crimson leaves
Of the maples have survived
Right through the autumn
That travellers may use them
In the worship of the god.[1]

For the Eleventh Month was this poem——

---

[1] As **nusa** for the worship of the God of the Pass.

. . . .
. . . .
. . . .
Then will I serve you during
A thousand generations.[1]

The picture for the Twelfth Month was of a lady
admiring the view from the window of a house in the
mountains in deep snow.

> Since the snow fell thus
> So deeply here, has no one
>   Been able to come
> To pay us a visit here in
> This mountain-village of ours.

To the walking-staff which was presented to the old
Chūnagon on this occasion was attached this poem—

> We intend this staff
> To help you in crossing your
>   Eightieth birthday,
> And to help you to attain
> Yet higher peaks of honour.

It was very delightful to see on the occasion of this
birthday celebration two barges, with musicians on board,
playing, as they floated on the pleasant, spacious, calm,
mirror-like lake. Courtiers of high rank and high officials
came in great numbers. The Minister of the Left was
present and made an uncountable number of presents.
The Empress-Dowager sent ten basted robes and the Chūnagon ten robes. Ladies and Maids of Honour in the

---

[1] The first part of the poem is missing in all extant copies.

service of the Empress came. The old Chūnagon felt better in health immediately. When all the guests were leaving late that night on the conclusion of the day's enjoyment, each was presented with a set of robes, and the noblest received some other gift in addition to the ordinary present. The Minister of the Left gave the old Chūnagon two very fine horses and two rare sō-no-koto. The retainers and servants were given clothes or silk cloth. The Echizen no Kami had been told to arrange everything at his own discretion; he had done his utmost, and everything had been arranged splendidly. Then, after staying a few days at Sanjō, the old Chūnagon and his family returned home.

The Lady said that she was very glad that all this had been done for her father, and the Lord was happy that his efforts had been so successful.

THE FOURTH BOOK

THE old Chūnagon's illness gradually became more severe, and the Taishō in his sympathy and sorrow had many incantations performed and prayers offered.

'Why is it?' said the old Chūnagon to the Kita no Kata of the Taishō. 'Now, I have nothing more that I desire in this world and so now I have no fear of death. Why then do you have all these prayers said for me? The time is fast approaching when I must die,' he went on for he realised that he was becoming feebler. 'If there is any reason why I should wish to live a little longer, it could only be because of the inferiority of my rank. I feel it a disgrace that I have been outstripped by many nobles but recently very junior to me. If I lived but a little while longer, I should be promoted through the all-powerful influence of the Taishō to the office of Dainagon. If I were to die now, it would be said of me that I was predestined never to rise to high rank. That is all I desire now, to rise to that rank. No one in the world could have a greater honour than I, if only I died a Dainagon.'

The Taishō was infinitely sorrowful when he learned all this. 'How very much I should like him to be made Dainagon!' the Lady said to him. 'I should like to be able to do this one thing for him.'

The Lord also wished that he could bring about this

promotion, but it was impossible for there were already the full number of Dainagon.[1] And it was impossible to dismiss one of them in order to give his office to the old Chūnagon. He therefore decided that he ought to give up his own position to the old Lord.

He therefore went to his father, the Minister of the Left, and explained what he thought of doing. 'I have several children,' he said, 'but the Chūnagon, their grandfather, will not live long enough to receive their dutiful attentions. For this reason, therefore, I wish to do this while he is still alive. Please have this approved.'

'Well, if you have decided to do this, then it would be better to do it at once. It will be quite all right for you to resign the office of Dainagon; you are still Taishō,' said his father, knowing that no question of getting the matter approved arose, for nothing was impossible for him to do now.

Infinitely pleased at this answer, the Lord resigned his office, and an Imperial decree was issued, promoting the old Chūnagon to the rank of Dainagon. When the old Lord heard this, he shed tears of joy, in spite of the pain he was suffering from his illness. To have given such happiness to their father would bring much happiness in the next world to the Lord and the Lady.

In his joy, the old Dainagon prayed that he might be able to rise from his bed once more and called his family

---

[1] By the Taihō Code, there were four Dainagon. Later the number was reduced to two. In the time of the Emperor Uda (888-897) the number was fixed at three.

together to pray that his allotted span of life might be prolonged. In response perhaps to these prayers, he became a little stronger. He therefore rose from his sickbed and ordered that a Lucky Day for his visit to the Court should be determined.

'I have seven children, but who has done so much for my benefit both in this world and the next, as the Lady of Sanjō has?' he commented as he ordered his preparations to go to the Court. 'It must have been my unfortunate Fate to have treated so unkindly, even for a short time, such a saintly person. I have two or three sons-in-law, and they have all been to this moment dependent on me for everything and have done nothing but bring disgrace upon me. As for the Taishō, I have never done the slightest things to make him happy and yet he serves me with such devotion. It makes me ashamed when I think of it. When I am dead, all of you, my sons and daughters, serve him faithfully in my stead.'

His words were very reasonable but the old Kita no Kata was offended by them, and wished that he would die soon.

On the day on which he went to the Court, he dressed himself very splendidly and first went to Sanjō, where he prostrated himself before the Lord and the Lady.

'You must not honour us so,' protested the Lord.

'It is not the Throne which fills me with any awe. It is the kindness of you, my dear children, which alone inspires me with reverence. I cannot serve you in this world sufficiently and my sole prayer is that I may be allowed to protect you after my death,' the old Dainagon replied.

When he left the mansion at Sanjō, he went to the house of the Minister of the Left and then proceeded to the Court. He made presents to everyone, but, though they were very splendid, we will not describe them here.

From that day, the old Dainagon's illness became much worse, and he had to take to his bed again.

'As I have not the slightest thing to desire further, I have no further desire to live,' he said from his sick-bed.

Learning how weak he had become, to his great joy, the Kita no Kata of the Taishō went to stay with him. His five daughters were all there to nurse him tenderly, but the old Lord thought nothing of anyone's services except those of the Lady of Sanjō. Her presence was the only thing which delighted him. It caused him to regain a little of his appetite and he was able to eat a little boiled rice soaked in hot water.

Feeling that he was sinking, he decided to divide his property while he was still alive. 'My children do not act like brothers and sisters to each other,' he thought. 'Even my daughters are not friendly with each other. When I am dead, quarrels are certain to arise among them.'

He therefore called to his side the Echizen no Kami and began to divide among his sons and daughters the heirlooms and the deeds of various properties, and as he distributed them, any which were rather better than the rest he bequeathed to the Kita no Kata of the Taishō.

'My other children should not envy her in the slightest,' the old Lord said. 'Even if you have all exerted yourselves to do your duty to me as my children, it is but right that I should give the things which are of a little higher value to the one who is of higher value than the rest. All the more so when all the others have been dependent on me for so long.'

Those who were present thought that what he said was quite reasonable.

'This house is old,' he went on, 'but it is large and nice.' So he gave it to the Kita no Kata of the Taishō.

When the old Kita no Kata heard this, she wept. 'It is good for you thus to express the gratitude you feel to the Lady,' she said, 'but how can I help being envious at what you are doing? I was married to you when I was still very young, and now I am over sixty and you more than seventy. All this time I have served you and have been dependent on you. We have had seven children. Then why do you not leave this house to me? You intend to neglect your children because they have neglected their duty towards you. But an ordinary father feels more anxiety about how those of his children who are less fortunate than the others will fare after his death. It does not make much difference to the Lady of Sanjō whether you give her this house or not. The Taishō is a man of great influence and can easily build three or four such houses as this. And their mansion at Sanjō is wonderfully furnished; we did it. Your sons will also be able to manage for themselves, and so will your married daughters, for even if they have now no splendid mansion of their own, it may be that they ought to build one. But where shall I and these two daughters of ours go to live, if we have not this house? Shall we have to wander along the streets? What you are deciding is unjust.' Thus she spoke without ceasing to weep.

'I am not neglecting you completely,' the old Dainagon replied. 'They will be able to live comfortably, if not in elegance. There will be no need for you to wander along the streets. In return for your loving care of your children for so long, they will take care of you. Echizen no Kami, take care of your mother in my place. The Sanjō house is not mine, is it? Truly it belongs to the Lady. The Taishō will have a very poor opinion of my gratitude, if I die without making him some fairly good present. Whatever you say, I shall not change my mind. Do not be spiteful to me, for I am now near to death. Do not make me speak more. The pain is too great for me to bear.'

The old Kita no Kata was about to remonstrate further but her children prevented her from saying anything more.

The Kita no Kata of the Taishō, hearing all this, was full of compassion for her. 'The words of the Kita no Kata are very reasonable,' she said. 'Do not give us anything at all. Give everything to my brothers and sisters. It must be a very unpleasant surprise for them to learn that they must leave the house where they have lived so long. Please do as I beg, and that quickly.'

She continued to urge him but the old Dainagon replied, 'No, I shall not give the house to them. When I am dead, you may do as you like with it,' and would not listen to anything further.

Next he gave to the Taishō several valuable belts which he had. The Echizen no Kami in his turn felt rather dissatisfied with this but did not grumble, for he thought that he ought not to complain as the Lady was his father's favourite daughter.

The old Lord then went on to speak of the arrangements to be made after his death, and thanked the Kita no Kata of the Taishō for the myriad happinesses which she had brought to him. 'Thanks to the influence of the Lord, your husband, I have gained much honour,' he said over and over again, 'I am leaving many daughters of poor promise. Favour them with your assistance.'

'I will,' answered the Lady. 'I will help them to the utmost of my power.'

'It makes me very happy to hear that,' said the old Lord. 'Obey her instructions, my daughters. Look on her as your mistress.'

As he said these wise words, it could be seen that he was growing more feeble, and all of them there were filled with sorrow.

Finally, on the Seventh Day of the Eleventh Month he died. His death was not untimely,[1] and yet though they realised it was natural for him to die at such an age, all the sons and daughters assembled and wept for sorrow.

---

[1] For he had reached the age of three score years and ten.

The Taisho had not gone to the Dainagon's house with the Lady but had remained at his own house with the children. Now, however, he went to the Dainagon's house every day and stood outside weeping as he directed what arrangements should be made. He thought of going to stay at the house[1] so that he could arrange matters more easily, but his father advised him not to do so as it would entail a neglect of his duties by such a long absence from Court which would be especially regrettable when the Mikado had not been long on the Throne.

The Lady also advised him not to do so. 'If you bring the children here,' she said, 'we shall have to hold a purification ceremony for them also afterwards, and that would be very troublesome. And if you left them in the Sanjō house while you were here, we should be anxious about them. It would be better not to come here then.'

So the Taishō in his house at Sanjō, as he looked at his children and played with them, felt it very lonely there in his unaccustomed celibate life. And when he thought of how soon the old Dainagon had died; he felt very glad that they had done for him so promptly what they had.

The funeral of the old Lord was held on the third day after his death for that was not an Unlucky Day. As the Taishō was the chief mourner, many nobles of the Fourth and Fifth Rank attended and joined in the funeral procession.

---

[1] If he had entered the house, he would have become 'unclean,' which would have prevented him attending the Court.

'He had the happiest of deaths,' the people said, one to another, just as the old Lord himself had said.

During the period of mourning, all the family moved to small huts which were erected in the grounds, for the main building was occupied by the many priests. Every day the Taishō came and stood outside to talk to the Lady about the arrangements to be made. It saddened him to see her look so pale through keeping the fast, and her black mourning robes made her look the paler still.

> The stream of my tears
> Has now joined itself to yours;
> Your sleeve now appears
> A deep, deep pool in the bed
> Of the River of Tears.[1]

The Lady replied—

> This robe is a robe
> Of **fuchi** called because—
> The stream of my tears,
> In which this my sleeve has soaked
> Till it rots, so deep appears.

So with the Taishō going to and fro between the two houses, the thirty days of mourning passed. 'Now come back,' the Lord said to the Lady. 'The children are longing for you.'

'Not yet. I will go home after the forty-ninth day,' she replied. So every night the Taishō came to stay with

---

[1] **Fuchi** in these two poems has the double meaning of 'a deep pool in the bed of a river' and 'the colour of mourning robes—light purple.'

her at the old Dainagon's house.

The seventh seventh day arrived. As this was the final ceremony to be held in the mansion where the dead Lord had lived, the Taishō had been making splendid preparations for it. The sons and daughters had also done so, and the religious ceremonies were therefore conducted in a stately and solemn manner.

'Now come away from here quickly, or they will shut you up in a room,' the Taishō said to the Lady when the ceremony was over.

'How terrible you are! Never say such a thing again. If they were to learn that you were still remembering how they treated me, they would not wish to have anything to do with us. I want them to love me for they have succeded to the place in my affections which my dead father held.'

'True. You must console your sisters,' the Lord answered.

When the Echizen no Kami learnt that they were about to return home, he went to them with the deeds of the various manors and the other valuables which the old Dainagon had left to the Taishō and the Lady.

'These are poor things but they are the things which the old Lord bequeathed to you,' was the message which he sent in with them to the Lord.

The Taishō looked at them; there were three belts, one of which he had himself given to the Dainagon and which was evidently more valuable than the other two, the deeds of various manors and the ground plan of the house.

'These are some very splendid places,' commented the Taishō to the Lady. 'Why did the old Lord not give this house to the Kita no Kata and your sisters? Is there another house for them?'

'No, there is not,' answered the Lady. 'And I refuse to take this house. They have lived in it for such a long time. I shall make a present of it to the Kita no Kata.'

'That is a good idea,' said the Lord. 'If you accept this house while we have already so many, every one will resent it.'

They therefore called the Echizen no Kami in to them. 'You know how your father divided his property. Why did he give us so much? Did he think that he must give me so much because of my rank?' the Lord asked with a laugh.

'No, he did not give you so much for that reason. He bequeathed all these things to you on his death-bed to show his gratitude to you.'

'That was very good of him,' said the Lord, 'but the Lady says, "How can we take away from them this mansion where they are all accustomed to live?" The Kita no Kata must accept this house. And as for these two belts, I give them to you and your brother, the Saemon no Suke. I will keep these deeds for the manor in the Province of Mino and this one belt, so that I shall not appear to be making of no avail your father's last will.'

'It is not right for you to do so. Even if my father

had not bequeathed all these to you, it would have been within your rights to have taken them all now. Much more so when he left them to you. We have each one of us been given something, and I should not like to act contrary to my father's will,' the Echizen no Kami said, and refused to accept the return of anything.

'Your words sound strange to me,' said the Lord. 'You cannot be blamed as being selfish, if you take the house. It is all one to the Lady whether she has the house or not. While I am alive, she will have enough, and she has children who will care for her when I die. The Third and Fourth Ladies have not yet anyone to provide for them, and I wish to do what I can for them. And I will do something for the husbands of the First and Second Ladies.'

The Echizen no Kami was full of joy and gratitude to hear this. 'I will convey your intentions to the family,' he said.

'However, even if they refuse to take back these things, do not bring anything back to me. Or that will make matters difficult. I do not wish to have to repeat my offer.'

'Would it not be better for you to take these belts so that you can present them to someone?' asked the Echizen no Kami.

'If I do wish to give them to anyone, I will ask you for them. I can do that as we are kinsmen,' said the Taishō and thus persuaded the Echizen no Kami to take the belts.

The Echizen no Kami went out and told the old Kita

no Kata and his sisters what had been said.

'I was very sorry to lose this house, and am very glad that we are to have it back again,' was the Kita no Kata's comment. However, she was very irritated at the thought of having to be grateful for the return of what she considered her own property. 'Isn't it a pity that it is the Lady Ochikubo who is giving us the house?' she said.

The Echizen no Kami was furiously angry to hear this. He snapped his fingers. 'Are you out of your mind?' he cried. 'Did you not act so cruelly to her that you made us all ashamed? Ought people to talk as you do? Do you want to spoil our careers? Call to your mind the disgraces we suffered when the Lord was angry against us and you will know how he can make us suffer again. And then you say such ungrateful things when he is trying to help us! And how badly you treated her formerly! It seemed outrageous to us and to everyone who heard about it. And then you say "Ochikubo" and things like that!'

'It is not we who have had any benefits from her,' the Kita no Kata said in reply. 'It was because the Great Lord was her father that she attended on him. It was a slip of the tongue calling her "Ochikubo." Why then must you blame me?'

'Oh, how sad this is! You have no feelings,' the Echizen no Kami exclaimed. 'When you say that we have received no favours from her, you mean that you personally have not. Who was it that brought about the promotion of my brother, the Daibu, to the post of Saemon no Suke?

And after I, Kagezumi,[1] became the Taishō's steward, who was it that brought about my promotion? You ought to know that the promotion of your sons depends on the influence of the Taishō. And if he had not given you back this house, where would you search for a dwelling? Consider all these things together and you will be grateful for all the kindnesses which the Lord has shown you. I, Kagezumi, have an income as a governor of a province, yet I have never helped my wife's mother, for I have said that I must provide first for my wife. Neither have I given you anything. That is due to my lack of filial piety. When you consider how poorly you are thus served by your own son, you ought to shed tears of joy to think with what affection the Lord cares for you.'

While he was thus explaining to her the whole situation, she said not a word but thought that what he said was true.

'What answer shall I make then?' the Echizen no Kami asked.

'I do not know. I can say nothing. Every time I speak, you cry out that I am spiteful. You are wise and learned. Answer what you think best.'

'It is for your own sake alone that I have said what I have,' he explained. 'The Taishō told me also that he was going to do what he could to help the Third and Fourth Ladies. No doubt he is doing that in accordance with the wishes of the Lady of Sanjō. Could she be more kind to them even if she had been born of the same

---

[1] The Echizen no Kami's personal name, here given for the first time.

mother as they?' he concluded.

'Did he say that he would do anything for me?' inquired the old Kita no Kata eagerly. 'What a pity it is that the manor in Tamba which was left to me will scarcely yield one to of rice a year![1] And the other is in Etchū, so far away that it will probably yield me no profit at all. The one which was left to the Uchūben has a yield of three hundred koku. It must have been through your roguery, Kagezumi, that I was thus given poor and distant places.' So she grumbled on—but all the family had seen the Dainagon distribute his property.

'How can you say that?' they said. 'You would be more grateful to the Lady of Sanjō for returning the house to you, if you considered how often quarrels arise between members of a family over such matters.'

'Stop talking like that,' the Kita no Kata cried. 'Don't try to corner me with that kind of talk. It is only because we are so poor that we must speak as we do.'

While this conversation was going on, the Saemon no Suke had come in. 'Even in poverty though, virtuous people act according to the rules of honour,' he now said. 'When the Kita no Kata of the Taishō lived here, she never grumbled. She cheerfully obeyed the harshest of orders, and I heard her say once in secret that she was quite contented.'

'Oh, how I should like to die!' exclaimed the Kita no Kata. 'If I continue to live, my children will continue to sin by speaking evil.'

---

[1] One to is nearly four gallons, and one koku nearly forty.

'True. All right then; all right. We will not speak of this again,' the two sons answered and left the room.

However their mother then tried to call them back. 'Wait a moment. Tell me about the answer to the Lord,' she called out, but they went out as if they had not heard her.

'Why is our mother so evil-minded?' the Saemon no Suke asked his brother. 'We can but pray for her that she may become more righteous. It is important we do so for our own sakes too.'

They wrote the answer to the Taishō together. 'I am very much obliged to you for your kind offer,' the letter read. 'I have only you on whom I can lean now. My sons did not wish me to accept the deeds of the various places which you offered me, thinking that it would be against their father's wishes to do so. However, I accept them lest I make your kindness of no avail. As for this house, it must have been after deep consideration that it was left to you, and therefore we should not be able to forgive ourselves if we acted contrary to his last wishes. Therefore please keep the deeds.'

When the Echizen no Kami was leaving with the deeds, the Kita no Kata, suspecting that he would return the deeds, called out to him. 'Why are you taking them? The Lord gave them to us, did he not? Bring them here. Bring them here.'

'Oh, she is crazy to speak so foolishly on an important

matter like this,' the son thought and went out with the deeds.

The Taishō read the answer. 'What she says might be true enough if it were a question of the house going into the possession of strangers. I intend the Great Lady to live there as long as she lives, and then for the house to be given to the Third and Fourth Ladies. Thus the will of your father will not be transgressed. Please keep the deeds.'

The Taishō and his family then left the mansion to return to Sanjō. 'I will come again soon,' said the Lady. 'Please come to visit us. I wish to do what I can to serve you in place of my father. Tell me about everything which troubles you. I shall be very delighted indeed if you keep nothing back from me.' With such loving words, she consoled them.

Splendid presents—ornaments for the Third and Fourth Ladies and more practical presents for the old Kita no Kata —were always being sent at every opportunity just as when the old Dainagon was alive. Gradually the old Kita no Kata came to a due appreciation of the devotion of the Lady of Sanjō as she saw how dutiful the Lady was to her and to her family, while her sons were indifferent about her welfare.

The old year passed away and at the time of the General Appointments, the Minister of the Left was appointed

Dajōdaijin,[1] and the Taishō became Minister of the Left.[2] His brothers were also promoted, but details need not be given here, as it would be too boring. The good fortune of the Kita no Kata of the new Minister of the Left was the object of the joy and the envy of her kinsfolk and the people at large.

The husband of the Second Lady, the Uchūben, sorry at being left in poverty for so many years, went to the Kita no Kata of the new Sadaijin to beg for promotion and was appointed Governor of the Province of Mino through her favour. The Echizen no Kami, as he was due to be transferred to another province that year,[3] was given the Province of Harima, on account of the excellent results of his rule in his former province. The Saemon no Suke was appointed Shōshō. Both of these attributed their promotion to the influence of the Lady and went together to report their good fortune to the old Kita no Kata.

'Do you not see here again evidence of the Lady's devotion?' they said. 'Do not grumble selfishly again.' And their mother said, 'I see.'

People said among themselves that the General Appointments that year had brought joy only to the kinsmen of the new Minister of the Left.

The Lord's influence was now increased so greatly that

---

[1] President of the Supreme Council of State.
[2] Sadaijin.
[3] After a five-year term of office.

even his father, the President of the Council, talked over
his plans with the Minister of the Left first. And if he
said, 'No good. Don't do that,' his father did not do it.
Many times therefore the President had not done what
he himself wished to do, and on several occasions he had
found it best to do what he had not wished to do because
he had been asked by the Lord to do it. At the General
Appointments even the humblest posts were given according to his wishes. This was due to his being the uncle
of the Emperor who had infinite respect for him, to his
holding the high office of Minister of the Left, and to his
unrivalled intellect. There was not a single high official
who had the courage to withstand him in his management
of affairs. Even his father, the President, held him in
great honour though he was his son. The son seemed
to be in the place of the father.

'We must try to please the Minister of the Left rather
than his father, the President of the Council,' people said,
'for to do that is the surest way of pleasing the father.'
Anyone who had any wish went to pay his respects to
the Lord, and therefore the mansion at Sanjō was always
crowded with supplicants.

The Kita no Kata of the Minister of the Left made great
preparations for the farewell banquet of the Mino no Kami,
infinite care being taken with the arrangements as he had
been so much associated with the Lord's family. A horse
with saddle and full equipment was presented to him.

'It is at the wish of the Lady that you have been so

well-provided for,' the Minister said to him. 'If I hear of any neglect of duty on your part, I shall not regard you with favour any longer.'

The Mino no Kami was highly delighted at his words and regarded him as a very gracious kinsman. He returned home and told his wife what had been said. 'As he advised me to perform my duties well, I am sure that I stand high in his favour,' he concluded. The Second Lady, his wife, was very glad to hear that.

'Now I have but to find two husbands for the Third and Fourth Ladies. I have been looking around, without telling any one my object, but I am sorry to say that I have not found anyone suitable up to the present,' the Lord said to the Lady some time later.

The Minister had provided the old Kita no Kata and her daughters, the Third and Fourth Ladies, with suitable robes for the different seasons and all their other necessities in a style far superior to that to which they had been accustomed when the old Dainagon was alive. And as he advanced step by step in rank, he arranged everything in grander style still.

Other children had been born and 'putting on the hakama' ceremonies had been held for each in turn, but we have no space here to describe them. The eldest son was now ten and grown quite tall and sturdy. As he was clever and would not be likely to make errors in his Court duties, he was allowed entry to the Palace of the Crown Prince. He was a good reader and very intelligent, so he was allowed to be the play-fellow of the still very young Mikado who was very fond of him and taught him to play the sō flute. His father was very proud of him. The second son, now nine years old, had been brought up in the mansion of his grandfather who was very jealous when he heard that the elder boy had been permitted to go to the Palace.

'I want to go too,' the boy said to his grandfather.

'Why didn't you tell me before?' his grandfather said, and went at once to the boy's father to get him to grant the boy's wish.

'But he is still too young,' the Minister replied to the request.

'What! But he is cleverer than his elder brother,' the President replied. 'He seems to be the elder brother.'

However, the father only smiled in answer.

The old Lord therefore went directly to the Court. 'This is the grandson I love most of all. Please favour him especially. Favour him more than his elder brother, I beg you. He has more talent than his brother.'

He also gave orders to his own household that the boy should be treated as the eldest son, and called him Ototarō.[1]

The next child was a girl now eight years of age, very beautiful and surrounded with loving care by her parents. The next two were sons, now six years and four years old. Another child was expected shortly, and naturally the Lady herself, as her family increased, was treated the more considerately.

---

[1] The younger eldest son.

The Lord's father, the President, was sixty years old that year, and the Minister of the Left arranged to celebrate it. Everything was done in a grand manner, but you are able to imagine it for yourselves. The Minister's two elder sons performed a dance, both equally cleverly, and their grandfather shed tears of joy as he watched them. Thus the Lord left undone nothing that could possibly be done for the pleasure of his father and did everything in such a splendid manner that his reputation was the more enhanced.

Time passed quickly and the Lady went out of mourning.[1] As the family of the old Dainagon was now very prosperous, the anniversary of his death was celebrated very splendidly. To the delight of the Lady, the Kita no Kata expressed her joy that her children had prospered so greatly by the Lord's iufluence.

All the while the Lord had been looking for a suitable husband for the Third or the Fourth Lady, and time had gone on without his being able to find one, until he heard of the sudden death of the wife of one of the Chūnagon who had been selected as Tsukushi no Sochi.[2] He was of fine reputation and would make a good husband for one of the ladies, he thought. So when he met this Chūnagon at the Court, he made a tentative suggestion

[2] One year after her father's death.
[3] Vice-Governor General of Kyūshū (actually Governor, for the Governor General was never in residence there.)

of the match, and the proposal was promptly accepted.

The Minister told the Lady of the proposal and the acceptance. 'He is noble in rank and character,' he went on. 'Shall we marry him to the Third Lady or the Fourth Lady? Which shall it be?'

'I do not know,' answered the Lady. 'Arrange the matter as you think best. Still, for my part, I should suggest the Fourth Lady. For she has suffered greatly and it would rouse her from her melancholy.'

'We must hurry the marriage for he leaves for Tsukushi at the end of the month. Write to the Great Lady and with her permission we will hold the marriage ceremony here.'

'How can I explain all that in a letter? And it would be inconvenient for me to go and ask her. It would be better for you to tell the Shōshō or the Harima no Kami yourself.'

However next morning, she called the Shōshō to her, and told him all the story privately. 'I should like to go to your house myself but I have things to do here. This is what the Lord has told me. What shall we do? "Although it may be enviable to remain single," he said to me, "evil is likely to befall a woman who lives alone. This lord is a man of high reputation, and if all the family agree, I would very much like her to be married from this house."'

'We should not refuse to agree to any proposal of the Lord, however distasteful it might be to us. Still less should we withhold our consent to such a gracious proposal. I will go and inform the family.'

He returned and told his mother what had been said, 'This is a very good match. There could be no thought of refusing a proposal which entails the Fourth Lady being married as the adopted daughter of a Minister in office. And such an influential Minister! He must have arranged this to cover the disgrace and ridicule the Fourth Lady has suffered through Omoshiro no Koma. The Tsukushi no Sochi is forty years old, and even if my father were alive he could not have made a better match for her. We ought to be grateful to the Minister for all his affectionate interest—more than that of a parent—in us. Let the Fourth Lady go to the Sanjō house promptly.'

'I have been anxious about what is to happen to the Fourth Lady after I am gone,' the old Kita no Kata said. 'I would have married her even to a Governor of a Province. I am glad therefore to find that this man is a noble and am most grateful to the Minister of the Left for his so careful regard for our welfare. He seems to behave more considerately towards us than the Lady does.'

'However, I am sure that it is only through the Lord's love for her that he treats us so kindly. "If you love me truly, look after my brothers and sisters," she says to him, and that is the reason why we are so well treated. Though even I, Kagemasa,[1] desire many wives, he seems not to know that there are other women beside his wife. He pays no attention to the pretty ladies whom he meets at

---

[1] The Third Son's personal name, here given for the first time.

the Court of the Empress. When he has finished his duties there, he returns home at once, even in the middle of the night or at dawn. She is the supreme instance of a woman truly loved by her husband,' he said, and then went on, 'Ask the Fourth Lady for her answer.'

The old Kita no Kata called for the Fourth Lady to come and the proposal was explained to her. 'It is a very fortunate thing for you after your having been disgraced by the affair of that fool. What do you think of the proposal?' the Kita no Kata asked her.

The Fourth Lady blushed. 'It may be a very happy thing' she answered. 'But if I accepted it, it would seem as if I were not conscious of having been disgraced, and people would consider that I had brought shame on this lord, and consequently on the Minister. That would be a great pity. In my sorrow, I have often thought of becoming a nun, but while you are still alive, I thought it was my duty to remain here and look after my child, the souvenir of my unhappy marriage. For that reason alone, I have remained here till now,' she concluded weeping. And her brother, seeing how her mind always ran on her own shame, wept also.

'Oh, how inauspicious!' said the old Lady. 'What reason is there to become a nun? You should lead a happy life while you can, so that people may not think that you were born to be unlucky. Please accept the proposal if only in obedience to my request.'

'How shall I answer then?' asked the Shōshō.

'Although the Lady herself is reluctant to accept, I

think it would be a very happy thing for her,' answered the old Kita no Kata. 'The Minister may therefore make any arrangements he pleases.'

'Very good,' the Shōshō said as he left.

The Shōshō returned to relate to the Lady of Sanjō what had been said, both by the old Kita no Kata and the Fourth Lady.

'Naturally the Fourth Lady thinks like that. But you must tell her that there are many living in this world who have suffered such shame as she has,' was the Lady's comment.

The Minister was then told of what had been said. 'As the Great Lady thus favours the match, I will disregard what the Fourth Lady says and will hasten the marriage, for he is a very fine man. He is leaving for his post at the end of this month, so the ceremony must be held very soon. Let the Fourth Lady come here to live at once.'

The Shōshō on being told this sent for a calendar and found that the next Seventh Day was a Lucky Day. The Minister agreed to this date and suggested that they should use the robes which were stored in the house. He decided that the ceremony should be held in the West Wing of his house and began the preparations for it.

The Minister then sent a message asking that the Fourth Lady should be allowed to go to the Sanjō house, and the old Kita no Kata and the others urged her to go at once.

'I am just going now,' she kept on saying in answer but did not start.

'Would you refuse to obey him in any other matter than this marriage?' her mother demanded of her. 'What an obstinate girl you are!' With such words, she forced her to start, and the Fourth Lady left accompanied by two older servants and one young maid.

Her child and Omoshiro no Koma's was now a pretty girl of eleven. She wished to go with her mother but that was impossible for it was being kept secret that she was the Fourth Lady's child. And this parting from her child added to her sorrow, and she wept bitterly.

The Minister of the Left welcomed her to his house and had a talk with her, telling her those things which it was necessary for her to know at such a time. The Fourth Lady was more embarrassed and shy than she had been on the occasion of her first marriage, and could not utter a word in answer to his explanations. She was now twenty-five years old, three years younger than the Kita no Kata of the Minister of the Left. She had been married to Omoshiro no Koma at the age of fourteen and had become a mother when she was fifteen. The Kita no Kata of the Minister of the Left was now twenty-eight.

For the next three or four days which had to elapse before the ceremony, the Lady of Sanjō looked after her with infinite care.

On the day of the wedding, the Seventh Day, the Minister of the Left and his Kita no Kata went together to the West Wing. Seeing that the attendants of the

Fourth Lady were not very splendidly dressed, he gave them each a set of robes. And as the attendants who had come with her were so few, the Kita no Kata of the Minister of the Left sent in three older servants and one young maid to help them.

The robes of the people and the furniture of the ceremony itself were most magnificent. The old Kita no Kata, the Fourth Lady's mother, and her sons and daughters arrived and busied themselves with the preparations, as the evening approached. The Shōshō, the Fourth Lady's younger brother, was filled with grateful joy as he looked around.

It was late when the Sochi arrived. The Shōshō ushered him in. The Fourth Lady thought that it now was too late to make any objection and, as the Sochi appeared to be a most estimable man and as the Minister of the Left had done so much for her, she went out to meet him. Her touch was so gentle and her appearance so elegant that he was enchanted. What he said to her we did not hear, and so cannot tell you. And at dawn the Sochi left.

The Lady of Sanjō was very anxious about how they were getting on together. The Minister of the Left soothed her as he replied to the fears which she expressed. 'There are many lovers who have not sent many love-letters but who remain constant afterwards,' he said. 'He could not have found her unworthy of his notice; however it was not wise of her to appear so reluctant. When I first began to write to you, I did not, as many lovers do, send you a continual stream of letters. I sent you one from time to time as I took it into my head to do so. Chance might have prevented our meeting at all. How thankful I was after our first meeting that this had not happened! It is interesting that our meeting can now be regarded in such a light.'

They spoke for a while in this way, and then both got up and went to the Fourth Lady's room. She was still lying in bed behind the screens. 'You had better get up now,' the Lady said to her, but just then a letter arrived from the Sochi.

'I should like to read this first of anyone,' said the Minister of the Left, taking it. 'But there are probably things in it which he wishes to remain secret from everyone but you. Show it to me afterwards.' He therefore pushed it through the screen and the young Kita no Kata took it. But the Fourth Lady refused to take it from her.

'Then I will read it,' the Kita no Kata said, and she opened the letter. The Fourth Lady was reminded of the time when Omoshiro no Koma had sent her such a letter and she dreaded that this one might be similar.

The Lady therefore read the letter to her.

> 'Since last night's meeting,
> My love for you has grown now
> So great that it is
> Immeasurable as the sands
> On the shores of Ariso.

"When I love you most." [1]

'Send an answer promptly,' said the Lady but the Fourth Lady would not write. Outside the screen, the Minister urged her to show him the letter.

'Why are you so anxious to read the letter?' the Great Lady asked, handing it out to him.

'He has not written a very long one, has he?' said the Minister. 'Write the answer now,' he said, as he handed it in again. He brought a writing case and paper and urged her to write, but the Fourth Lady was too shy to answer it for she knew that the Minister would also read it.

'Oh, this is not proper. You must write an answer quickly,' the Lady also urged her, and so oblivious to everything else, she concentrated her attention on the answer.

> 'Without doubt, you have
> Many lovers beside me,
>   And therefore your heart
>   Has now no more grains of sand
>   Left for counting out your love.'

She wrote her letter, folded it and passed it out.

'How I wish I could read this letter! I am sorry that I shall never be able to know your answer,' the Minister

---

[1] Referring to the poem—

> Is there any time
> When my longing is greatest?
>   Although but at dawn
>   This morning did I leave you
>   Yet my love seems stronger now.

commented in a humorous manner. The messenger was given a reward and sent back with the answer.

As it had been decided that the Sochi should sail on the Twenty-Eighth Day of the month, the day of his departure from the Capital was close at hand. The Minister of the Left made grand preparations for the Third Night, as grand as if she were being married for the first time.

'A man's constancy depends very much on the hospitality the lady's family show him,' he said. 'And as she has no father, I must do the more for her. Look after her carefully,' he said to the Lady. 'It will be a great pity if the marriage proves a failure for we have arranged the affair from the beginning.'

All this talk reminded the Lady of the beginning of their own love. 'What was it that attracted you to me at first when Akogi tried to hide the miserable conditions under which we were living' she asked. 'What made you constant in your love for me?'

The Minister laughed. 'What nonsensical things you talk about!' he exclaimed, and then he drew nearer to her so that no one could overhear and said, 'My love for you grew strong on the night when I heard your step-mother torment you and call you 'Ochikubo.' And what I planned that night as I lay in bed with you has now nearly all been realised. I resolved then that I would avenge you on your step-mother, and that after having had my revenge, I would amaze her with our favours towards her.

That is why I have done all this for the Fourth Lady. Is the old Kita no Kata grateful for all that we have done for her? I think Kagezumi is.'

'Yes, she has said many times how thankful she is to you,' the Lady replied.

After dusk, the Sochi came. As this was the Third Night, his attendants were given presents and entertained to dinner. Next morning he did not leave till it was broad daylight, for this was the Fourth Morning. All saw then how very elegant and handsome he was; Omoshiro no Koma could not be mentioned in the same breath.

'The day of my departure for my post is very near,' the Sochi said to the Fourth Lady as he left. 'I have many things which I must arrange before I go, and if I go to you every night and return in the morning, I shall have to neglect something. There is no one at my house; will you not go there to live? Also, would you please gather together servants to go with us? Begin to prepare yourself also. We have only ten days more.'

'How can I go to such a distant place leaving behind all my dear friends?' the Fourth Lady answered.

'Must I go alone then? And do you wish our intimacy to end, after this one or two days of meeting?' he asked, laughing heartily in a good-humoured way.

However, as he went away, he was feeling dissatisfied wondering whether her intelligence matched her beauty. Still, as the greatest noble of the time had arranged his marriage, and as the day of his departure was at hand, he decided that he could not think of giving her up. He therefore sent a message to her asking her to go to his own home.

'What a rare son-in-law! To send for the Lady so soon!' was the Minister's laughing comment on this. The Minister therefore sent her with three of his own carriages and some of his own men.

'Are we expected to go also?' asked the servants of the Sanjō house who had been appointed to help the attendants of the Fourth Lady.

'Yes, you must,' answered the Kita no Kata of the Minister of the Left, for she thought it not fitting that she herself should accompany the Fourth Lady.

Meanwhile, the servants of the Sochi also had their complaints. 'Now all in a moment we find ourselves with a new mistress,' they were saying to each other. 'What will she be like? It will not prove a change for the better for the sons and daughters of our late mistress. The new one will have everything her own way as she is from the family of the most influential noble of the day.'

The eldest son of the Sochi by his first wife was now Vice-Governor of a Province, and the third son, a Kurōdo official, had just been promoted to the Fifth Rank.[1] The Sochi's second wife who had just died had left a girl of about ten and a boy of two; their father loved them with a love it would be foolish to attempt to describe. His

---

[1] After six years of service,

elder sons, the Vice-Governor and the Shikibu no Daibu,[1] had both been given permission from the Court to accompany their father to Tsukushi.

For the presents which the Sochi had to give and for the robes of his attendants, he obtained two hundred rolls of silk and dyes and left the work to the Fourth Lady. She did not know what to do with them; she only put them in order and did not put a finger to the work. Instead she wrote to her mother explaining everything. 'I have the silk,' the letter went on, 'but I do not know what to do. All the servants whom I brought from the house are too young to be able to help me. How I long to see you and how I yearn to see the young child also! Please come and bring her to me secretly.'

The old Kita no Kata called her son, the Shōshō, in to her and told him what the Fourth Lady had written. 'I think I shall go and see her in secret tonight. So I shall need the carriage for a little while.'

'You think to keep it a secret but how can that be done?' replied the Shōshō. 'Also, it would not be proper for the Fourth Lady to take her child with her in the brilliant procession of the Sochi to his post. The Sochi also is taking with him his second wife's child also about ten years of age. And the sight of the Fourth Lady's child will look all the more strange. Still, ask the Kita no Kata of the Minister of the Left, and if she consents,

---

[1] A noble without office, attached to the Ceremonial Department.

you can take the child to the Fourth Lady.'

The old Kita no Kata did not think it a reasonable suggestion. 'Must I wait for her permission before I see my child, when we are about to part?' she burst out in anger. 'Oh, it seems as if no one can do as he likes while this Minister is alive. How sad it is that just as formerly I made others submit to my will, now I must submit in all things to the will of others! And not one of my children will support me in anything I say!'

The Shōshō saw that, as usual, opposition to the old Kita no Kata's will had offended her. 'Why are you so angry? I suggested that we consult her because we have no one else whom we can consult. I am very sorry that you have spoken as you have done, and that you are so angry at my suggestion,' he said and left the rocm.

For the most part, the old Kita no Kata was very grateful to the Minister and the Lady of Sanjō for the favours which they had shown her family, but it was her sad habit thus to rail against them when she was offended.

The Shōshō then went to the Lady of Sanjō and explained that the old Kita no Kata was very desirous of seeing the Fourth Lady and taking the child to her mother, but he said nothing of how offended his mother had been at his suggestion of consulting her.

'It is quite natural that she should wish to see her. You should take her there at once,' the Lady replied.

'However, is it not rather improper for my mother to visit her when the Sochi is not expecting a visit?'

'Yes, that is true. Then I suggest that you go yourself and give her the message in the presence of the Sochi. Say how her mother longs to see her, if only for a moment, on the eve of her departure to such a distant province, of how lonely she feels at the prospect of their separation, and that she wishes that the Fourth Lady would start her journey from her mother's house so that she could remain with her mother while she is in the Capital. You could then see whether the Shochi agrees to this. If the Sochi agrees then you can take her mother to her, or take her to her mother. As for the child, do not allow the Sochi to know that she is the child of the Fourth Lady. Say that the Kita no Kata is sending her to be a companion to the Fourth Lady on her solitary journey.'

The Shōshō was overjoyed to realise this fresh instance of the wisdom of the Lady of Sanjō shown in the way she arranged this while it is not necessary to say how it saddened him to think of the obstinacy and bad-temper of his mother. 'That is a very good plan,' he said. 'I will do as you suggest.'

The Shōshō did not like the errand he was on, but felt impelled by his sympathy for the Fourth Lady and his mother who longed to see each other to go to the house of the Sochi. He found the Sochi and the Fourth Lady sitting together. 'I have something I should like to speak to the Fourth Lady about,' he said.

'If you do not mind my hearing, please come in and tell her,' answered the Sochi. The Shōshō therefore came in and gave the message.

'How I should like to see my mother!' the Fourth Lady exclaimed. 'I long to see her, and yesterday I wrote a letter to her asking her to come to see me.'

'If you were to go to your mother's house, it would be very inconvenient for me having to go to and fro. It would be better for your mother to come here, although that is rather troublesome for her. There are no people here so she should feel no constraint in doing so. There are only the children, and if they are a nuisance, they can be moved into one of the detached buildings. We have only a few days before we leave and we must let her have an opportunity of seeing you first.'

The Shōshō was very glad to see that everything was going as pre-arranged. 'That is why my mother is so anxious to see the Fourth Lady,' he said.

'Let her come as soon as it is convenient to her. It would be most inconvenient for the Lady to have to go to her mother's house,' the Sochi said.

'Then I will convey your invitation to her,' the Shōshō said and rose to go.

'Be certain to persuade her to come,' pleaded the Fourth Lady.

'I will,' he said, and left the house.

The Shōshō then returned to detail to his mother all that the Lady of Sanjō had said, though he feared all the time he was speaking that his mother would take offence and become furious at something which had been said. 'It is a trifling matter,' he concluded, 'but you can see from the advice she gave me how far superior she is to ordinary people. Was not that a wise suggestion of hers? How gifted she is!'

The old Kita no Kata was infinitely glad that she was to go to see her daughter. 'That is a good plan. Let us go then, Third Lady. He will not mind us going tonight at once.'

'That is being in too great a hurry. It would be better to go tomorrow,' counselled the Shōshō.

Next morning, they busied themselves about the preparations for the visit. 'What a pity we have no new clothes. Are there any in the store-room?' the old Kita no Kata said.

The Kita no Kata of the Minister of the Left, knowing that they were going to stay at the house of the Sochi, and thinking that they most probably had no new clothes suitable for such a visit, had sent a set of finely made robes for the old Kita no Kata, and one for the young grand-daughter. 'I am sending robes for the little one, for on such a journey one is apt to be stared at.'

The old Kita no Kata was infinitely delighted at this. 'Step-children care for one more than one's own children do,' she declared. 'I have seven children of my own and not one of them cares for me as tenderly as she does. How infinitely glad I am that I do not have to take the child there on her first visit clad in those old garments!' She was infinitely pleased that she was going to the Sochi's house, and therefore she expressed her gratitude so unusually.

In the evening of that day they went to the Sochi's mansion in two carriages. The Fourth Lady was delighted to see her mother and told her how she had been faring during their recent absence from each other. She looked very lovingly at her little daughter; she smoothed down her child's hair and thought how tall she had grown since she had seen her last, though it was such a short time before, and how pretty she looked in her new dress. 'It fills me with agitation when I wonder how I can manage to take her with me. I am ashamed to tell the Sochi that she is my child,' the Fourth Lady said to her mother.

The old Kita no Kata then explained to her the plan which the Lady of Sanjō had suggested. 'I think it would be a good plan to do that,' she went on, and added, 'My robes and those of the child are presents from the Lady.'

'Why did we formerly so despise her who now cares for us so tenderly?' said the Fourth Lady. 'She cares for me more tenderly than a mother. Just imagine, she gave me a set of table-bowls for the house, and robes for the servants and screens and curtains. If she had not given me all these things to bring here, what would the servants here have thought of me? How glad I was to get them!'

'I have come at last to realise how good step-children are to one. Do not forget that. Do not neglect your step-children here. Care for them more tenderly than your own. If I had not treated the Lady of Sanjō so badly in former times, I should not have had to suffer the shames and disgraces which for a time I had to endure.'

'Yes, that is true,' agreed the Fourth Lady.

The old Kita no Kata saw that the Sochi was very grave and elegant, and was very grateful to the Minister of the Left and thought that he had obtained as good a husband as even he, the most influential noble of the day, could have done.

The day for their departure was drawing near. Everyone was very busy and every day two or three new servants were engaged. The Shōshō was even more grateful to the Minister when he saw the grand style of the mansion now.

The Fourth Lady's elder brother, the Harima no Kami, was in his province, and a message had been sent to him to tell him of the wedding and how kind the Kita no Kata of the Minister of the Left had been. 'They sail on the twenty-eighth of this month,' the letter went on, 'and will touch at the place where you are. Entertain them well, please.'

The Harima no Kami was infinitely delighted to hear this. He had not taken as much trouble as this to find a husband for the Fourth Lady, although she was his own sister; he thought that the Minister of the Left must be Buddha or a god, made incarnate to assist the members of his family. He made great preparations to welcome the party. He was a very good-tempered man, not at all like his mother.

The servants of the Sanjō house who had gone with the Fourth Lady to the mansion of the Sochi now sent to ask for permission to return to the service of the Lady of Sanjō, but she refused them leave. 'Attend on the Fourth Lady while she is in the Capital, and if any of you wish to accompany her on her journey, you may do so.'

'Service here is quite good, but it is obvious even to us who have been here such a short time only that the people here cannot be compared with our own master and mistress. If we had been in the service of these people from the beginning, we could not avoid going with them to Tsukushi. Even if they were of the same rank as our own master and mistress, we should prefer our own master and mistress, for they are of a much pleasanter nature. And our master is of much higher rank than this noble. We should therefore be mad to leave our own master's service, in so many respects a Paradise, to go down to Tsukushi with these people.' So all of them thought, down to the lowest of the servants, and none of them would enter the service of the Fourth Lady. It had been decided that thirty older servants, four young maids and four inferior servants should accompany them to Tsukushi.

As the day for their departure drew near, the Fourth Lady's sisters assembled at her house and spoke together sadly, regretting that they had to part.

'Next to the Kita no Kata of the Minister of the Left, the Fourth Lady is the most fortunate of us all,' some said, as they gazed round at the splendid attire of the maids.

'And to whom is all this due? Her good fortune is due to the good fortune of the Lady of Sanjō,' others answered.

Two days before their departure, the Fourth Lady decided to pay a farewell visit to the Lady of Sanjō. They went in three carriages, thinking that more would be troublesome. What the Kita no Kata said in this interview we will not detail; it can easily be imagined. She provided each of her own maids who had been attending on the Fourth Lady with a fan, a comb of mother of pearl, and a gold-lacquer toilet-powder box in order that they might give them as parting presents to the servants who were accompanying the Fourth Lady to Tsukushi. Those who gave the presents thought how kind it was of the Lady to think of doing this, and those who received them were very grateful and promised her that they would serve the Fourth Lady with devotion.

'We all thought this place a good one to serve in,' they said to each other in secret when they returned to the Sochi's mansion, 'but now that we have been to that house we can see that this place is far inferior to that in all points, even in etiquette. It has taken the place of this house in our thoughts. How we should like to serve there!'

The next morning the Fourth Lady received a letter from the Lady of Sanjō. 'Last night,' she wrote, 'I had thought of talking with you at length about the time that is coming when we shall be absent from one another. However the evening seemed too short. When I think how soon our life passes, I am filled with horror.

> You are leaving us
> And going far away now
> As does the white cloud
> Which parts from the mountain peak.
> Until you return, how long!

I shall be delighted if you can use these on your journey.'

She sent with the letter two gold-lacquered chests, one of which contained a robe and a **hakama** to give away as presents, and the other a set of robes for the Fourth Lady herself and cloth of many different kinds. Besides there was a bag, as large as a chest, containing **nusa**[1] and one hundred fans. There were also two small chests for the little girl, one containing a robe and the other a little comb-box and a gold casket for toilet-powder. But we will not describe these things in detail for that would be too tiresome.

'You have only a day or so to stay here,' the Lady of Sanjō's letter to the little girl read, 'and what must my feelings be!'[2]

---

[1] For the worship of the gods of the road.
[2] Quoting the poem—

> Because I love you,
> I think of you as precious
> Now you are leaving.
> What must my feelings be when
> You leave me like a white cloud!

> You are leaving me,
> Although my desire is that
> You go not away.
> My sorrow is the greater
> Because my heart goes with you.'

'There are too many,' the Sochi said when he saw all the presents which the Lady of Sanjō had sent. 'She ought not to have sent so many.' He rewarded the bearers and sent them away.

'I would that I could express my thoughts,' the Fourth Lady wrote in answer to the Lady.

> In my sorrow that
> I must leave you now, feel I
> Like to a white cloud
> Parting from the mountain peak
> To wander it knows not where.

Our excitement in the preparation for the journey is heightened by the people's delight in gazing on the presents you have sent us.'

The little girl also wrote an answer: 'I also had been wishing to write to you while I was still in the Capital.

> Were it possible
> For me to leave half myself
> With the one I love,
> You and I would both be happy,
> Though I go away from you.'

It would be foolishly inadequate to say only that the old Kita no Kata wept as she read these letters and the answers; she was so moved because the Fourth Lady was her favourite daughter. 'I am nearly seventy years old,' she said, weeping bitterly. 'How shall I be able to live for six or seven years? I shall not be able to see you again before I die.'

The Fourth Lady was also weeping for sorrow at the parting. 'It was because I did not wish to part from you that I was so unwilling to marry the Sochi. But you forced me into the marriage. Now it is impossible for me to stay with you. Still, do not be sorrowful; our parting is not necessarily for ever.'

'Did I plan this marriage? The Minister of the Left planned it; and he did it with the base object of bringing this sorrow of parting on me. Oh, why was I so grateful then to him for doing it?'

'It is of no use talking like that now,' the Fourth Lady said, trying to soothe her. 'It was my Fate that I am compelled to part with you thus for a time.'

'You ought not to speak thus and weep so wildly at bidding farewell. People do not do it. It is not becoming,' the Shōshō rebuked the old Kita no Kata.

The Sochi went to say good-bye to the Minister of the Left. 'I felt very friendly towards you before we were ever acquainted,' the Minister said to him. 'All the more affection do I feel now that we are kinsmen. Take care of the little girl who is going with you. Her father, the old Dainagon, loved her most of all his children. We wished to adopt her ourselves, but the old Kita no Kata wished her to go with the Fourth Lady, whom she does not like to travel so far alone. That is why she will not let us have the child.'

'I will do what I can for her,' answered the Sochi.

The Minister was very friendly and when at dusk he left, he was presented with a robe and two fine horses.

When the Sochi returned home, he related to the Fourth Lady all that had been said. 'How old is your youngest sister?' he then asked.

'Eleven,' the Fourth Lady answered.

'Strange that the Dainagon should have had a daughter when he was so old.' It was most amusing that he should wonder that.

'What presents did you give to the servants who came from the Minister's house to help us?' the Sochi then asked.

'You did not give me anything to give them. So I have given them nothing.'

'You talk nonsense. Were you going to let them return with nothing after they had helped us so long?' he said rebukingly; and to himself he said sadly that she did not seem to be very clever.

He therefore gave each of the three older servants eight rolls of silk, two rolls of damask silk and a pound of violet dye, to each young maid six rolls of silk and dye, to each of the under-servants four rolls of silk and dyes from what was remaining of the presents. 'How generous he is!' the servants thought.

Preparations still went on busily and noisily for they were to set out at dawn next morning. The old Kita no

Kata leaned on the shoulder of the Fourth Lady and wept in her misery, unwilling to return to her own house.

Just then a servant brought in a large gold-box with perforated sides, as large as a dress-chest, decorated with five-coloured braid and wrapped up in brown gauze. 'When I asked the man where it was from, he replied that you would be able to tell when you saw it, and then he went away,' the servant explained. They thought this was very strange and opened the box. Inside there was a gold carving of sand-hills on an island, set on a piece of blue silk for sea, and on the sea was set a boat of agilawood. The island was covered with trees and the sand-hills were finely worked. They looked for a message and found a letter, folded very small and attached to the boat. They opened it and read—

> 'Sad sight to see you
> Waving me good-bye, as now
> Further and further
> The boat in which you are
> Is rowed away from the island.[1]

I must not speak of my love for you, and for that reason alone do I remain silent.'

The handwriting was that of Omoshiro no Koma, the Fourth Lady noticed with horror, for it was so unexpected. The old Kita no Kata was also amazed. The Fourth Lady had but rarely thought of her former husband for she had never had any love for him, and their relations had been

---

[1] The poem quoted refers to the incident of the Lady Matsuura Sayo waving her sleeves in farewell to Ōtomo no Satehiko.

so unusual. Now this letter reminded her of him.

'Give this as a present to the daughter of the Minister of the Left,' the Shōshō advised.

'No, it is a nice thing. Keep it,' the old Kita no Kata said.

But the Fourth Lady, thinking of all the kindnesses she had received from the Minister of the Left, agreed with the Shōshō. 'That is the best plan,' she said.

'There is no better,' said the Shōshō. 'I will take it myself,' he said as he went out with it.

Omoshiro no Koma had not thought of sending this present himself; it was his sisters who had sent it, thinking it improper not to send a present to the lady who had had a child by their brother.

Late that night, the old Kita no Kata returned to her own home. And at four o'clock in the morning, all the party started in over ten carriages. The Sochi had been given fresh orders to hasten to his post, so they made no stop at Yamazaki[1] and hurried on their way at once, those who had accompanied them thus far returning to the Capital with the rewards which the Sochi had given them.

The servants who had been attending on the Fourth Lady returned to the Sanjō house and told the others of the events they had witnessed at the mansion of the Sochi. When the Minister of the Left and the Lady heard of how the old Kita no Kata had said, 'Did I arrange the

---

[1] Farewell banquets were held at Yamazaki on these occasions.

marriage?' they laughed with great enjoyment of the joke.

The old Kita no Kata wept most bitterly, too bitterly, with longing for the Fourth Lady, but it was but for a short time; she soon forgot about the parting.

We will not write of how splendidly the Harima no Kami entertained the Sochi's party on their journey.

'I have made one of the ladies happy; now I would like to do the same for the other,' said the Minister of the Left.

Thus the time passed on and happy events followed one after another.

The Sochi arrived safely in Tsukushi and sent presents to the Minister of the Left.

The eldest son of the Minister reached the age of fourteen and 'put on the hat'; the daughter 'put on the skirt' at twelve. The second son was allowed 'to put on the hat' at the same time as his elder brother.

'My father allows my second son to rival his brother always, does he not?' commented the Minister with a laugh.

The daughter had been trained to become an Imperial consort and in the following year in the Second Month she entered the Court. The splendour of the ceremony may easily be imagined and we will not describe it. By her infinite beauty, she gained the love of the Emperor and through that and by the assistance of the Empress-

Dowager, her aunt, she was soon in greater favour than any of her fellow consorts.

The Harima no Kami was promoted Chūben.[1]

Emon's husband, the Mikawa no Kami, became Sashōben.[2] Emon was now the mother of several children and living with much dignity she often came to visit the Kita no Kata of the Minister of the Left.

The President of the State Council, the Minister's father, had many times asked permission to resign, but the Mikado had always refused. 'I am getting very old,' he now said, 'but I should be very sorry if I neglected my duties by not appearing at Court every day. This year is an Unlucky Year in which I ought to withdraw myself further from active life, and I should therefore like to resign my office. I should consider it most improper of me to be absent from any important Court affair while I hold my present office. Let the Minister of the Left be appointed in my stead. He is very talented and can guide your counsels better than an old man.'

The President also asked the Empress-Dowager to further his request, and the Emperor at last consented. 'Why do I try to persuade him not to resign?' the Mikado said. 'I consider it a blessing to me if only he remains alive.'

The Minister of the Left was therefore promoted Dajō-daijin in place of his father.

[1] Vice-Controller.
[2] Deputy Vice-Controller of the Left.

'He is not yet forty years of age and has risen to the highest rank possible,' was people's amazed comment on this.

His daughter was appointed Empress.

The Shōshō was appointed Chūjō and Miya no Suke.[1]

The President's two sons had both been promoted Hyōe no Suke;[2] the elder was now appointed Sakon-e no Shōshō.[3]

'Why was my Hyōe no Suke not promoted at the same time?' the President's father asked him.

'It would be unjust, especially at the very commencement of my administration, to promote both my sons at the same time.'

'He is not your son; he is my fifth son. No one can censure you for promoting him then. You have promoted your own son to be Sakon-e no Shōshō. Promote the other Ukon-e no Shōshō.[4] It is outrageous for a nephew to be promoted to a higher rank than his uncle.' Then as the President made no reply, he went on, 'All right. All right. I can see that you are not willing to do it.' He therefore went to the Court himself and the result was that his favourite grandson was promoted Ukon-e no Shōshō.

'That is good,' the old man said then. 'If this boy had been older, I would have left the Presidency of the

---

[1] Vice-Steward to the Empress.
[2] Colonels of the Military Guards, of the Left and Right.
[3] Major General of the Bodyguard of the Left.
[4] Major General of the Bodyguard of the Right.

State Council to him.' Was not this more than ordinary grandfather's love?

How can we describe the happiness of the Kita no Kata of the Dajōdaijin?

'When she wore an unlined **hakama** and lived in the Lower Room, who would have thought that she would become the Kita no Kata of the President of the State Council and the mother of the Empress?' those who had known her in former times said to each other in secret.

The Third Lady was appointed Directress of the Imperial Wardrobe.

The Sochi and the Fourth Lady returned safely to the Capital at the end of his term of office,[1] to the great joy of the old Kita no Kata, her mother. It seemed designed by the will of the gods and Buddha that she should still be alive at over seventy years of age to witness how her kinship with the President had blessed her family.

'You are now very old. You should turn your thoughts to the practice of religion,' the Kita no Kata of the President now counselled her step-mother, and consenting she entered the Religious Life.

The old Kita no Kata was extremely pleased at having been given this advice. 'Let no one in the world hate their step-children. Step-children are the most valuable of children,' she said.

But when she was angry, she said, 'She made me be-

---
[1] Of five years.

come a nun. And she knows how fond I am of fish. Step-children are very crafty.'

Finally, she died and the President gave her a splendid funeral.

Emon was made an official of the General Affairs Bureau of the Empress, and we shall learn soon her later history.

The President's two sons kept pace, step by step, in their promotion. The old Lord, his father, was dead, but on his death-bed he had kept on saying, 'If you love me, do not treat the younger as inferior to the elder'. So the President kept his father's wishes in mind and took care to treat them equally in all things. When the elder became Sataishō, the younger one was promoted Udaishō. The happiness of their mother, the Kita no Kata of the President, was unparallelled.

The Sochi was promoted Dainagon by the President's influence.

Omoshiro no Koma had fallen seriously ill and having entered the Religious Life, nothing further was heard of him.

The Tenyaku no Suke had never recovered from the beating he had received at the hands of the servants of the President and had died long before.

'How sad I am that he never lived to see the Lady's happiness!' the President said: 'Why ever did I allow them to kick him so violently?   How I wish he had lived a little longer!'

The Empress, when she was an Imperial consort, had appointed Izumi no Kami, the husband of Emon's aunt, Steward, and he was now very high in rank.

And she who was formerly called Akogi became Naishi no Suke.[1]   And it is said that the Naishi no Suke lived to the age of two hundred years.

---

[1] Vice-Directress of the Bureau of General Affairs (of the Empress.)

APPENDIX I

i. THE TITLE

The title of this story is explained in the opening words; it is the history of the fortunes of the heroine, forced by her 'wicked step-mother' to live in a room on a lower level than the rest of the house—ochikubo naru tokoro. From this fact she is given the name of Ochikubo no Kimi, a title here rendered in English as 'Lady Ochikubo.' However it must be remembered that the title **kimi** was more appropriate to an upper servant in a noble's house than to one of the daughters of the house, **himegimi.** The title **kimi** at once expresses the heroine's inferiority to the legitimate daughters, her half-sisters; she is 'The Lady of the Lower Room' while they are spoken of as 'Eldest Lady' or 'Second Lady'; she is addressed as a chief attendant might be—Ochikubo no Kimi.

ii. THE AUTHOR

'Ochikubo Monogatari' is the work of an unknown author of the second half of the tenth century. Ancient tradition attributed it to Minamoto no Shitagau (910–983), a famous scholar of the age, to whom also were attributed 'Taketori Monogatari' and 'Utsubo Monogatari." There are certainly similarities of thought and expression between 'Taketori Monogatari' and 'Utsubo Monogatari' which favour their attribution to

the same author, but there is no resemblance of any kind
between them and 'Ochikubo Monogatari.' This traditional attribution has been dismissed by Japanese scholars
of the last two hundred years as having no evidence in its
favour, and as being based solely on the fact that he was an
eminent scholar of the period when the story was written.
Instead of this attribution, various suggestions were made
as to the identity of the author. The famous critic of the
eighteenth century and a great lover of 'Ochikubo Monogatari,' Kamo no Mabuchi, attributed it to Fujiwara no
Tadahira, the 'cuckoo dilettante' and Regent (Kwanpaku)
in the reigns of the Emperors Shujaku (931–946) and
Murakami (946–967). Still, this and all the other at-
tributions have as little evidence (or less) to support them
as the traditional one of Shitagau. The critics of the Meiji
Era, therefore, contented themselves with ascribing the
book to an unknown author. However, recently the
traditional ascription to Shitagau has found its defenders,
though very little additional evidence can be brought
forward in support of it. A comparison of his known
writings, a score of his poems included in the anthology
of poetry, the 'Shūishū,' compiled between 999 and 1011,
and the poems in 'Ochikubo Monogatari' show no identi-
ties of matter or style. Though the poems in 'Ochikubo
Monogatari' are, like Shitagau's poems in the 'Shūishū,'
often humorous, they show no traces of deep study of
Chinese philosophy as the poems of Shitagau do. As
poems, those of 'Ochikubo Monogatari' are perhaps
rather poor. That seems to be the main argument of the

modern defenders of the traditional attribution; the poems in 'Ochikubo Monogatari' are poor enough to have been written by Shitagau. Further than that, there is no positive evidence to support the attribution to Shitagau or to any other writer. The author is unknown.

Nevertheless all the commentators agree on one point —the story was written by a man. The style is too direct (they say) and too 'outspoken' and not verbose and vague and wordy enough for it to have been the work of a woman writer. Further (they say) the humour sometimes becomes too coarse and vulgar for a woman to have written the story.

If the reader forms the opinion that the writer portrays the character of Akogi, the Lady Ochikubo's attendant, with more autobiographical feeling than the rest of the characters and that a hint to the same effect is given by the closing words of the story, his feeling will agree with my first impression. Many details of style and expression certainly do point to a man as author, yet still I feel reluctant to give up my first impression that a woman of the same station in life as Akogi was the author, even though the whole weight of the opinions of all the experienced commentators is against that conjecture. And of all characters of the book, it is Akogi who shows the greatest appreciation of that coarse and vulgar humour which leads the commentators to ascribe the story to a man!

iii. THE DATE

The eminent critic, Kamo no Mabuchi (1697–1769) concludes that 'The Tale of the Lady Ochikubo' was written during the reign of the Emperor Reizei (976–979). We may well question such precision of dating. No doubt Mabuchi, having decided that Tadahira was the author, comes to this conclusion by a study of the life of Tadahira. His dating must fall with his attribution. With absolute certainty we can say that the story must have been written before 1001. This date is fixed by an allusion to Ochikubo in 'Makura no Sōshi.' Matsuki Kin-en, a critic of the period immediately preceding the Meiji Era, was of the opinion that it must have been written before 967. His more famous pupil, Nakamura Shūkō,[1] the greatest modern authority on 'Ochikubo Monogatari,' places it between 946 and 986. Some modern critics have given it a later date than this, but still before 1001, as some poems are quoted in the story which are included in the collection, 'Shūishū' of 999. However to date it, as it must then be dated, between 999 and 1001 seems most improbable; the poems are quoted in the story as being already well-known to everyone, and the allusion in 'Makura no Sōshi' also depends on Ochikubo being already well-known by 1001. We must, I think, assume that the poems quoted in the story were

---

[1] Nakamura Shūkō's editions of 'Ochikubo Monogatari,' especially his 'Ochikubo Monogatari Taisei,' have been mainly used in making this translation.

well-known before their inclusion in the 'Shūi Anthology.'[1] Some commentators also consider that the poem on page 220 of the story, written in honour of the eightieth birthday of the old lord, was written under the influence, conscious or unconscious, of a poem by Onakatomi Yoshinobu; both use the imagery of the hope that a walking staff presented to the old man may also help him to climb to yet higher peaks of honour. If the poems have any interrelation and if the poem in 'Ochikubo Monogatari' is the borrower, then we should be able to fix the earlier limit for the writing of this novel with this assistance, for it is known that Yoshinobu's poem was written in 969 in honour of the seventieth birthday of the Regent Fujiwara Saneyori. This would give a date between 970 and 1000 for 'Ochikubo Monogatari.' This date seems most probable on other grounds also and allows us to conclude that 'Ochikubo Monogatari' was written before the end of the tenth century, probably during the last quarter of the century.[2]

---

[1] The date of composition of the two poems quoted in the story which are included in the 'Shūishū' is unknown. The Gonchūnagon Atsutada, the author of one, died in 943; Taira no Kanemori, the composer of the other, in 990.

[2] It might be thought possible to fix the date of 'Ochikubo Monogatari' by some reference to the history and conditions of the time in which it was written. However this is of little use. We see in the story nothing of the turbulent politics of the age, nothing of the revolts of the great families in their struggle for supremacy. The author writes of a political situation which had already disappeared; there is, for instance, no mention of the Kwampaku, the minister who, as Regent, controlled the whole administration from the time of the Emperor Uda (888-897).

iv. OCHIKUBO MONOGATARI AND
HEIAN LITERATURE

The most famous work of fiction of the Heian Era,
Murasaki Shikibu's 'Genji Monogatari,' was written soon
after 'Ochikubo Monogatari,' probably within twenty or
thirty years. Though it is difficult to make any comparison
between two works in such very different manners, we
must conclude that 'The Tale of Lady Ochikubo' is inferior as a work of literature. 'Ochikubo' has neither the
poetic prose nor the lyrical spirit nor the stylistic refine-
ments of its more famous successor. There is not a word
of appreciation of the beauties of nature such as form a
distinctive characteristic of 'The Tale of Genji,' as it does
also of the earlier **monogatari** such as 'Utsubo Monogatari.'[1]

Though we must conclude that 'Ochikubo Monogatari'
is on a lower level of literature than Genji Monogatari, we
can see at the same time what great advances were made
by the author of 'The Tale of the Lady Ochikubo' on
the literature of the preceding age. Here for the first time
we have a novel. Before it there were fairy stories such as

---

[1] Whether 'Ochikubo Monogatari' definitely served as a model for
Murasaki Shikibu must remain as a matter of some doubt. Most of the
commentators say that undoubtedly it did, and mark a number of similarities between the story of the Lady Ochikubo and that of Lady Murasaki in the story of 'Genji.' Both are step-daughters with a 'wicked
step-mother.'. Both celebrate their father's birthday in the same splendid
manner. In both stories, the son-in-law, the Kurōdo no Shōshō and the
Higekuro no Taishō, become alienated from their wives, the half-sisters
of the heroines. In both there is a quarrel over the precedence of
carriages on the occasion of the festival of the Kamo Shrine.

'Taketori Monogatari,' tales of wonder such as 'Utsubo Monogatari,' poem-romances such as 'Ise Monogatari' where short prose explanations serve to link together a series of poems, and diaries, stray notes on many topics or narratives of journeys such as 'Tosa Diary.' In 'Ochikubo Monogatari' for the first time we have a novel with a plot and dramatic situations told vividly, with humour and with careful regard to characterisation and consistency. Its realistic dialogue, its dramatic power, and its life-like characterisation make 'Ochikubo Monogatari' a master-piece unique in Japanese literature, a work of fiction second only to 'Genji Monogatari' among the novels of the Heian Era and a fitting link in the development of the novel from the poem-romances of 'Ise Monogatari' to the full development in 'The Tale of Genji.'

APPENDIX II

THE POLITICAL ORGANISATION OF JAPAN IN THE TENTH CENTURY

The Political Organisation of Japan at the time of 'Ochikubo Monogatari' was that prescribed by the **Taihō-ryō**, the Code of the Taiho Era (702) and added to very considerably at intervals. The date of creation is given for those ranks (**Ryōge Kwan**) created later than the Taihō Code.

The following note is a summary of the organisation intended only to facilitate identification of ranks and offices mentioned in the story, especially necessary because through disuse of personal names the characters are referred to throughout by their titles.

The Government System is outlined under

      (1) The Two Offices,
      (2) The Eight Departments,
      (3) The Imperial Bodyguard,
      (4) Local Government.

(1) THE TWO OFFICES

(I) JINGIKWAN, The Department of Religious Ceremonies.

(II) DAJŌKWAN, The Council of State, to which the Eight Departments were responsible.

The members of the Council of State were—

1. DAJŌDAIJIN, The President of the Council of State.
2. SADAIJIN, The Minister of the Left.
3. UDAIJIN, The Minister of the Right.
4. NAIDAIJIN, The Minister of the Centre. The first appointment to this office was in 777.
5. DAINAGON, The Great Counsellors. Originally four in number, later two and finally fixed at three in the reign of the Emperor Uda (888–897).
6. GONDAINAGON, The Counsellors of Junior High Rank, created 828.[1]
7. CHŪNAGON, The Counsellors of Middle Rank, created 705, three in number.
8. GONCHŪNAGON, The Counsellors of Junior Middle Rank, created 756.[1]
9. SHŌNAGON, The Minor Counsellors, three in number.
10. SANGI, Members of the Council of State, eight in number; also called SAISHŌ and SHŌKŌ.
11. SADAIBEN, The Controller of the Left.
12. UDAIBEN, The Controller of the Right.

The Sadaiben and the Udaiben controlled the Government Departments by means of bureaux headed by the SACHŪBEN and the UCHŪBEN, the Vice-Controllers of the Left and the Right.

The KURŌDO-DOKORO, the Department of the Imperial Archives, created 810, gradually usurped the duties of the Shonagon.[2]

---

[1] Holders of these titles do not appear in 'Ochikubo Monogatari.'
[2] One of the minor officials of this bureau, the Kurōdo no Shōshō, appears in the story.

(2) THE EIGHT DEPARTMENTS

1. NAKATSUKASHŌ, The Intermediary Department.
2. SHIKIBUSHŌ, The Ceremonial Department.
3. JIBUSHŌ, The Department of Civil Administration.
4. MINBUSHŌ, The Department of Popular Affairs.
5. GYŌBUSHŌ, The Department of Justice.
6. HYŌBUSHŌ, The War Department.
7. ŌKURASHŌ, The Treasury Department.
8. KUNAISHŌ, The Imperial Household Department.

The highest officials of these Departments were KYŌ, Minister, TAIYU and SHŌYU, First and Second Vice-Ministers.

Each of these Departments controlled a number of Bureaux. The Imperial Household Department, for instance, had eighteen bureaux, one of which, TENYAKU-RYŌ, the Bureau of Medicine, is mentioned in the story.

At the head of these bureaux were KAMI, Director and SUKE, Vice-Director.

(3) THE IMPERIAL BODYGUARD

The Imperial Bodyguard was divided into six divisions in 811 in place of the five divisions of the Taihō Code.

1. SAKON-E, The Bodyguard of the Left,
2. UKON-E, The Bodyguard of the Right.

These guarded the innermost part of the Imperial Palace, between the Kayō and Immei Gates.

The highest officers were the TAISHŌ, General, CHŪJŌ, Lieutenant-General, and two SHŌSHŌ, Major-Generals.

    3.   SAHYŌE, The Military Guards of the Left,
    4.   UHYŌE, The Military Guards of the Right.

These guarded the middle part of the Palace, between the Kenshun and Gishū Gates.

The highest officers were the KAMI, Commander and SUKE, Colonel.

    5.   SAEMON, The Gate Guards of the Left,
    6.   UEMON, The Gate Guards of the Right.

These guarded the outer part of the Palace, between the Yōmei and Impu Gates.

The highest officers were the KAMI, Commander and SUKE, Colonel.

(4) LOCAL GOVERNMENT

Each KUNI, Province, was headed by a KAMI, Governor.

The Principal Provinces had a special organisation. The Province of TSUKUSHI (modern Kyūshū) was governed by a KANZUKASA, Priest, and a resident SOCHI, Governor.

KOKORO

Natsume Soseki

When the old values meet the new in Japan

In Tokyo a lonely young student from the provinces is befriended by a sophisticated older man. Yet the man himself is lonely too. For a dark shadow from his past makes him feel like a mummy left in the midst of living beings. Even the man's wife has never penetrated this tragic mystery.

Then one day the student is dramatically taken into his mentor's confidence . . .

In this beautiful, evocative portrait of Japan at the turn of the century, Natsume Soseki explores the tragic conflicts between old and new, love and duty, friendship and self-interest.

Natsume Soseki is regarded as the greatest novelist of the Meiji era, when Japan began to blend Western culture with oriental traditions.

'One of the most important Japanese writers of the modern period'   *The Times Literary Supplement*

'Exquisite. The novel represents the moment at which the limitations and gifts of the native genius triumphed over an alien literature' *New York Times*

WINTER'S TALE
Mark Helprin

A haunting rhapsody of imagination –
A white horse that learns to fly
A chase that lasts one hundred years
A beautiful consumptive girl asleep on a mansion roof
A mile-long ship to build a bridge of light to infinity
An apocalyptic fire that heralds the millennium
A dazzling epic of lovers and dreamers, eccentrics and
    beauties, madmen and geniuses . . .

'Massive fantasy-saga . . . this extraordinary work,
defying synopsis, vaults time and space'
Sunday Telegraph

'Utterly extraordinary . . . a piercing sense of the
beautiful . . . funny, thoughtful, passionate'
New York Times

'Prodigiously inventive imagination and dazzling use
of words . . . a cascade of brilliant, sensuous images'
Publishers Weekly

VIRGINIE
Her Two Lives
John Hawkes

She is in her eleventh year and at the eleventh hour of her innocence. She lives in two worlds, two centuries apart; parallel lives in which dream and reality fuse as one, in which purity and decadence, innocence and knowledge, heart and mind must meet.

VIRGINIE

'Hawkes' serene, inviolable prose is so precise, luminous and evocative as to make this novel seem dreamed rather than read . . . troubling, strange, a marvel'
Angela Carter

'This is the stuff of fable and romance . . . a celebration'
New York Times Book Review

'Lyrical and elegant' *The Literary Review*

'A lush, erotic masterpiece' Robert Coover

'Funny, sad, and intensely moving, it is a joy to read from beginning to end'   AUBERON WAUGH

LETTER TO SISTER BENEDICTA
Rose Tremain

From Rose Tremain, author of *The Cupboard*, a hauntingly memorable novel of pathos and humour

LETTER TO SISTER BENEDICTA

Ruby Constad has loved her husband and her children, and they have all abandoned her. Ruby Constad has always had money, and it has made her fat and silent. But during the first stretched-out days of aloneness, waiting to see if Leon, her husband, will die, Ruby finds her voice at last – her own voice, her own humour, and her own will to live.

'A fine novel' *Scotsman*

'A most impressive book' *Listener*

'It deserves to be mentioned in the same breath as Paul Scott's *Staying On* . . . Miss Tremain does something to restore my faith in the vitality of the English novel'
Auberon Waugh, *Evening Standard*

AKÉ
Wole Soyinka

'What if V. S. Naipaul was a happy man? . . . What if Vladimir Nabokov had grown up in a small town in Western Nigeria and decided that politics were not unworthy of him? . . . *Aké* locates the lost child in all of us, underneath language, inside sound and smell, wide-eyed, brave and flummoxed. What Waugh made fun of and Proust felt bad about, Mr Soyinka celebrates . . . Brilliant'   John Leonard,
The Sunday Times

'A superb act of remembrance . . . dazzling reading . . . *Aké* has an enchanting effect . . . Soyinka's memoir makes everything seem wondrous'
Village Voice

'Enchanting' *The Observer*

Winner of the BBC Bookshelf/Arrow First Novel Competition

LORD OF THE DANCE
Robin Lloyd-Jones

'A picaresque novel of astonishing imaginative brilliance'
The Times

In India, in 1575, Thomas Coryat, English surgeon and rationalist, searches for a cure for his dying wife. With him is his boyhood friend, Frog, a lustful priest seeking to save the souls of those he loathes. Confronting them is an alien world: the exotic, violent India of the Moghul Empires, a world of peasants and lords, courts and villages, warriors and travelling players, warlords and princesses.

Colourful, rich, erotic and mysterious, funny and tragic, *Lord of the Dance* is a magnificent creation, at once a brilliant picaresque adventure and a profound literary achievement.

'A marvellously readable, richly colourful adventure . . . written with style, character, and deft touches of philosophy, humour and irony!'
Sunday Express